"You sure don't act like a virgin," Sophie said.

"That's just it, I'm an actor," Kenny admitted with a touch of pride. "Had you convinced that I was a man, didn't I?"

"Mm..." Sophie nodded. "And I wanted you then, too."

"More than now?"

"No." Sophie leaned back and looked down the length of Kenny's body. "Definitely not more than now."

The words and the look were like a physical touch on Kenny's hot skin. Tentatively, she reached out and put her hand on Sophie's thigh. Her skin also felt hot — it burned through the sheer cloth of Sophie's nightgown. Kenny rubbed lightly, moving her hand in small circles, moving her hand higher up Sophie's thigh.

Sophie looked down at her. Her lips were parted slightly and her breath was quickening. Abruptly, she leaned down and kissed Kenny on the collarbone. Her hair cascaded over Kenny's face and Kenny inhaled deeply the scent of that dark curtain.

⤷ ⤷ ⤷

AND LOVE
CAME CALLING

BEVERLY SHEARER

RISING
TIDE
PRESS

Rising Tide Publishers
65161 Emerald Ridge Dr.
Tucson, AZ 85739
520-888-1140

Printed in the United States on acid-free paper.

Publisher's note:
All characters, places, and situations in this book are fictitious, and
any resemblance to persons (living or dead) is purely coincidental.

Publisher's acknowledgments:
Special thanks to Edna G. for believing in us, to the feminist and gay
bookstores for being there, and to the Tucson lesbian community.

First printing: June, 1999
10 9 8 7 6 5 4 3 2 1

        Shearer, Beverly 1963-
        And Love Came Calling/Beverly Shearer
                p.cm

ISBN 1-883061-22-9

Library of Congress Catalog Card Number 98-73138

DEDICATION

To Shizuko, Julie, and Rhoda:
For each of you
in your own time.
My love and gratitude always.

AND LOVE
CAME CALLING

BEVERLY SHEARER

Prologue

Nothing is as silent as a knife across the throat in the dead of night. She stood over the sleeping man with the knife held in her trembling hands. The tip of the curved blade hovered an inch above his pale skin. The faint, smooth line of his throat was visible in the moonlight, the line so similar to her own, but without the marks of anger that she carried.

Her feet were growing cold on the rough plank floor. She waited for him to wake and make a move that would force her past her indecision. But this night, like every other, the man slept with the comfort of knowing he ruled his house. Never had a hand turned against him and never would one turn. She knew that as well as he did.

But something was different tonight and she could feel it deep in her soul. Something was building within her, some emotion, some push to action. It wasn't the cold desire for murder rising inside her, she understood that. Still, something was changing and it wasn't until she nervously turned away from his bedside that she realized what it was.

Her shaking fingers reached out to touch what she saw draped over the footboard of the bed. The rough denim of her father's pants felt soft to the calluses on her hand. She carefully laid the knife down next to his foot and silently stepped into his pants. It was right. A surge of laughter filled her chest, but she suppressed it, same as she'd pushed down all the emotion in her life. After sliding her nightgown off over her head, she sought his shirt and found where it had fallen from the bed. Working the buttons with one hand, she picked up the knife with the other and backed out of the room.

On the rack by the door hung a single hat. A large, black Stetson, it was the pride of a stingy, yet vain man. She jammed it on her head and her smile glinted coldly through the darkness. With the faintest rustle of denim she was out the door and gone. Her escape was perhaps not as silent as a knife across the throat, but it was just as satisfying.

One

I don't much care for the thought of you livin' here."
Narrowing her eyes, Sophie ignored her brother-in-law's
voice and continued to scrub her laundry against the
washboard. Robert had been bitching at her all morning, his
hard words punctuated by the solid beats of his hammer as he
worked, despite his desire to the contrary, to make the small
shack ready for her to move in.

It was not like she cared to be here either. Anywhere
within a thousand miles of this man was just too close, and
Sophie felt her hatred for him building with every word he
said.

"My brother was a damn fool to marry you. I told him
so. Now I'm the fool who's stuck with you."

Sophie gritted her teeth and swallowed the insult
silently. Allen, her late husband, had been no prize and she
only appreciated her loss when she compared him to his
brother. The men seemed to have nothing more in common
than their surname. McLaren...and it was her name now and
forever, but she knew she would never be a part of their family.
And that knowledge pleased her no end.

A brief smile came to her lips, not much more than a
dimpled line beside her mouth, but she suppressed it quickly.
It would not do for Robert to realize how little she was impressed
by his tirade. Oblivious to her contempt, he went on.

" — but I can't have you stayin' in the main house any

more, the only woman among us men. I'd have had you out sooner if the weather had warmed." Robert either had no concept that his words might be hurtful, or he knew and just didn't care. "As it is, I'll have to let someone off work long enough to ride out here and check on you every damn day."

"That won't be necessary." She turned her dry eyes full onto his face and refused to look away from his glare.

Standing silent for a moment, his irritation evident in the tense lines of his body, Robert then threw down his hammer and stalked away. Sophie returned to her laundry. A trickle of sweat ran down between her delicate shoulder blades then lost itself in the thick cloth of her underskirts. As soon as he was gone, she was going to lose at least three layers of clothing. It was simply ridiculous to expect a woman to dress this way in this weather and these surroundings. Dirty water splashed over her knees as the thought lent new vigor to her scrubbing. The harsh soap stung her wrists and knuckles and she welcomed the pain. It was proof that she could still feel, that although she would never cry over her husband's death, she was not herself dead.

Allen had died senselessly, an innocent man caught in the cross-fire of a stagecoach robbery half a state away. In the tense, endless months since his death, Sophie found herself at the mercy of his brother. She had no idea what Robert had expected his brother's Eastern wife to be, but Sophie had apparently not lived up to one single expectation. Perhaps he imagined she'd be cultured, or maybe he thought she would be weak-willed. She did have culture, more than the McLarens would see in a lifetime, but she had no interest in showing it off to them or the townsfolk. And her will was anything but weak, as Robert learned when he tried to lord it over her as if she was his wife as well.

That was the one thing that Allen had supported her in. She looked at him with a bit more respect after that, revising her opinion that he was completely spineless. Perhaps if Allen had tried a little harder to be her friend, not just her husband, she could have felt some sadness at his death. Maybe then she could have wrapped herself in a cloak of grief that would have satisfied her brother-in-law's expectations of a dutiful wife.

A shadow fell across her hands. Her muscles tensed and she looked up quickly. Robert's ability to walk without a sound unnerved her, though she refused to let it show.

"The door will lock from the inside now. Tomorrow I'll bring out some dried beef and flour."

Silence filled the space between them until she realized he was waiting for her gratitude. "That's very kind of you, Robert."

The precise, unemotional words caused a frown to deepen the weathered lines around his eyes. He stood with his feet wide apart, his heavy frame seeming to root his legs deep into the earth. The stance made his possession of the land unmistakable. "Don't plan on makin' this your home. I'll need it for the fence crews come next spring."

At her brief nod, he turned away.

"Robert, please." The words were out before she could stop herself. She hated being reduced to asking this man for anything. Impatiently, he waited for her to finish. "Lend me a horse. Then you won't have to worry so much about me."

"I don't have a sidesaddle," he said with contempt. His hatred for her, for women in general, filled the air with a sense of lightning about to strike.

"I don't need it — " she began, then hastily amended her words. "I can ride sideways with just a saddle blanket. That's how I learned," she lied.

Robert wanted to refuse. His annoyance increased as he visibly searched for the slightest reason to deny her request, but her suggestion made sense. Reluctant agreement was in his curt nod. "I'll bring a horse out tomorrow. If you don't care for it right, I'll take it back."

"Of course you will," Sophie agreed, without revealing any bitterness. "Thank you."

She turned away from him. Going back to her washing, she listened intently for any sound that would tell her he'd gone. The silence gave no hint of his movement until the dull thuds of his horse's hooves proved he had walked away. When the horse approached her, she raised her eyes and looked straight into the black barrel of his rifle. It was pointed at her forehead.

Hair raised on the back of her neck, her muscles tensed. She slowly sat back onto her heels, her stomach threatening to turn at the sight of his cold smile.

The passage of time wavered in the thin morning as Robert waited until he felt satisfied that she was frightened. "Do you know how to use this?"

Not trusting her voice, Sophie nodded.

"How to clean it?"

Again, she nodded.

"Then take it. Don't use it unless you need to. Bullets ain't free."

Standing on trembling legs, she wiped her hands on her apron. As soon as her hand grasped the cold metal, Robert let go of the gun and urged his horse forward. He rode without a glance behind him. If he had looked, he would have seen her standing with the rifle to her shoulder, taking careful aim at his broad back, and calmly imagining how good it would feel to pull the trigger.

Despite her contempt for Robert, he was soon forgotten as she worked to make the line shack into her home. The sun struck deep shadows in the creases of her forehead and the thin lines in the corner of her eyes; Sophie frowned too often, but was unaware of the severity of her expression. A serious woman, she nevertheless carried a strong streak of humor hidden under that seriousness. The humor was like the curls of her long, dark hair; no matter how strictly she tried to keep it restrained, there was always a contrary strand that would slip out to tease her.

Now that she was alone, she let her hair go free and let the late April sun shine directly on her face and arms. Her skin was becoming a nice, honey-brown color. She liked it — it felt so much healthier than the faded, deathly white shade of her friends back in Boston. The color made her look common, but she believed that her status had fallen plenty far enough to consider herself as common as they come. Working without thought of complaint, she wasted no time reflecting on the changes that had brought her here. When the orange light of sunset struck the weather-beaten gray walls, she straightened up and looked around her.

Her new home was well located. Regardless of the view of the shack itself, the view away from it was beautiful. The variety of landscape offered by her western Colorado home always amazed her. To the west, a low range of mountains whose name she had not bothered to learn ridged up from the earth, black against the fading light. Many men from Jackson were employed in mining those mountains of their gold. Beyond the mountains were the red rocks of the desert that stretched across Utah. To the south and east, pine forests gave way to juniper as they encroached upon her small meadow. Northward ran the fence line, coming ramrod straight from the southern woods and running as far as she could see across the flatlands beyond.

"Robert's fence," she said with a bitter twist to her lips. She wished she could dismantle the shack and rebuild it on the other side.

She turned back to face her new home. It was a dilapidated line shack; the walls were bleached and dried out from sun and wind, and the roof wasn't much better. It would be an insult to anyone who had any other place to go. But she had no such place, and this was all she would ever get from her dear brother-in-law. This and three-quarters of a year in which to decide on a new life. By then, her time of mourning would have passed, and Robert probably knew to the day when he would be free to set her packing. What he didn't know was that his brother had not been so tightfisted and, maybe just to impress her, Allen had once shown her where he hid a small pile of shining coins behind the headboard of their bed. The coins were now wrapped and tied tightly in an old, red-checked bonnet. It was not a fortune by any count, but it was enough to keep her until she could get out of Colorado.

Sophie picked her way through the gathering darkness and pushed open the wide plank door. The night pressed into the room and against her chest as she fumbled a moment for the matches to light the oil lamp. When its soft, yellow glow reached the corners of the shack, she breathed deeply and looked around the single room with a critical eye.

The poorly built stone fireplace looked as if several years had passed since it was used for anything other than a place to throw trash. But, incredibly, the room was blessed by the luxury of a battered cook stove. She had inspected it earlier in the day, hauling out bucket after bucket of ash and tapping the stove pipe with a poker to sound out any obstructions. It had seemed clear, but she wouldn't risk a fire tonight.

The oil lamp sat on a rough-hewn table which was accompanied by a long, low bench on one side and a stool and a rickety rocking chair on the other. The only other furnishings were the four wooden bunks, top and bottom, that were attached to the walls farthest from the fireplace.

Sophie let her weary body down into the rocking chair. It did not rock as much as lurch forward and back upon the uneven floorboards.

"It's just you now, Sophie," she said aloud, the sound of her own voice making her smile. All alone, miles from the nearest house or town, she should have been afraid. But instead, she felt an excitement welling up inside — an indescribable feeling of anticipation. Something was coming...Coming to her, and she had to be ready for it.

*A*round ten o'clock, the stage rattled down the main street of Jackson, Colorado. The creaking of the harnesses and the jangling of the braces were quiet compared to the competing sounds of the out-of-tune pianos and the laughter of whores from the town's two saloons. A thin slice of moon faintly lit the two dust-covered figures that slumped in the bench seat built on top of the coach. Passing the saloons and the darkened general store, the stage rolled to a stop next to the livery stables. The driver leaped down, then staggered on shaking, tired legs. The old man riding shotgun chuckled.

"I hate that run," the driver said with passion, in a voice rougher than trail dust could account for.

"Well, I like it." The old man grunted as he climbed down from his high seat. His skinny bones seemed to rattle and creak within the ragged frame of his clothes. Pushing his upper lip against his nostrils, he scratched the tip of his nose with the bristly hair of his mustache and watched the driver lean down to touch the ground. He felt no sympathy for the tension in those lean muscles; the driver would recover strength long before he would. A bottle of whiskey and sleeping in tomorrow were the only things that would iron the kinks out of his old body. "Yep, I like it," he repeated. "No whinin' passengers. Smooth road most all the way out to the mine."

"I don't like hauling payroll."

"Ya scared, Kenny?" He laughed again at the scowl that wrinkled the young driver's face. In a kinder voice, he said, "It does get yer blood going the first few times, but ya get used to it. No one's ever bothered a coach on this line."

"Don't mean they never will, Frank."

"Now don't you talk like that, you'll be turning our luck." He took off his hat and used it to slap the dust from his pants. "Let's go get a whore."

Kenny blushed from the bandanna up and was suddenly intent on checking the lead horse's harness. The old man's laughter rang out yet again; it was a familiar sound on the streets of this small town.

"Ya got to do it sometime, boy. There ain't no shame in bein' scared of women, most men are at first. But soon enough curiosity gets the best of that fear. Ain't ya curious?"

Frank elbowed the driver's ribs but got no response. "I know by that voice of yours that you've passed over into bein' a man, so ya should be real interested in what I'm saying. How old are ya, anyway?"

"Not old enough, I guess." The rough, deep voice put the lie to those words.

The old man hesitated, then spit decisively. "Your choice, son. I think you'll be changin' your mind soon enough, but I ain't gonna stand here waitin' for it."

"Good, 'cause I've got to find the livery boy and get these horses taken care of. I don't have time to fool with you and..." The driver stopped, realizing that Frank had already stepped through the swinging doors of the closest tavern. Kenny moved closer to the lead horse, body shielded from view of the street. Quick, slender fingers unbuttoned the center of the faded red shirt and reached inside to swiftly wipe away the itching sweat and trail dust that had collected beneath the wide band of cloth that served to hide the driver's breasts. The quietly approaching footsteps almost went unheard as the driver scratched with deep contentment. When the sound eventually sank into her tired brain, she jerked her hand out and struggled with the buttons.

"Sorry I'm late," a thin, reedy voice came from behind her. "I fell asleep."

"Again?" Kenny smiled as she turned to the boy. She looked down at his tousled hair; stalks of hay stuck out of the yellow tufts.

"Sorry, Kenny..." The boy looked down at his boots in shame. He idolized the young driver, and Kenny knew it.

"That's all right, Tyler." Reaching out, she started to gently pull the straw from his hair, then caught herself. The tender gesture was transformed into a light cuff upside the boy's head. He ducked, laughing, and ran to tend the horses.

Kenny hitched up her belt and swaggered down the dusty street, her stride as long as any man's. Walking comfortably now that her legs had regained their strength, she loved the feel of the baggy woolen pants that brushed her thighs as she moved. The pants were striped gray and black; they were her uniform, given to her by the coach company, and she wore them proudly, cinched to her narrow waist with a wide, black belt. As soon as she got her next paycheck she was going to buy the fine black shirt that tempted her from the window of the general store. With that shirt and her customary black hat and blue bandanna, she knew she'd cut a fine figure in the streets of Jackson.

A weathered and buckled boardwalk separated the storefronts from the street. Kenny stepped up and kicked the dirt from her low-heeled boots. She could smell the old wood combined with the odor of cow manure and years of rainfall. It was a smell that blanketed the town on calm days. When the spring wind blew down from the mountains, still carrying the hint of lingering snow, the scents of pine and juniper freshened the air. Kenny enjoyed the smells and she had grown accustomed to them. They told her she was home.

As she crossed the boardwalk, a gust of laughter from the tavern breezed out before her. She moved up to the door frame and cautiously peeked over the swinging doors.

Inside were about twenty men. Most leaned their tired bodies against the bar, drinking without much talk. A few sat at several low tables playing cards, and another five or so danced awkwardly but enthusiastically with the bar's offering of fallen angels. Kenny watched Frank dance, his boot heels striking sharply against the rough plank flooring. The woman he spun around the room was young, maybe no older than Kenny was herself. Kenny knew that if it weren't for her voice and her sense of determination, she might have become that woman. Pushing down the knot of fear that rose in her stomach, she moved to walk on by. As she stepped blindly into the street, she collided with a softly plump, sweet-smelling body.

"Watch it, you damn fool boy!"

Kenny didn't even look up at the man who cursed her.

Her bright green eyes were fixed on the ample cleavage exposed before her. Swallowing hard, she forced her gaze upwards to the woman's face. The man shoved her shoulder, pushing her to the side.

"Leave him be, Carl. He didn't hurt me." The prostitute took Kenny's arm and smiled kindly. "You're the new coach driver, aintcha?"

Kenny nodded. Her face was burning red — she hoped that it didn't show in the dim light that spilled from the tavern. "I — I'm sorry, ma'am," she whispered, her voice not more than a squeak.

Carl laughed and walked through the doors, leaving Kenny and the woman alone in the street.

"Don't worry 'bout it. Like I said, you didn't hurt me none." She still held Kenny's arm lightly. "What's your name?"

"Kenny."

"Kenny? Just Kenny?"

"Kenny Smith."

She chuckled with delight, a sound that raised Kenny's hairs and made her feel warm inside. "My name is Belle. Belle Smith. You don't s'pose we could be related, do you?"

Kenny laughed, a jarring sound in the suddenly and temporarily quiet street. Belle's thin, painted eyebrows rose at the harshness of it. "No. I don't s'pose so."

"Where do you live, Kenny?"

"The boarding house."

"I thought so. You know, the girls and me been talking about you — "

"Girls?" Kenny blurted.

Lifting a long, painted fingernail, Belle pointed to the interior of the saloon where Kenny could see the piled and powdered hair of the women dancing inside.

"Sarah, the blonde, she thinks you must be a virgin. She can spot 'em a mile away, she says. Me, I'm not too sure."

"Don't talk like that," Kenny protested, backing away as far as she could with Belle still latched onto her arm.

Belle smiled to reassure, but did not let go. "Hmm...I guess I could be wrong." Sliding her grip down to Kenny's wrist, she lifted the slender hand, then abruptly placed it on her breast.

Kenny's breath left her in an audible rush. She was shocked speechless, but somehow could not find the strength to remove her hand from the warm lace. Belle leaned forward, pressing herself into Kenny's palm.

"I got a rule," Belle whispered into her ear. "The first time's free."

Kenny turned her head to avoid the tickling breath and Belle quickly brushed her lips against Kenny's open mouth. Kenny pulled her hand away as if Belle's breast had become fire. She staggered backwards, stumbling off the boardwalk and out into the street.

Belle was kind enough not to laugh at Kenny's consternation. She just stood, silently watching, her hands on her hips.

"I — uh, thank you, I just can't — " Kenny continued to back away, fighting the urge to turn and run. "Oh God..." she whispered as the other woman walked toward her, matching her steps. She was humiliated to picture herself in this situation, being backed down by a whore. A man would never allow it. Setting her jaw in a firm line, she stopped, not looking away from Belle's eyes as she approached.

"That's better," Belle said as she stood before Kenny. "Now why are you so afraid? I don't hurt anyone who don't ask for it, and don't pay extra."

Kenny wished she could call Belle's hand and take her into the small, dirty room she rented at the boarding house. She imagined pushing the woman down on the bed and watching her face as she slowly undressed, revealing a leaner version of the same soft curves that Belle advertised so prominently. But she knew she could not afford to destroy the identity she had built in exchange for a pointless revenge.

"I just can't," Kenny said resolutely. "I have a girl..."

She let her voice trail away.

"Oh, that's it, huh?" Belle pursed her crimson lips in thought. "Well, I hope she's as faithful to you."

"I'm sure...I'm sure she is."

"Well, my offer still stands if you change your mind."

Kenny stood calmly without flinching as Belle leaned forward to kiss her cheek.

"So smooth," Belle exclaimed, reaching up to rub the back of her hand against Kenny's skin. "Don't you ever have to shave?"

Kenny ducked her head, feigning embarrassment to hide the grin she could not suppress. "Not often, ma'am," she admitted.

"Well, don't be ashamed. It feels better than the grizzled animals I got to sleep with." Belle gathered her skirts with one hand and patted her hair with the other. "Look me up...you'd be a nice change for old Belle," she called over her shoulder as she swayed back toward the saloon.

"Like you could not imagine," Kenny said quietly to the woman's departing back. After Belle had disappeared safely inside the smoky barroom, Kenny slapped her hands against her hips and laughed out loud. Spinning around on her boot heel, she felt daring, she felt so very cocky. She could pull this off and fool them all, the last week had proven that. The family she'd never truly belonged in would never find her now. She had it made; a strong, twenty-year-old woman with a man's clothes, a man's job, and best of all, a man's freedom. Kenny Smith would never again be Kendra Anne Nelson. She promised herself that.

TWO

Robert kept his word and grudgingly brought Sophie a gentle, brown mare.

After spending a week getting to know each other, the woman and the horse had bonded, Sophie feeling that they shared a mutual dislike of Robert. Already in love with the animal's peculiarities, Sophie had the sudden urge to ride her into town. The mare frisked and trotted, seeming to enjoy the opportunity to go with such a light weight upon her back. Sophie let her have her head and the horse went through her paces quickly, then settled into a smooth gallop. Leaning forward, Sophie laughed, loving the feel of the wind in her unbound hair and the strong muscles moving beneath her. Bravely, she tightened her legs on the horse's sides and closed her eyes, trusting her mount to carry her safely down the rough wagon track of a road.

Long before she was ready, she felt the mare slow to a canter. She opened her eyes to see that they had reached the small farms that lay just outside the flat, dusty ground of Jackson. Pulling the horse to the side of the wagon tracks, she dismounted near a tall tree stump and studied the town before her. Jackson was not an old town; established not more than ten years back, it nevertheless looked next to ruin. The buildings weathered quickly, battered each turn of the year by the harsh western Colorado winters and the blazing sun of summer. It was not a wholesome town; its purpose was obviously to provide entertainment for the cowhands and miners rather than safe, virtuous lives for its residents. There was no law.

Stomping her feet and brushing her palms down the front of her skirt, Sophie paced back and forth quickly. But her efforts did little to flatten the wrinkles formed when the cloth had bunched up around her thighs as she rode astride. When the dress looked as good as she thought it could without an ironing, she led the horse to the stump. She climbed up on its jagged top, then slid over to sit sideways on the horse's broad back.

As the mare ambled forward at a more sedate and ladylike pace, Sophie gathered the heavy mass of her wind-tangled hair and tucked it up under her bonnet. The dust of the road tickled her nose and she frowned to hold back a sneeze.

Jackson was very busy; Sophie thought she had never seen the place so crowded. Buckboards jammed the streets, the hitching posts were all taken, and people crossed the dirt streets at their peril. Sophie turned off the main street and rode to the general store from behind. The back ways were empty in comparison to the commotion she'd just escaped.

"What's the occasion?" Sophie asked the back of her horse's head. The mare very slightly twitched one ear. "If you don't know, you could just admit it," she grumbled, not willing to admit that she herself had lost track of the day of the week.

Sophie slid to the ground and wrapped the reins lightly around the store's back drainpipe, hoping that the horse was not one that liked to roam. It was wiser to allow the mare to pull loose easily if she wanted, instead of taking the chance that she would rip the pipe from the wall. Sophie glared sternly into one liquid brown eye and commanded, "Stay." The horse was content to dip her head into the rain barrel beneath the drain and drink.

Sophie entered the narrow alley between the store and its neighboring building. Must be a saloon, the young widow surmised as she picked her way through the litter of empty and broken bottles. The tavern was silent, although she remembered it standing open earlier than this. Perhaps today is Sunday, she thought, but doubted that the town banned drinking on the Sabbath. But that would explain the crowds of people...She nodded decisively, feeling a little less out of touch now that she imagined she knew what day it was.

Sophie stepped out of the alley and edged along the crowded boardwalk. Not since the long ago and hardly imaginable days of living and teaching school in Boston had she been around so many people. The isolation she had endured during her marriage and subsequent widowhood had made the press of people offensive to her. Pausing in front of the screen door, she appraised the interior of the busy store. It seemed less crowded than the street, so she ducked inside.

The store was airless and stifling. The huge, high-ceilinged room had no windows. Oil lamps were lit in their holders, spaced evenly down the lengths of the side walls. The wares were arranged in tall stacks that threatened to overflow into the narrow walkways. Sophie slipped down an unoccupied aisle, one that was clearly unpopular this time of year owing to its offering of galoshes, woolen socks, and other winter supplies.

She stood fingering the corner of a thick blanket until her breath came easier and her ears grew accustomed to the din.

"Mrs. McLaren."

Sophie looked up at the sound of the pleasant voice. A lanky man with a sliver of waxed mustache smiled down at her. He was wearing a cap that apparently set him apart as a clerk.

Startled at being recognized, she spoke tensely. "Who are you? How do you know my name?"

"I'm Abe Black, I'm a clerk here, and I make it a point to remember names and faces," he explained cheerfully. "You came in with your husband last — " his voice stopped abruptly and his ears turned a deep red. He swallowed and spoke again, "I saw you here last October."

Sophie nodded slowly, ignoring the clerk's discomfort at mentioning her departed husband. The situation seemed to upset him more than it had ever bothered her.

"Can I help you find somethin'?" he asked uneasily.

"Just point me toward the needles and thread."

"You'll find those in the northwest corner, right under that stuffed moose head."

Sophie peered over the stacks at the poor, startled-looking animal. It was not what one would call a fine specimen, possibly having died of mange prior to being mounted on the wall. She tried to soften her expression before she turned back to the clerk.

"Thank you," she said softly. "I think I can find the rest on my own."

"Suit yourself." He sent her a grateful smile before loping down the aisle toward another customer whom he undoubtedly knew by name.

Two hours later Sophie had finally collected the small pile of things that she needed. She could safely say that she would never again have to ask for help in finding anything here. Except for bullets.

Her long skirts brushing the shelves to either side, Sophie carried her choices to the narrow counter that ran along the back wall. A different clerk stood behind it. He appeared harassed and surly, but he spoke politely enough.

"This'll be all?"

Sophie imagined him thinking that she should have bought more after taking up space for two hours. "Just that and a box of bullets."

"What kind?"

Sophie looked at him blankly.

"What kind a gun are they for?" He spoke slowly, clearly, as if he suddenly doubted her ability to understand English.

Sophie knew she would regret her words even as she spoke them. "A rifle?"

*K*enny's head ached with a dull throb. Another night had passed with her again asleep in her chair at the window, her forehead resting against the frame. It was her habit to straddle the chair backwards and prop it against the wall to view the street below. She had never lived in a town before and she was fascinated by the parade of people that came and went at all hours of the day and night. Even living on her father's small piece of land in the desolation of the Utah desert, Kenny found herself wanting to stay awake later and later into the night. There was something about darkness. The way it made the familiar so strange and exotic intrigued her. Had she known that, in a town, so much action continued on after nightfall, she would have much sooner tried to escape the constraints of that lonely life.

Dressing slowly, she wound the cotton band tight around her chest. She made a futile search for her striped pants, even cautiously getting down on all fours to look under the bed before she remembered that she'd left them with the landlady to be cleaned. Sighing, she pulled on her denim jeans and hoped that she wouldn't forget to pick up her work pants before the afternoon run.

Her headache faded as her blood got moving. She pulled a fresh blue bandanna out of her drawer and tied it securely over the deep scar that crossed her throat and trailed down past her collarbone. The long, curved knife that hung from her belt dug into her hip as she sat down on the window sill to pull on her boots. While shifting the knife to the side, her attention was caught by a figure on the boardwalk across the street.

A slim, brown-skinned woman sidled past the storefront, avoiding contact with the other pedestrians. Her skirts were full, but the dress seemed old and plain, and her looks were nothing outstanding. Kenny noted the long, wispy curls of black hair that escaped the confines of a tattered

bonnet and dangled down her slender back. Wondering why
her attention had been drawn to the unassuming figure, she
continued to watch as the woman hesitated at the door, then
quickly stepped inside.

Kenny shook her head as if clearing away mental
cobwebs and pushed her feet into her boots. The big, black hat
she had stolen from her father during her escape would top off
her outfit. Kenny was sure she looked good, but she wished she
could check herself in a mirror. Why did women assume men
would not want to look at themselves? The landlady had
intentionally picked a room without a mirror when Kenny first
came to the boarding house. She ran her fingers through her
close-cropped, brown hair one last time before angling the hat
down over her forehead.

The hallway echoed her footsteps as she clattered down
the stairs, and as soon as she hit the street, she was running.
Her long legs felt strong as her muscles pumped. I could pull
that stage myself, she bragged to herself, feeling proud and
outrageous and not the least bit ladylike. Not that, never again.

Her pace slowed as she passed the undertaker's parlor.
Through the front window she could see the large, shadowy
bulk of what at first glance seemed to be a long narrow coffin,
but was actually a grandfather clock. It was 9:30 and she had
more than three hours before she had to meet the stage. Plenty
of time for a leisurely breakfast at the hotel restaurant, and then
perhaps a stroll or two past the cribs.

When she'd first come to Jackson, she had no idea what
the cribs could possibly be. She'd slunk past the row of tiny,
narrow shacks lined up behind the saloons as she learned the
lay of the town. The buildings confused her. They were
obviously too nice for pigs, but much too small for people.
Why, those rooms wouldn't hold much more than a bed for
furnishings, she remembered thinking, not realizing how close
she was to the truth.

Frank had educated her not long after they began to
work together. Since then, she had spent plenty of time

thinking about the prostitutes taking their customers to those little rooms, but her imagination stopped just outside the door. She understood the act of sexual intercourse, she just couldn't picture those soft, white women with any stinking man. Her revulsion didn't prevent her from walking that street and seeing what she could see.

Lost in her thoughts, Kenny was halfway past the restaurant before she knew it. Backtracking, she jumped the steps, and pulled open the screen door. Her favorite table was free, as usual, and the waitress sent her a friendly wave as she hooked a chair with her boot and pulled it to face the window. Three weeks and Kenny had already established a comfortable routine. Within five minutes Hannah, the waitress, would bring Kenny three eggs, some slices of plain bread, and coffee with honey. Kenny would smile shyly, not speaking until Hannah found a clever way to make her say something. Kenny suspected that Hannah found her voice attractive and she had learned long ago not to give away anything that someone else really wanted.

Kenny ate slowly, watching the people walk back and forth on the street before her. This was her town, she told herself, not for the first time. The realization always came with a little tingle of pleasure that made her grin. People of the town were getting used to seeing her on the streets. They sometimes even acknowledged her by name. Kenny loved to tip her hat at the ladies and receive their friendly, and occasionally flirting, smiles and nods. She was learning to appreciate her own worth, and just the look in the waitress's eye when Kenny came through the door was more kindness than she'd ever gained at home.

Hannah brought her a third cup of coffee and the bill. Kenny signed it for the coach company, as always adding on an extra nickel for Hannah. The food was free to her, but the tip would be taken out of her wages. It was a small price to pay for the welcome Hannah made her feel.

Back out on the dusty street, Kenny smiled up into the

already blazing sun and let its warmth soak into her bones. She was ambling toward the back streets in a mood of lazy contentment. Just as she reached the general store, she hesitated. The image of wispy black curls came to her mind. Before she could think twice about it, she'd entered the shop.

The woman was in the third aisle Kenny tried. She was studying a stack of fabric bolts, lightly touching the different textured cloths, touching and rejecting. Kenny studied her profile. Her initial impression did not change. The woman was plain, almost severe in her concentration, and her skin was a little too brown for Kenny's liking. Probably hasn't smiled for a year or two, Kenny decided, ready to find a reason to dismiss her from notice.

But then the woman turned to face Kenny. Well, she was better looking from the front, Kenny allowed. Her eyes were light-colored, blue or gray, and they were contrasted nicely by her dark brows. Kenny smiled her most winning smile as she approached, and was startled as the woman seemed to look right through her. The woman's elbow had actually brushed along Kenny's side, and yet, she evidently took no notice of Kenny's presence.

Kenny stood in the aisle for several minutes after the woman had gone. Somehow Kenny had gotten used to being noticed since she'd become a man. She wasn't actually vain at this point, but her pride had certainly found a new life. The hardest thing for her to accept at this moment was that the woman had not been rude, she had just been completely unaware that another living being had stood between her and the next item on her shopping list.

Kenny waved off the approach of a lanky clerk and rounded the aisle she suspected the woman had taken. For the next half hour she followed her, never attempting to avoid notice, never being noticed. Occasionally she asked herself what the hell she thought she was doing, but did not receive much in the line of an answer.

After touching and practically smelling every item in

the store, the woman finally gathered her choices and walked to the back of the room. Kenny followed, just within earshot. When the woman said, "A rifle?" in a voice that pained Kenny to hear, she stepped forward and spoke before the man behind the counter could.

"He means the caliber of the gun, ma'am."

The woman turned and her eyes met Kenny's for the first time.

Kenny felt a shiver of dread along her backbone, and suddenly wished that she could do something, anything to take back her words and remain unseen by that gaze. She felt she was being inspected, sized up and measured, and she was sure she didn't want to know the results of that appraisal. For the first time since taking on her new life, she was seriously afraid that her masquerade would be exposed.

"The caliber of the gun," the woman repeated. Her expression had not changed, giving no clue to the judgment she had made of Kenny's appearance. "I'm afraid I don't know what that is."

The precise words heightened Kenny's uneasiness. The woman's voice was educated, cultured, with an accent Kenny had come to associate with Easterners. Feeling like a crude barbarian, she tried to breathe deeply and relax a little. After all, she wasn't the one with no idea what caliber meant. "Maybe it'd help if you looked at some of the different bullets," she suggested. "Maybe you'd recognize them from the size."

The woman cocked her head slightly. The gesture conveyed doubt, but the clerk had already placed several open boxes on the counter. She turned reluctantly and picked out a bullet at random. A long moment passed as she studied it, then slid it gently back into its box.

Kenny watched her silent movements. When she finally hesitated at a certain size, Kenny spoke again. "That's for a 30.06. That caliber's very common."

"Thirty ought six..." the woman murmured, then looked at Kenny with the most articulate expression of skepticism that Kenny had ever seen.

Kenny realized the woman thought Kenny was making fun of her. The woman had not said anything to make Kenny think that, but she had no doubt that it was true. At a loss for what to say, she pointed to the numbers on the box.

"30.06," she stated defensively.

The woman nodded once, a shallow acceptance of Kenny's truthfulness. "I think it would be best if I returned with the gun."

Kenny and the clerk agreed. The man licked his pencil tip and mumbled as he began adding up her purchases. Kenny stood for an awkward moment, then started to back away. The woman's look stopped her.

"Thank you for trying to help me," she said with a tone smooth as honey, but with no apparent depth. She then held her hand out to Kenny. "I'll be better prepared next time."

Kenny took her hand and pressed it lightly, wishing she had the nerve to drop a gentle kiss on the slightly rough skin. "My pleasure, ma'am." She gave her best smile one last shot and was rewarded by the appearance of a small, dimpled smile line on one side of the woman's face. She was charmed.

Kenny spent the rest of the morning on a cloud, feeling elated. She walked, but couldn't say where. Several people said hello, but she couldn't say who they were. When the time came to make the run to Stockton, she went to the stable in her blue jeans and Frank had to hold the stage while she ran home, collected her striped pants, and got changed.

As she drove the team out of town, whistling happily over the mumbled complaints of her hung-over shotgun man, she could have sworn she saw a woman galloping astride a brown mare. Just before the two disappeared over a grassy ridge, Kenny caught sight of a mass of black curls streaming out into the wind. Kenny grinned, mentally repeating the last words the woman had spoken to her. She had shyly, a little ruefully, asked, "Could you tell me the day of the week?"

*R*obert reined in his horse as they crested the small ridge that overlooked the line shack. Holding the animal still, he studied the house and yard below. The place, already showing the subtle touch of a woman's hand, seemed deserted. Robert pushed his hat back and spat to the side. His face was dark with an angry scowl, even darker than his usual mood. Instead of taking the time to contemplate why he found himself returning to the line shack, he just let himself be angry at his inability to resist coming. His desire was a weakness. A weakness caused by the evil of that woman. It was getting to where he could hardly close his eyes without seeing her body.

Robert shifted uncomfortably in the saddle. He sat with his legs taut in the stirrups, a position that pressed the front of his jeans hard against the saddle horn. The pressure on his crotch made him feel powerful and in control. It had become such a habit with him to sit that way that he no longer even realized he did it.

A sound that had been growing at the edge of his consciousness finally revealed itself as the pounding of hooves. Without thinking, Robert spurred his horse and sent it trotting into the cover of the woods that surrounded the clearing. When he was in far enough to be concealed from the rider, he swung his leg over and dropped down from the back of the horse. After tying the reins to a tree branch, he walked silently from the protection of one tree to another until he had a clear view of the shack below.

Sophie was just sliding down from the back of the mare when he got sight of her. The edge of her dress caught on the horse's rump and pulled back to expose the white skin of her leg. Robert sucked in a hard breath and narrowed his eyes. The woman was a slut. His stomach burned as he watched her rub the horse's head fondly. Her dark hair hung loose around her shoulders; even at this distance he could see the way the sunlight glinted on it. He thought of its softness and how it would feel twisted in his fingers.

Unconsciously, he tugged at the inseam of his jeans to relieve the pressure that was growing there. The memory of the morning he'd brought her to the shack flashed into his mind. Seeing the fear in her eyes when he'd pointed the gun at her had given him such a stab of pleasure that he'd thought he would fall from the horse. He liked that look, that feeling of domination. He wanted it again.

Sophie pulled the bridle from the mare's head and shooed her away. The horse ambled over to the water trough, bent her head to drink, then raised it suddenly as if she'd heard a sound beyond Sophie's range of hearing. Sophie listened intently for a moment, but heard nothing in the clearing or from the forest beyond. After a few seconds the horse dropped her head, apparently satisfied that there was nothing amiss. The apprehension was as quickly gone from Sophie's mind.

Hefting the small gunnysack of provisions she'd bought in town, Sophie crossed the porch and pushed the door open with her foot. The interior of the shack was dark and seemed incredibly dingy to her at that moment. She dropped the bag on the table and then propped the door open with a rock. If only she had the luxury of glass windows — the furnishings had too long been deprived of sunlight. Standing in the dim room, Sophie herself felt stifled and wished she had found an excuse to linger in town. The young man at the general store seemed about ready to ask her something, maybe to drink a cup of coffee or to take a stroll. Would she have done it? Sophie wrinkled her nose doubtfully. Certainly, at that moment, she would have said no, no matter what she was feeling now. Suddenly annoyed with herself, Sophie stripped down to one underskirt. Someone like that man would have no interest in a woman like her. She wasn't flashy enough, or to put it simply, she wasn't pretty enough.

Her hair was tangled from her reckless ride and she thought some sunlight would do her good as well. What she needed was a relaxing afternoon and a good hairbrushing. Taking her hairbrush from the small wooden box that served as her nightstand, she headed out the door. Suddenly, before her mind could make out the rushing shape that approached from the sun's glare as that of a man, she was grabbed and shoved face first against the wall.

Sophie found she couldn't scream or even gasp in pain as her arm was twisted behind her back. The force of her chest hitting the wooden beams had driven the air from her lungs. She tried to turn her head to see who held her, but the man grabbed her hair and pushed her face back against the bare wood. A sudden image of the rough young man in the store came to her frightened mind. His body pressed along the length of hers and she could feel the heat of it and the dampness of his sweat. Closing her eyes in an attempt to shut out her fear, she struggled to catch a breath.

"Stupid bitch," the man growled. His breath was hot against her ear. "I told you it wasn't safe for a woman out here alone."

"Robert?" she whispered, still unable to find her voice.

"Shut up." He pulled her body several inches away from the wall just to slam it back against the boards.

Sophie was prepared for that shove and managed to hold onto the breath she'd finally drawn, but her cheekbone struck the wall painfully. "Robert, what are you doing?" she screamed, unable to hide the desperation in her voice.

Roughly, he jerked back on her hair. Her neck bent and the sharp whiskers on the side of his face scraped her cheek. "Didn't I tell you to shut up?"

Sophie knew better than to speak again and he held her too tight for her to be able to nod her head. Closing her eyes again, she let her muscles become slack, and hoped he would be satisfied by her submission. He twisted her arm tighter to try to force her to cry out. Clenching her teeth against the pain, Sophie silently waited for whatever he had in mind.

"I came here to teach you a lesson." The words were

hoarse and grating. He was breathing hard and Sophie was horrified to realize it wasn't because of his exertions. "I told you to pack that rifle and I told you to lock that door. You didn't do either. Now I gotta wonder why."

Sophie felt a burning in her throat and was afraid she was going to be sick. Her legs had begun to shake. She prayed that she wouldn't faint.

Robert continued his accusations. "Either you are a stupid bitch...or you like this."

"Oh God, no!" The words were out before Sophie could stop them.

Robert laughed. The sound was more frightening than his voice had been. He rubbed his body against her back.

"Robert, please." Sophie tried to pull herself closer to the wall to avoid his touch. "I'm your brother's wife."

"My brother's dead. Remember?"

Sophie searched in desperation for the words to say to make him stop. "Allen told me you were a good man," she lied, trying to summon a calm to her voice. "I see what you're doing, Robert. I — I didn't pay attention to you before. I'm sorry."

Robert had stopped his movements as he listened to her speak. She quickly went on, "This was a good lesson for me, Robert. I understand now. Thank you."

Unbelievably, Robert released her and stepped back. Wincing at the pain in her muscles, Sophie pulled her arm around to press her hands tightly together. Suppressing a sob of relief, she leaned her forehead against the wall. When she was finally able to turn around, she found herself alone. Robert had, as silently as a ghost, disappeared from the room. The tears that had not come before suddenly poured from her eyes. Blinded, she groped for the door and slammed it shut. Her shaking hands fumbled with the latch. As it clicked into place, her strength gave out and she collapsed to the floor. Drawing her legs in close to her body, Sophie wrapped her arms around her knees and cried without a sound. Her eyes were open wide as she waited for his silent shadow to come back over her.

Three

D river, why are we stopping?"
Frank grinned at Kenny through his tobacco-stained mustache as the strident voice bellowed once again from the interior of the coach. Kenny bared her teeth and dragged her finger across her throat before saying pleasantly, "Just checkin' the horses, sir."

Frank tipped his hat to Kenny and crawled down from their high seat. The stage creaked and swayed as the weight shifted. He hurried up to stand in front of the lead horse and unbutton his jeans. Kenny laughed as his expression changed to one of immense relief.

"Isn't this the third time you have had to check the horses?" The voice was that of a preacher or banker, Kenny couldn't tell which by the man's appearance. With his attitude of moral superiority and well-fed laziness, he could be either. "Are the animals in such poor physical condition, or did the two of you harness them improperly?"

Kenny pressed her lips together to keep back the sarcastic remark that sprang to mind. Frank scuffled back to the coach and peered past the faded curtain into the side window. Standing silently, he eyed the man's girth. He belched from the depths of his belly, then said, "Could be we took on too much weight."

The passenger sputtered incoherently and Kenny had to quickly pull her hat down over her face to muffle her laughter.

Frank casually boosted himself back into his seat and settled back.

"You need to check yer own horse?"

"Nah. I can wait," she assured him.

"Well, you're a tougher man than me," Frank allowed. "I used to could handle it when I was younger. I guess the roads weren't as rough then."

With a click of her tongue, the horses pulled forward. "And the nights weren't as long, and bottles weren't as full, and the whores weren't as — "

"Now where'd ya learn to talk like that?" Frank interrupted sternly.

"From you."

"Well, all right then." Frank wiggled around trying to find a comfortable position for his skinny backbone. The coach hit a rut, jostling him over into the corner of the seat. "Perfect," he exclaimed, sighing with contentment.

"Driver! How long before we reach Stockton?"

"Did you hear somethin'?" Kenny asked.

"Not a thing," Frank assured her. "Although the woods through here are filled with jay birds. Sometimes they set up an awful racket. Just ignore 'em." Following his own advice, Frank closed his eyes and pulled his hat down low. Kenny drove ahead with a smile.

The road between Jackson and Stockton was not that rugged, but it was slow going due to the range of mountains that separated the two long valleys in which the towns nestled. Kenny let the horses choose their own pace up the grade; once they reached the down side she would encourage them to step it up. The only experience Kenny had driving, previous to this job, was the time she had spent on her father's buckboard. She'd learned by driving back and forth to town to pick up the supplies demanded by her father's wives. That responsibility had taught her to be patient with the horses. But what really made her a good driver was her willingness to look at the road from the horses' perspective and not force them to tire themselves too early in the journey.

As they crested the pass below the mountain's shoulder, the desert beyond the range opened to her view. She hated to even look in that direction. Her consolation was the beauty of the setting sun and the knowledge that the road crooked south at the foot of the mountains and wouldn't turn back toward the red rock canyons until well beyond Stockton. Kenny lifted her chin defiantly at the expanse of sand and sagebrush and whistled the horses into a trot. They headed down the slope eagerly.

The stagecoach arrived at Stockton by nightfall. With a new team of horses and a new driver, it would continue on through the night toward Price. Kenny and Frank would spend the night in Stockton, then relay the eastbound stage back to Jackson first thing in the morning.

Kenny sat on the edge of her bed in the town's only hotel and contemplated a bath. She was covered head to toe with road dust and she couldn't stand the thought of crawling into clean sheets as filthy as she was. Prying off her boots, she regretfully wiggled her tired, dirty toes. The men's bath house was not private and there was no way she could go near the women's room. She eyed the corner washstand with its basin and pitcher of lukewarm water. A small square of cloth hung from a peg. It would at least remove the top layer of dust, a reasonable compromise.

After closing the curtains, Kenny undressed fully and scrubbed her skin with the wet washcloth. Being naked had always felt like freedom to her, and now, having her breasts unbound felt purely liberating. She rubbed until her whole body was a bright pink, then stood in the middle of the room to air dry. Refreshed, she pulled back her blankets and lay down on the cool, clean sheets.

As she rested, her muscles slowly began to relax. Kenny stretched her arms out above her head and sighed. She closed her eyes and waited for sleep to come. What came instead was the image of a woman, the woman Kenny had encountered at the general store. Kenny smiled to herself, remembering the faint, sweet scent that had reached up to her nose from the woman's hair. She let herself wonder if the woman had a husband. If they were lying in bed as well...

Kenny took a deep breath and opened her eyes. Probably, she should have been ashamed of her thoughts, but she wasn't. Crossing her long legs, she wiggled her toes happily. She liked thinking that way.

Looking down at her own small breasts, Kenny thought that woman's had been larger. They had strained against the cloth of her dress as she breathed. Kenny had been hard pressed not to stare. She wondered what they looked like without clothing. Were her nipples as dark? Did they change and get tight when she was excited? Kenny touched a light fingertip to her own nipple and wondered what it tasted like and how it would feel inside her mouth. She imagined opening the front of the woman's dress and bending her head down. What she would do, she told herself, would be to let her tongue just glide across the woman's breast and then lightly tease her nipple. It was easy to envision the woman's breath quickening and her hand reaching up to hold the back of Kenny's head. Kenny would then lead her to the bed, which always happened to be nearby in her fantasies, and carefully guide her down onto the sheets.

Kenny had the long-held desire to run her hand up under a woman's skirts and along the inside of her thigh. She pictured the woman's face: it would be framed by her dark hair, and her stern expression would change as Kenny touched her. Those blue-gray eyes would burn with desire...

The fantasy could have gone on through half of the night. Could have and would have if an urgent pounding on the door hadn't startled her. Quickly, she sat up, scrambled for the blankets, and clutched them to her chest. She couldn't recall if she had locked the door.

"Kenny!" a familiar voice yelled from the hallway.

"Frank? What the hell do you want?"

"You, ya dumb ass," Frank hollered. He had clearly taken no time at all to begin a drunk. "What are ya doin' in there?"

"Tryin' to sleep. It would be a good idea for you to do the same." She let her irritation fly.

"Bullshit!"

Kenny's stomach dropped as the doorknob rattled. Frank cussed at the door, but it did not open. Taking a chance, Kenny jumped out of the bed and struggled into her pants.

"Open the damn door, kid. I want to talk to ya." Frank's loud whine set her teeth on edge.

With shaking hands, Kenny grabbed up her breast band. There was no way she could get it wrapped around herself quickly enough with Frank out there banging on the door and he was likely to force it open at the worst time. She shoved the band under the mattress and pulled on her shirt.

"Just give me a minute!" she yelled, trying to button her shirt properly. Unfortunately, the material wasn't thick enough to hide the fear-hardened points of her nipples. She looked down at herself, then hunched her shoulders forward so the cloth stood away from her breasts.

"This better be good," she warned as she opened the door.

Frank stood leaned against the doorjamb, a sloppy smile stretched across his drunken face.

"What is it?" she asked with no pretense of patience.

"What is what?" Frank's expression showed his confusion.

"What the hell do you want?"

The old man worked up an attitude of hurt feelings. Kenny didn't fall for it and continued to glare at him. "I just wanted to talk to ya, maybe come in fer a drink." A half-empty bottle appeared before her face.

"No," she stated firmly. There was no way she would let him into her room — she couldn't hold this posture for long. But getting rid of her persistent old friend did not prove to be easy. Their argument continued for several minutes before she finally made the compromise to meet him in the saloon.

"In fifteen minutes," Frank repeated as he staggered down the hall. "Or I'm comin' back for ya."

Thirteen minutes later, Kenny stood in the doorway of Stockton's best saloon. It was a long, narrow building, lit garishly by innumerable oil lamps fastened along the walls. Dark smoke from the oil mixed with the lighter haze of cigarette smoke and rose in a cloud. Since the saloon had no ceiling, Kenny could see right up to the angled boards that formed the roof. There was no telling if the floor was wooden; six inches of filthy sawdust covered it from wall to wall. Peering through the bright light and haze of smoke, Kenny found her partner leaned against the end of the bar, arguing with an old cowhand who seemed only slightly less sober than Frank himself. Their voices rose over the raucous sounds of a piano and other drunken voices. She worked her way carefully through the crowd of drinkers.

Frank didn't recognize her until she was standing next to him. "There ya are," he shouted triumphantly, waving an indignant finger under the cowhand's nose. "This guy'll back me up."

The cowhand snorted with laughter. "If I ain't stupid enough to believe you, I'm surely smart enough not to believe any friend of yours."

"What are you arguin' about?" Kenny knew she would probably regret asking.

"You ain't gonna believe it," Frank assured her. "But this damn fool says...he thinks that..." He scratched his head for a moment, then turned back to the cowhand. "What was it you said?"

"I didn't say nothing! It was you that bought it all up in the first place."

"You sayin' I started this?" Frank was incredulous. "You're the one who called me a liar."

"I did no such thing, you — "

Kenny shook her head and turned away from the two

blustering old men. Leaned back against the bar, she looked around at the saloon's other patrons, careful not to allow her gaze to rest on any one man for too long. To do that was to invite trouble. But she had no such hesitation with staring openly at the room's few women. After some minutes of intense study, she was forced to conclude that Jackson's whores were much more beautiful.

"What'll you be drinking?"

Kenny turned around at the sound of the voice. A short, broad-shouldered Irishman stood at the other side of the bar and looked at her expectantly. His posture suggested that he was guarding the long line of glass bottles behind him. Half of them appeared to be full of dirty water and Kenny was not the least interested in sampling their tastes.

"Uh, nothin'. Thank you, sir," Kenny said quickly.

"Give him a shot of whiskey," Frank demanded.

"No, Frank. I done told you I don't drink."

"Ya gotta drink." Frank's words were slurred, making his sentence sound like one long word.

The bartender waited patiently for their argument to finish.

"Why do I have to drink?"

"Because...because it's my birthday," Frank proclaimed.

"Well, congratulations," the bartender laughed.

Kenny glared at him in doubt. "Why didn't you mention that before now?"

"I just plain forgot." Frank leaned smugly into her face. His breath was overpowering — she could get as drunk from the smell of him as she could from a drink. "Now, are ya gonna refuse to celebrate with me?"

"Just one?" she asked. Frank nodded. "If you buy me more than one, I'll dump it right out," she warned.

"Just one. I couldn't bear to see no good liquor wasted like that."

Frank had finally said something tonight that Kenny could believe. The bartender poured two generous shots of a pale brown liquid. He handed her one of the glasses and she sniffed it cautiously. It smelled like autumn, when the leaves were piled thick and wet on the ground and the air had that sharply pleasant bite to it. She brought her lips to the edge of the glass and started to take a sip. Frank grabbed her hand and pulled the glass away.

"No, no. Ya don't drink it that a way." He shook his head in exasperation. "Like this…" The glass disappeared under his furry mustache and he tilted his head back quickly, drinking down the contents in one gulp.

Kenny raised her eyebrows doubtfully, but the bartender nodded encouragement. Shrugging, she tilted back her own glass.

Liquid fire burned from her lips, seared past her lungs, and gathered down into the pit of her stomach. She gasped one short breath and began to choke. Frank leaned her over and pounded encouragingly but ineffectively on her back. She tried to push him away, but every time she almost got a breath he knocked it out of her.

Frank and the bartender were laughing at her. The sound made her furious, but she was incapable of doing anything except struggle for a breath that didn't reignite that fire.

When she finally straightened up and wiped the tears from her eyes, the two of them had assumed sober, concerned expressions. The bartender slid her another glass, a taller one filled with a bubbly yellow brew. She shook her head and pushed the glass away.

"It's just beer," the bartender assured her. "It don't taste near as good, but it'll put out that fire."

Frank slid the glass back over to her. "I'm sorry, pard. That was a mean trick to pull on ya, but it's kind of a tradition."

The bartender agreed. " 'Twas the way I got my first taste of whiskey."

"And was it your last?" Kenny wheezed.

The two men laughed. Kenny reached out cautiously

and lifted the glass, taking a very small, cautious sip of the cool beer. It was bitter on her tongue, but it felt good going down. She took a longer drink and sighed. It didn't taste half bad.

Reaching into her pocket, she pulled out a handful of coins. It was all the money she had. The coins rang as she dropped them on the bar, but the bartender shook his head.

"Your friend has already set up a tab," he explained. "And I've been told to add your drinks to it."

"I think this one will do it for me."

He shrugged. "Suit yourself," he added, before heading to the other end of the long counter.

Turning to face the room, her elbows on the bar and her boot heel hooked over the low metal rail that ran the length of the counter, Kenny was beginning to feel warm and friendly inside, almost to the point where she could forgive Frank for dragging her out of bed. She looked over at him and smiled.

"What?" Frank asked suspiciously.

Kenny just laughed.

Wary, Frank watched her until he decided that she was not going to seek vengeance on him. "Do ya want to dance?" he asked abruptly.

His question shocked her speechless. The first thought in her mind was that he had seen through her disguise. But wouldn't he be angry at her passing herself off as a man? She finally managed to stammer, "You — you want to dance with me?"

"Not with you, ya idiot!" Frank gave her a cuff upside the head that knocked her hat off onto the sawdust-covered floor. "With them." He swung his arm out to point at several prostitutes who lounged near the battered piano.

When Kenny leaned over to scoop up her hat, she had to fight to get upright again. The walls swayed and the temperature seemed to be rising rapidly in the crowded room. The beer was cool; it would help to reduce her body heat, she reasoned, as she finished off the glass.

"Dancin' is thirsty work," Frank warned her. "We'd better get you another 'fore we get started."

Kenny hesitated for a moment, wanting nothing more than to walk across the room and take one of those women into her arms. But she was damned if she even knew how to dance.

Frank signaled the bartender and he quickly brought them two more beers. Kenny took hers with a shrug. It couldn't be too bad for her — it was so mild she wasn't even sure it had alcohol in it.

Frank clinked his glass against hers. "Shall we, then?" he asked before pushing her out to walk just ahead of him.

They crossed the room slowly. Weaving carefully between the tables, she avoided looking up at the faces she approached. Her belly filled with dread. Would the women laugh at her, thinking she was too young to even be in here? Would they expect her to know how to dance? Would they touch her in a way that would give away her secret?

Suddenly, her fears became overwhelming. Kenny turned to escape but Frank caught her by the arm and propelled her forward. The smell of his sweat filled her nose and she was thankful that she had at least cleaned herself up after work. She stared at the toes of her boots as Frank greeted the women. He elbowed her in the ribs and she instinctively pulled off her hat and crushed it to her chest. Their voices went on speaking, but the words were muffled by the pounding of the blood in her head. Startled, she looked up when someone took the beer from her hand.

A plump, blonde woman, probably old enough to be Kenny's mother, stood holding her drink and smiling. The woman was dressed in faded blue satin and lace and her heavy breasts were pushed up beneath the lace until they formed a broad shelf of pearly white flesh.

"Do you want to dance?" she asked kindly.

"No, ma'am," Kenny whispered. Seeing the woman's frown, Kenny quickly added, "I mean, yes, ma'am. But, I don't know how."

"I never yet met a man that did," she informed Kenny with a smile. "Just watch your friend there." Taking Kenny's

arm, she stood close to her, pointing out to the dance floor
where Frank was stomping his feet with abandon. His partner
appeared out of breath and dizzy already.

"You want me to do that?"

"No. I want you to do anything but that. Really, all
you got to do is relax and I can show you how to step."

In an effort to relax, Kenny let out a shaky breath and
nodded.

"First, put your hat back on and drink your beer."

Following orders, Kenny gulped the drink down and
turned to face her partner. The woman took Kenny's left hand
and put it on her smooth waist. Holding her right hand, she
tried to pull Kenny's rigid body closer to her. Kenny balked.

"I don't know your name," she stalled.

The woman laughed. "You're a young one, ain't ya? Just
call me Sally."

"Sally...Smith?"

"Now how'd you know that?" Sally teased.

"Lucky guess." Kenny took a deep breath and wiped
her sweating palm on her striped pant leg before again moving
close to Sally.

"That's better," the prostitute encouraged. "Now, we're
gonna do what's called the two-step. It's easy, just two steps
forward, then one back." Moving smoothly, she dragged Kenny
along with her.

Kenny stumbled on the back step, took the two forward
much too quickly, and almost stepped on Sally's foot. Sally
stopped on the edge of the dance floor.

"Let's count the steps together," she suggested. "It is
one, two, then back one. One, two, one. One, two, one."

Kenny whispered the count under her breath, her body
held out at an angle from Sally's as she looked down to watch
their feet. The women made a complete revolution of the dance
floor without a misstep.

"Now stop countin'."

The counting stopped and the dance continued

smoothly. Kenny grinned.

"Now stop lookin' at our feet."

Looking up into Sally's friendly eyes, Kenny promptly stomped on her foot.

"No, don't stop," Sally said with a grimace as Kenny tried to pull away. After an awkward moment of getting their steps back in time, they danced smoothly again. "That's better. Later we'll try followin' the music."

A smile warmed her face as they danced, Kenny slowly allowing herself to be pulled closer toward Sally's body. The sweet perfume that Sally had bathed herself in drifted around them; the woman smelled like lilacs and something else that Kenny thought she should recognize but did not. It was a wonderful smell. Women themselves were wonderful. Kenny snuggled in closer and allowed Sally's breasts to press against her chest. Dancing was the most wonderful thing ever invented.

"Hon," Sally whispered in Kenny's ear. "The music has stopped."

They danced and drank long into the night. Frank had disappeared hours ago, but before he left he had pulled Kenny aside. Yelling in what he thought was a confidential whisper, he told Kenny that "everything was taken care of, if Kenny decided this was the time."

"The time for what?" Kenny had asked.

Frank had shaken his head sadly and walked away.

Ultimately, Kenny figured out what milestone Frank had meant. Comprehension came as she was sitting at a corner table with Sally's arms wrapped around her and her tongue teasing Kenny's earlobe.

"I'm too drunk," she thought aloud.

Sally pulled her lips away from Kenny's throat and asked, "Too drunk for what?"

"It's my first time."

"First time drinkin'? Or first time makin' love?"

"Both," Kenny confessed with a mournful expression.

Sally tried to hide her laughter, but did not succeed. "I'm sorry," she gasped. "There's really nothin' to be ashamed of though."

"I'm not ashamed, ma'am. I just want my first time to be...well, special. I don't want to be too drunk to do it right."

The laughter disappeared from Sally's face and was replaced by a look of tenderness not often seen on the faces of women like her. "Oh, that is so sweet."

Leaning forward, Kenny put a poorly placed kiss on the side of Sally's mouth. "So, you wouldn't mind if I didn't...you know?"

"Of course I wouldn't mind," Sally swore. "I shouldn't have let you drink so much anyway. You wait right here, I'm gonna have the bartender brew you up some coffee."

Sally was up and gone in a swirl of satin before Kenny could protest. The hard slats of the chair dug into her back as she sat up and tried to bring the room into better focus. That struggle lasted a very short time before she gave it up. Suddenly, she was very tired. With a sigh, she crossed her arms on the table and rested her head on her forearms. Her mind wavered between consciousness and sleep.

The sound of a chair scraping the floor across from her made her raise her head. Expecting to see Sally with a cup of hot coffee, she was instead faced by a hulking, hard-featured man she had never seen before. He reached over and put a glass of beer down in front of her as she stared at him wordlessly.

"I wanted to buy you whiskey, but the bartender said you don't care much for it," the man said without introduction.

Kenny didn't care to drink the beer either, but something in his eyes said he wouldn't be pleased if she refused his offer. Raising the glass, she took a small sip. "Thank you, sir."

He nodded. "You work for the stage line."

"How'd you know?" Her voice was sharp with suspicion.

With a sound much more pleasant than the look in his eyes, the man laughed. "Those pants you're wearing ain't too common."

Kenny looked down at the gray and black stripes and smiled back at him.

"So, what kind a work do you do for 'em?"

"I'm a driver," Kenny stated with drunken pride.

"Is that right?" He raised his eyebrows, and Kenny thought that he looked at her with a little more respect.

"That's right. I work out of Jackson."

"Nice town. I know some men who work the mines in that area," he said casually, stretching his booted feet out to the chair next to her. "You ever been out to the mines? Leeland's Glory and them?"

"Yeah, I make the run out there every other Friday."

"Drivin' the coach? Guess you don't get to see much, goin' out there at night."

"We don't go at night. We leave Jackson late afternoon, usually get to Leeland's 'bout seven o'clock." Kenny began to feel a bit uncomfortable and wished Frank were still around. Maybe she had said too much. She suspected that this man's questions were not as innocent as his manner tried to make them appear.

"How many of you make that run?"

Kenny stood up and struggled to stay balanced on her feet. The man looked up at her, his expression inscrutable. "I don't think I should be talkin' to you, sir."

"You 'fraid of something, boy?" the man taunted her.

"No, I ain't afraid of nothin'," she lied. "But I ain't stupid either."

"Is that right?"

Looking down at the long-barreled pistol the man wore on his hip, Kenny kept her mouth shut. As drunk as she was, it was obvious to her that the man was trying to make her do something foolish. She didn't know if she could just walk away from him without him following her into the street. Scared and indecisive, she stood there as the man just smiled, waiting for her to make a move.

Just then, Kenny felt a light touch on her shoulder. Her reflexes were so slowed by alcohol that she didn't even jump. It was Sally. Kenny was afraid to turn away from the man to look at her.

"Kenny, I brought your coffee. Now why don't you come over to the bar and join me?"

Tension roughened Sally's voice. The man put his feet on the floor and stood up slowly. Kenny took a deep breath and hoped that Sally had enough sense to walk away. She held her ground as the man stepped up to her, his thumbs hooked over his belt buckle.

"Next time, you buy the drinks," he said softly, then walked out of the saloon.

Staring at the door, Kenny batted her eyes several times in confusion. Next to her, she heard Sally release a tight breath. "What the hell was that all about?" Kenny asked her in a low voice.

"I was just goin' to ask you that," Sally said gruffly, trying to hide her concern. "I didn't know that I couldn't leave you alone for a minute."

"But I didn't — " Kenny tried to protest.

"Get over there and drink your coffee, then I'm taking you to your room," she ordered, aiming Kenny's staggering steps in the right direction. "Didn't know I was getting into baby-sittin' this late in my life."

"I'm sorry. I can take care of myself — "

"Just shut up and sit down." Sally sat next to her and shook her head reproachfully. "If you wasn't so damn good lookin'..."

The compliment went right past Kenny as she cradled the hot cup between her shaking hands. "I got a bad feelin'," she whispered into the rising steam. "A really bad feelin'."

Four

Sophie drank her morning coffee out on the front porch, her feet propped up on the wobbly railing and the rifle beside her. She had awakened before daybreak, troubled by insubstantial bits of her dreams. All during her morning ritual she was plagued with the feeling of almost remembering what she'd dreamed, but if she stopped her actions to concentrate on the feeling it would dart away from her, only to return when she gave up trying. A nagging sense of foreboding kept her sitting on the porch longer than usual.

Putting the cup on the floor beside her chair, Sophie leaned back against the wall. A faint blue bruise shadowed the line of her cheekbone. The nervous tension that had gripped her shoulders since Robert's "lesson" would not be relieved, no matter what position she took. She could not get comfortable, but still she sat.

There were chores she could be doing. But what did it matter, really? she asked herself. She could sit here until nightfall, if that was what she pleased. Robert could take his browbeating and go to hell. A shadow of a grin crossed her lips. The idea of answering to no one was new to her, and the pleasure of the situation had a guilty taste to it. Breathing deeply of the late morning air, she closed her eyes and determined to be as lazy as she wished.

Allen had not asked much of her, she thought in response to a fragment of her dreams. But he had not given much either. He never seemed to want to know her, only to know that she was there. Where, didn't matter — in his kitchen, in his bed — just somewhere in his life.

He had never been able to read her or respond to her moods. They never talked about their feelings, but that was no different from the rest of Sophie's life. No one had ever touched her deeply or reached inside her, past the layer of coldness she wore around her emotions. In turn, she responded by moving farther and farther inward as the years went by. Her speech became slower, her reactions slower, and oftentimes she didn't bother answering when someone spoke to her.

Suspecting that Robert thought she was stupid or addled in the brain, Sophie hoped he would continue to think of her that way; it somehow seemed much safer for her to be underestimated by him. Oh, but she despised him. If she had met Robert before she had become betrothed to Allen, she would have refused the marriage. Then where would she be now?

The memory of where and who she'd been before coming west flashed unbidden into her mind. The life she had lost because of her insatiable curiosity could never be regained. She'd lost Boston, a good teaching job in her father's private school, and all the money she had stashed away for her future. Even intelligent women make bad choices, she consoled herself. Really, she had just been unlucky.

Her downfall had come from her curiosity about sexual intercourse. Never feeling compelled by the desires that seemed to befall her friends, she felt, nonetheless, that she should see what the fuss was about. One time was enough to leave her convinced that sex was highly overrated. Unfortunately, that one time was also enough to leave her pregnant. Her family was scandalized. Sophie found herself relieved of her position and made a prisoner in her own family's home. For seven months she was locked in an upstairs room and given food and water, but very little else. No one spoke to her. She was refused even the temporary escape of a book.

Her mother could not help but hear Sophie's screams when the baby came, but the door never opened. Sophie had no idea of the number of hours it took for her to deliver. She kept losing consciousness. Certain that the baby had died inside her, she just wished to stop and die herself. But her body labored on, still intent on carrying out its duty. The last hours of that struggle were mercifully lost to her.

When she awoke, an indeterminable time later, all the evidence of the birth had been disposed of and her own body washed and dressed in a clean nightgown. She got to her feet and staggered to the door. It was still locked.

Three days later, her father appeared. He spoke to her in the voice he used for strangers, explaining that the remainder of her savings had gone to buy her a ticket west to Colorado. There she would meet her future husband, a man who was generous enough to overlook her immorality, and who had even reimbursed the family for the troubles they had undergone in her behalf.

"So, you're selling me?" she asked bitterly, just to see the expression that crossed his face. Those were the last words she meant to say to any of her family.

Sophie stood up from her chair and forced her mind to return to the present. She was even more irritated by the mood that had seemed to overtake her this morning. As far as she was concerned, contemplating the past was as useless as planning for the future.

Just then, the mare, whom Sophie had named Twitch because of her habit of twitching her ear when Sophie spoke to her, ambled into the yard. The horse innocently stretched her neck toward the forbidden lilac bush that grew near the corner of the house.

"Do you really think that's a good idea?" Sophie asked her.

The horse twitched her ear and walked over to the pile of hay Robert had dumped in the yard. Sophie shook her head. Twitch had proven that she didn't need to be tied or penned, and Sophie was glad to give her the freedom to roam around their little patch of land. But the lilac bush was an issue between them, and they had this conversation every morning. As far as Sophie could tell, not a single leaf was ever taken in the night, although if Twitch really wanted to she could strip the plant clean within five minutes.

Sophie picked up her cup and went inside. For a moment, she hesitated over the coffee pot, then decisively poured herself another cup of the strong liquid. Despite her wishes, today had made itself a day for contemplating instead of doing.

Sitting down at the table, she thought again of Allen. She recalled the last time she had seen him; she stood silently in the yard as he rode out from the barn on a horse she'd never seen before. He waved to her and left without telling her where he was headed. Three days later, Robert brought his body up from Durango and buried it before bothering to tell her that her husband was dead.

She knew little about his death...only that he had been murdered on the stagecoach. Instinctively, she'd known not to ask Robert for additional details. But that didn't stop her from wondering why Allen had been a passenger when he had taken a horse. And why was he on the stage traveling away from home? Patiently, she had gathered those questions, mused over them, then buried them deep inside. She could tell herself that she wasn't at all curious anymore, but the wondering still seemed to surface in her dreams.

Looking down into her coffee cup, she studied the distorted reflection of her face. It looked like an image seen in a mirage or a nightmare. As she swirled the liquid she saw other faces — Allen, Robert, the young man from the general store.

Suddenly she realized she had dreamed of that man with the strangely pleasing voice, the one she found so unsettling. She thought of how she stood in the store amazed that he seemed to react to each of her thoughts and feelings. The experience had been disturbing. He had made her feel that she was actually there — a real, living, breathing person like the rest of them. Sophie was not convinced she liked the feeling.

She lifted her face from her cup and allowed the fragment of dream to come to her. It was night and she faced him across a small fire. They did not speak, but he never looked away from her eyes. Sometimes he would smile and nod as if she'd said something to amuse him.

He was doing something with his hands; Sophie could see his shoulders moving smoothly, rhythmically. Caught by a strange fascination, she watched the movement for a long time, feeling it in her own body before looking down at his hands. He was sharpening a brutal-looking knife. The long blade flashed in the firelight each time he turned it, drawing it down the whetstone. Suddenly, the movement stopped and the young man stood. Sophie didn't move; she could not, or would not, stir as he stepped around the fire and knelt down before her. He held the knife just below her chin. The agonizing thrill of danger quickened her breath.

In defense, Sophie raised her hands, not realizing until that moment that they were tied. She stared in surprise at the thick coils of rope that held her wrists. The knife blade flashed into view and sliced through her bindings as if they had been formed of smoke. She separated her hands and flexed her fingers gratefully, waiting for him to speak in that voice that touched like a caress. The man handed her the knife, then Sophie watched as he silently faded into the night.

Shifting uncomfortably back into real time, Sophie touched her fingertips to the table top, the house feeling like home for the first time since she moved in. She shivered, trying to dispel the remnants of emotion that had followed her from the dream. Despite his kindness, that man had been the first she suspected when Robert had attacked her: obviously, there was an air of something not quite right about him. Without any clear reason for doing so, she decided that she did not like that man.

*K*enny shifted the reins to her left hand and tugged the wide brim of her black hat down over her eyes. "Frank, would it be askin' too much for you to stay awake just this once?" she barked, clearly annoyed with him.

The old man sighed heavily and spat over the side of the coach. His red-rimmed eyes fixed on Kenny. "Yer the one who's spooked, why does that mean that I gotta stay awake?"

"'Cause, for one thing, it's your job." Kenny braced her feet against the boot rail and half stood, twisting around to look back the way they had come. "You'd be spooked too if you'd seen that man. He was so...cold."

Frank hid his grin as Kenny shivered in the bright afternoon sun. "I've seen plenty of those characters; they don't surprise me none any more. But I am surprised at you. Most people get brave when they drink. Looks like you got a shade more yellow."

Turning on the old man in indignation, Kenny shouted, "I ain't yellow!"

Frank laughed at Kenny's expression. "I'm just foolin' with you, son," he soothed as Kenny continued to look angry. "Ya still got that headache?"

Kenny nodded; it was miserable. She was still feeling the remnants of her first hangover.

"Next time won't be so bad," Frank promised. "As it is, you'd feel better now if ya took some hair of the dog that bit you." He pulled a pint of whiskey from his vest and offered it to her.

"No. And there ain't gonna be a next time," she vowed. "I learned my lesson." Just the sight of the alcohol was making her queasy. All she hoped was that she could make it to the mine office before needing to stop and be sick. Getting this payroll unloaded safely would do plenty to ease her hangover. This run had always made her uncomfortable and her encounter with the man in the Stockton saloon had only intensified her uneasiness.

The road to Leeland's Glory was well-maintained. The ore wagons that went out twice a week were loaded so heavily that the road needed to be as smooth as possible. Still, it was a narrow track, bordered on both sides by dense stands of trees. When there was a break in the forest Kenny could look ahead and see the road winding up the side of the low mountain. Sometimes she could get a glimpse of the portal to the mine, its wide black opening aproned by a triangular slope of blasted rock.

On this run, Kenny always tried to keep a watchful eye on her surroundings. She also knew that she was prone to getting caught up in the beauty of the landscape. There was always something new to be seen: flowers, the way the light glinted off the creek, the animals that sat up straight at the sound of the stagecoach then darted away quicker than the eye could follow. Competing with the sights were the sounds and smells that also delighted her. As much as she loved living in town, Kenny knew that someday she would make herself a home in a forest like this. It suited a deep, quiet part of her.

They rode in silence for half a mile before Kenny noticed Frank's chin nodding down to his chest again. His ability to sleep on the hard seat had always impressed her, but today she found herself annoyed by his carelessness. As she leaned over to elbow him in the ribs, a bright flash of light from the edge of the forest momentarily caught her eye.

"Frank — " she yelled, trying to warn him. In the same instant a crash of gunfire burst from the woods and a flash of agony hit her in the left shoulder. The leather reins burned across her palms as she was knocked backwards off the side of the coach, landing flat out on the dirt-packed road.

Frightened by the sudden gunfire, the horses screamed and broke into a run, dragging the coach around a corner and out of sight. Through a red haze of pain, Kenny saw three horses and their riders break from the trees and follow.

Gasping harshly, Kenny fought for air — the impact of hitting the ground had knocked the wind out of her. Unable to move, she lay on her back in the roadway and listened to the sounds she could not block out.

Frank's gun roared, once, twice, then was answered by a hail of gunfire. She heard Frank yelling, then screaming, then silence. Nothing had ever terrified her as much as that silence. It gave her the strength to get to her feet and run.

She stumbled to the edge of the road, every pounding step like a knife in her shoulder. In panic, she shoved her way blindly through the underbrush and fell forward over the bank of a shallow creek running snow melt from the mountains. The water was freezing cold. Thrashing loudly, Kenny struggled to her hands and knees. Her hands slipped on the smooth rocks as she pushed herself up and tried to crawl out of the stream. The pain almost caused her to pass out each time she attempted to shift her weight to her left arm and hand. Finally, the agony immobilized her. She rolled onto her back and lay panting in the frigid water.

Kenny felt her body and her mind going numb as she lay there. The water around her was a pale pink: it was the strangest thing she had ever seen. She couldn't imagine what would cause that color, and it was troubling to her. Leaning her head back, she looked at the sky instead.

After a few minutes, her breathing finally calmed to almost normal and the pain in her shoulder was becoming bearable. But she knew that she was not safe. She had to get out of the freezing water and hide among the trees, but her body was not yet capable of movement.

Suddenly, a shadow fell over her, and at the same moment, a voice said, "You forgot somethin'."

Kenny looked up into the cold eyes of the man she had encountered at the Stockton saloon. He held his pistol in one hand and her father's black hat in the other.

*T*he sound of distant gunfire woke Sophie from her late afternoon nap. The echoes brought her bolt upright in instant fear, but she forced herself to become calm. The sounds had come from too great a distance to be a danger to her or

Twitch. Shaking her head at her unusual reaction, she got out of bed and walked to the open door. After a brief pause, the shots began again.

The sounds were coming from the west, from the direction of the mines. Still feeling uneasy, Sophie whistled for Twitch. The mare came to her immediately, looking unconcerned at the distant noises. Sophie shaded her eyes and looked toward the fading sun. The carpet of trees covering the foothills blocked Sophie's view of where she guessed the Leeland's Glory mine was located. She put her hand on Twitch's shoulder, grateful for the warm, comforting strength, and glanced around her small clearing. Of course, nothing was amiss here. There was no reason for her to be worried.

"What do you think that's all about?"

The mare gave her stock answer as Sophie rubbed her mane.

"I suppose it's just the miners celebrating the weekend," she said with a false lightness to her voice. Because she'd been keeping better track of the days since she last went to town, she knew today was Friday, possibly even payday, and that was indeed reason to celebrate. Still, Sophie was ill at ease. The guns boomed again, then stopped abruptly.

"I'd like to have all the bullets they're wasting," she said, thinking of the small handful Robert had grudgingly left her. "Maybe this is a good time for us to take the rifle to town and get some ammunition."

The longer Sophie thought of that idea, the better it sounded. She was getting awfully bored — maybe she would even spend the night at the hotel. It would be a nice change.

Hurrying back inside the cabin, she quickly packed the things she would need. The rifle felt comforting to her as she checked to make sure it was loaded. Back outside and bridling Twitch, she was surprised to notice that her hands were trembling. She struggled to fit the bridle over the horse's ears as Twitch shook her head, catching the feel of Sophie's agitation. Sophie mounted and immediately urged Twitch into a run.

As Sophie rode away, she reassured herself that she was not afraid. It was mere coincidence that town lay in the direction away from the sounds of gunfire. She gave Twitch her head and leaned forward as the horse stretched herself out in a ground-eating pace. Sophie was tense. She felt an itching between her shoulder blades, as if she could feel an unknown gun sighted on her back.

Five

A s she lay in the stream, Kenny felt a rushing chill that made the water feel warm by comparison. She had a sense that this situation was all so unreal; part of her mind cooperated and clung to that thought. But she also knew the wish was beyond hope — no nightmare she'd ever awakened from had held this amount of clarity and sheer terror.

If the man was waiting for her reaction, he was to be disappointed. Kenny could do nothing but stare at him blankly. He held her hat up by the brim and looked at it in disgust. With a sudden movement, he lifted his arm and sailed the hat into the air. Helplessly, Kenny's eyes were drawn to follow its high arc. Raising his pistol, he fired quickly three times. Kenny flinched at each thundering shot. As far as she could tell he'd hit it with all three bullets. The hat dropped out of sight into the deep woods on the far side of the stream.

A small shower of rocks falling into the water next to her brought her attention back to the man. He was sliding carefully down the steep embankment toward her. Suddenly she was flooded with adrenaline, enough to make her pain-racked body move. Frantically, she dug her boot heels into the gravel of the stream bed and shoved, pushing herself backwards and away from him.

Over the splashing of the water, she heard his mocking laughter. He jumped down the last few feet of the bank and landed at her side. Patiently, he kept pace with her as she struggled to get out of the stream. Finally, her hand slipped on a moss-covered rock and she fell back.

"I knew you were yellow, boy. The minute I laid eyes on you, I knew."

Despite the immobilizing pain in her shoulder, despite her fear, Kenny felt a hot rush of anger burn through her. He smiled, his eyes holding hers like a snake staring down a mouse. Kenny struggled to keep her face still, to keep his eyes locked with hers while she inched her hand toward the long knife at her belt.

"And you're a no-good bushwhacker." Her cold fingers clutched the slick handle of the knife and she prayed that the running water would hide the glint of steel as she pulled the blade from its sheath.

"You think you're insultin' me?" Bending down over her, he laughed in her face. "I tell you, boy, it pays a damn sight better than drivin' that stinkin' stage. Ain't as dangerous, either."

Before he could raise his body back up and away from her, Kenny whipped her hand out of the water, slashing with the knife in a path headed straight for his stomach. He was a big man, but his reflexes were quick. As if he'd been warned by the look in her eye, he was already jumping away from the path of the razor-sharp blade. But the stream was as much his enemy as it was hers — his boot slipped and he staggered — and the tip of the knife bit through the thick leather of his gunbelt and tore a long gash in the front of his shirt.

Kenny used the force of her movement and his momentary hesitation to struggle to her knees. Reversing the blade, she swung it back toward him. This time, she was rewarded by the feel of the knife catching his forearm and cutting flesh. He yelled, a furious howl, and staggered back again. The pistol raised, suddenly filling her sight. She ducked her head and slashed at his knees.

He evaded her thrust easily this time and regained his balance. His laughter was gone. Kenny took another desperate stab at his belly, but he simply lifted his foot and kicked the knife from her hand. It fell with a clatter onto the rocky embankment.

"You little bastard!" The man's voice was filled with rage. He smashed the long barrel of the pistol against the side of her head and she was knocked back into the water. As she fell, he stepped forward and stomped his boot down hard on her left shoulder.

Kenny cried out, a hoarse scream that made him laugh again. White-hot pain ripped through her body as he continued to shove at her shoulder, trying to push her head under the water. Kenny's head hit hard against the rocks but the stream was too shallow to fully cover her face.

He stopped pushing and held her still. Leaning over slightly, he aimed the long barrel of the pistol at her forehead just above the bridge of her nose. "Guess I gotta waste another bullet on you," he said, with no regret in his voice.

Kenny was nearly pushed beyond her ability to endure. Her breath came in short, painful gasps, and she felt her strength slipping away. She looked past the barrel of the gun and into his eyes. As he stared back at her, she thought she could see a bit of annoyance in his expression.

"Now's the time for you to beg for your life," his icy voice informed her.

Kenny's mind raced through possibilities, all the while knowing that there were no words she could say and nothing she could do to stop him from killing her. Still, she could die with what little dignity she still possessed. Not that she had much left to her at this moment, lying on her back at this stranger's feet in the middle of a muddy stream.

"Piss off. I won't give you the pleasure."

"Little bastard," he cursed her again, his finger tightening on the trigger. "This is your last chance."

As she began to shake her head in a refusal to speak, a flash of light blazed before her eyes, followed by a sea of blackness — then dead silence.

A gentle breeze billowed the white lace curtains adorning the window facing Main Street. The noise from the street below allowed Sophie to feel connected in some strange way to the world around her. She spent much of the afternoon sitting in her small hotel room reading a handful of religious tracts she had found in the lobby. They were an entertaining read; Sophie had actually laughed out loud at several of the writer's more imaginative prophecies. Some of the doom predicted had, in her opinion, already come to pass. But there was nothing like hindsight to lend credence to one's cause.

Sophie was not herself religious, but she did take every opportunity to learn what she could when she could. If she had a soul, and she was not convinced she did, it was long past redemption. Not that she had ever outwardly lived a life that could be called sinful; her appearance and demeanor had always been as proper as the times would allow. But inwardly, Sophie was another story. Her mind delighted in what she knew would be considered sacrilege and blasphemy. And the more she read about religion, the more rules and commandments and holy writs she absorbed, the more irreverent she became. She did not dare go to church, certain that if she ever found herself there, surrounded by all that sanctimony, she would probably burst, and all the years of silent scorn would pour out of her in a raging flood strong enough to overturn the pews. Smiling, she dwelt on that thought for a moment. Too easily, she pictured the upturned hoops of billowing skirts and the brief, frantic fluttering of the hymnals before they sank like drowned pigeons into the overflow.

Suddenly, the sounds of pounding hooves and incoherent yells from the street tore Sophie from her daydream. Curious, she walked quickly to the window, where she cautiously pulled the curtain aside to peer down at the rapidly growing crowd. Below, two riders shouted into the anxious faces that surrounded them. The thick, wavy glass of the window muffled their words, but she didn't need sound to understand their gestures. Something terrible had happened somewhere in the direction of the mines.

Her first thought was of a cave-in, then came the memory of the gunfire that had spurred this trip to town. A robbery? But who would want to rob the mines? All anyone could hope to get would be unprocessed ore, and several tons of that would make a clean getaway improbable.

A handful of men broke away from the crowd and ran toward the stables. They returned almost immediately, mounted and riding with rifles drawn. So it was a robbery, Sophie thought as the posse quickly formed, then galloped out of town toward the mines.

No sooner had the riders disappeared into the forest than another man on horseback emerged. He rode quickly toward the town, but without the same urgency. A short rope ran from his saddle to the harness of a pack horse behind him. The animal carried an awkward burden, and it was not until the rider had drawn up beneath her window that she realized the bundle was a man's body.

Sophie stepped back from the window as a wave of nausea washed over her. She held the sides of her face and shook her head from side to side. The presence of death carried by the pack horse created a horrifying reality for Sophie.

She sat down heavily on the bed and pressed her shaking hands together. The answer had come to her — surely it was the stage that had been robbed. The dead man draped across the horse outside suddenly wore her dead husband Allen's face; the light hair matted with blood was Allen's hair, and the rough hands dangling down became the same hands that Allen had used to touch her body.

A chilling film of sweat broke out on Sophie's skin as she forced her imagination to be still. That...that was not Allen. He was long gone from her, beyond anything she could see or touch. He would not enter her life again for good or evil.

Unsteady on her feet, she walked to the wash basin and splashed cool water on her face and wrists. Her room had become stifling and from outside the unintelligible sounds of crisis continued to irritate her. Though filled with a sense of dread, she had an uncontrollable urge to know what was happening out there.

Once down the stairs and in the lobby, Sophie regretted her decision to learn more. The street was far too crowded for her comfort; people pressed and jostled against each other without apology. The crowd had lost its initial sense of hysteria, but excitement still ran high. She edged out the hotel door and tried to keep herself on the fringe of the crowd. There were many voices, but she could not put faces to the words being said.

"That's Frank Buckland, he was the shotgun man."

"But where's the driver? Did they find the driver?"

The man who had brought in Frank's body shook his head meaningfully, his expression twisted with anger and suspicion.

A brief hush fell over the crowd — then, just as suddenly, everyone seemed to speak at once. Sophie could make out little of their talk, except that the driver of the stage was missing and the sole topic of speculation.

"Kenny Smith, the new man..."

"Did he do this?"

"He and Frank were friends. I don't believe — "

"I never trusted him. He was strange, different..."

"He was just a boy. He was kind to everyone."

"Oh Hannah, you've never been a good judge of character. He killed Frank!"

Sophie stood on her toes and tried to catch a glimpse of the woman she had heard named Hannah. The woman turned and Sophie recognized her as the waitress from the hotel restaurant.

Sophie's level of discomfort was rising too high to allow her to stand there any longer. She backed away from the crowd and ducked into the narrow alley between the hotel and the post office. In the cool shade, with her back leaned against the wall, she tried to breathe slowly and deeply. The voices from around the corner still assaulted her ears, but she no longer wanted to try and decipher what was being said. Later, she would talk to the waitress, when things were more settled, when, hopefully, there would be more facts than opinions to discuss.

Once calmed, Sophie walked to the stables where she had boarded Twitch. She was feeling the need for some quiet companionship and Twitch was the only being in this town that she felt bonded to. The horse gave her a sense of security that no human being had ever provided.

Hidden in the cool, dark stall, Sophie stayed with the horse until she estimated that the dinner hour at the restaurant was almost over. After brushing the hay and horse hair from her dress, she walked the back street to the hotel. Her stomach was admitting that it had been hungry for some time, though Sophie had been afraid that she would not be able to eat for days. She rinsed her hands and face at the water pump behind the hotel, then made her way again through the alley.

The hotel windows were well lighted and Sophie could see that the restaurant was almost cleared out. The woman she recognized as Hannah was standing behind a short counter filling the small table containers with salt. Hannah did not look up when Sophie stepped through the door.

"Am I too late for dinner?" Sophie asked quietly.

Hannah raised her head and looked at Sophie without comprehension. Sophie repeated her question.

"Oh, no. You're not too late," Hannah assured her. "I'm sorry, my mind was elsewhere."

"Yes, I understand," Sophie sympathized. "The whole town is that way."

Hannah led Sophie to a table by the counter. "So you know what happened?"

"Well, I was here in my room when the news came," Sophie admitted. "But I have not heard all of the facts. I'm not comfortable with crowds, or excitement, so I..."

"I understand what you're sayin'." Hannah patted the back of Sophie's hand while expertly slipping her a menu.

"Have they caught the men who did it?"

Hannah's kind and open expression was suddenly slammed closed. She spoke again, but her words were clipped. "Don't you worry about that none; they wired to Stockton for the sheriff. He'll be here tomorrow mornin'." She bustled off before Sophie could answer or apologize for offending her.

Sophie studied the menu Hannah had given her. The choices were limited, but Sophie reveled in the idea of eating a meal she didn't have to cook herself. Hannah eventually returned, pouring her an unasked-for cup of steaming coffee and taking her order without further conversation.

Sophie waited until her dinner was served before she tried to speak to Hannah again. "I understand that everyone's blaming the driver of the coach, and that you don't believe he did it." Sophie spoke quickly while Hannah poured her a second cup of coffee. "I don't know anyone in town well enough to form an opinion. I'd just like some information." A weak smile formed at the corners of Sophie' full, unpainted lips.

The waitress studied Sophie for a moment, her face shadowed with suspicion. Finally, she let out a deep breath and relaxed her expression. "I'm sorry about givin' you the cold shoulder, ma'am." Hannah looked around the room, then bent down closer to Sophie's face. "I just can't believe that Kenny Smith was behind any robbery, no less this one, and I'm tired of people accusin' him," she said, confidingly. She straightened up and put her hand on her hip.

Sophie motioned for Hannah to sit down on the chair beside her. After a moment's hesitation and a glance toward the kitchen, she sat stiffly on the edge of the chair.

"Was — is he your boyfriend?" Sophie asked kindly.

"Oh, no." Hannah almost laughed at the question. "He's much too young for me. But he came in here every mornin' that he was in town, and he was just so kind." Hannah shook her head, obviously remembering the last time she had seen him. Leaning toward Sophie, she whispered meaningfully, "Why, Kenny never even carried a gun."

Sophie raised her eyebrows. That was unusual, especially for a man in his line of work. But he may have intentionally not carried a gun just to prevent anyone from suspecting him. Sophie ate a few bites thoughtfully, without really tasting the food. A soft noise from the woman beside her brought her attention back to their conversation. Sophie was surprised to see that Hannah was crying.

"I'm sorry. I can just remember the last thing Kenny said to me," Hannah apologized needlessly, taking in a gulp of air before sobbing again. "And his voice..."

"His voice?" Sophie blurted the question, then quickly gained control of herself and asked in a calmer tone. "What do you mean about his voice?"

Hannah apparently had not noticed Sophie's sudden interest. "It's just strange. Very rough, but still sweet."

Sophie knew with conviction that she had heard that same voice. The young man in the general store had spoken to her in a voice that could be described exactly that way. That voice...she had never heard anything like it before that day and there could not be two men in this town, even in the whole state of Colorado, who spoke with the same soft huskiness.

Hannah and her sorrow were forgotten momentarily as Sophie thought back to the day she'd met the stranger in the general store, less than a week ago.

He had acted very kind, trying to help her when he did not even know her name. Was he capable of cold-blooded murder? She didn't know, but she seriously doubted it. But there was that something...something strange about him that she could not put her finger on.

Sophie suddenly blushed under the oil lights of the dining room. The dream she'd had of him came back to her with startling clarity. She had dismissed it as meaningless, but with the events of the day, the dream seemed to take on a sinister meaning. As she remembered his movements, she realized how sexual their rhythms had been; she thought of being bound and then freed by his hand. Recalling the glint of the knife in the firelight, she could not prevent a shudder of fear.

Sophie stood and groped in her bag for some money to pay for her dinner. She placed a few coins on the table and, ignoring Hannah's sounds of concern, Sophie fled the restaurant. She picked up the front of her dress several inches and ran to her room. Once safely inside, she locked the door. Throwing herself down on the bed, she squeezed her eyes shut tight and tried to banish the image of Kenny Smith from her mind.

Sophie fought to clear her vision of the handsome stranger, but the harder she tried, the sharper his image became. She rolled over on her back and stared at the ceiling, willing herself to calm down and breathe slowly. Thoughts could not hurt her, nor could the insubstantial impression of a man who visited her only in a dream. Sophie could close her eyes and look objectively at the memory of his long legs, flat stomach, and strong shoulders without fearing that he would somehow appear in her room. She could and she did.

Remembering both the man and the dream, Sophie felt herself relaxing. His face had seemed so soft. Not exactly kind, but understanding. He had a firm chin and a strong gaze, but not one of those looks that made a woman feel like she was an object to be possessed. Sophie had sensed the stranger to be a caring person. He had a warmth she never expected to see in a man's eyes. The events of the day made her wonder how she could have been so wrong.

Despite her misgivings, Sophie realized that her body was responding to the thought of him. Feeling slightly betrayed by the warm sensation spreading through her lower body, Sophie again closed her eyes. She could clearly see him standing before her. It did not take her long to notice that her thoughts could give him motion. If she thought that maybe he was softly kissing her parted lips, then he would. If she imagined his strong hand caressing her shoulder and sliding down to pull away the cloth that covered her breasts, then it happened. And if she reached up and held the back of his head, well then, the kiss would never stop.

Carried away by the fantasy, Sophie moaned quietly. She was possessed by the lips on her mouth and the strong body that covered hers, pressing her down, holding her a willing captive on the bed.

Six

The early evening light left long shadows at the forest's edge; the dark bands of shade lay across the creek and crept slowly up the rocky embankment. From nearby came the sounds of searchers. Men called to each other through the tangling brush and horses' hooves pounded dully along the ground. The sounds of the posse came and went.

A body lay unseen in the shallows, motionless until an occasional ripple of current moved the long fingers of a slender hand or brushed a strand of dark hair against the rocks. There was life in the body, but it was waning.

Kenny woke long after the posse had given up on finding her trail and had ridden away. It took her several moments to force one of her eyes open. The left one refused to budge and Kenny did not have the strength to reach up and find out why. Her situation was all too clear to her. She knew why she was lying in the water, why her body would not respond to her wishes. The only thing she didn't understand was why she was still alive.

The black shape of her hat hung in the air above her and that was confusing. Evidently, the bandit was still here, still playing with her. Kenny had not begged for her life, so he must be waiting for her to say the words. She licked her lips and tried to speak but no sound would come.

Her hat glided back into view, then split into two pieces. The bandit had shot it in half, she reasoned. Slowly, the realization came to her that she had not heard any more gunshots after that. She squeezed her eyes shut tight and then tried to open them as wide as she could. Her left eye finally opened a narrow slit, but she felt her eyelashes being torn from the upper lid.

Her vision at last brought the dark objects into focus. They were, of course, not pieces of her shot-up hat but the black bodies of vultures circling overhead. Their circling told her that something dead or dying was in the area, that they were waiting patiently for the chance to feast. Their graceful gliding was soothing to watch.

Kenny watched the vultures, as she gathered together the last of her strength. Comprehension came to her in a painful jolt — these scavenger birds were waiting for her! Suddenly splashing wildly, she flailed at the water and managed to draw herself to the bank of the stream. The water ran cold from her body except for a painful area of her shoulder where the moisture felt as hot as fire. Her left arm was useless. With one hand, she crawled up the slope toward the trees. The small rocks covering the bank dug into her palms and bruised her knees.

Kenny could not rise to her feet until she reached a tree whose broad trunk and gnarled roots gave her something to pull against. With her aching head resting on the rough bark, she tried to collect her thoughts. The evening air had become colder than the temperature of the water and soon Kenny was shivering uncontrollably. She pulled her wet shirt away from her chilled skin and considered taking off her clothes, but she had no way of making a fire to warm herself and dry her clothes. Her only hope of getting warm was to start walking.

Confused, she was not sure in which direction to head. The road was on the opposite side of the stream and Jackson lay to the southeast, but each time she thought of setting foot on the roadway she was filled with an unreasoning panic. *He* would find her if she did not stay hidden.

Kenny knew the thought was ridiculous and cowardly.

The man who had robbed the stage and left her for dead would be miles away by now, but the thought of his chilling eyes looking down on her was too much for her to bear. Her only hope of safety was to stay hidden, moving cautiously until she could find help, someone who would protect her and get her to a doctor. Kenny reached up to rub her forehead and was shocked by a stab of pain and the feel of a blood-encrusted groove running the width of her forehead and down across her left eyebrow.

The pain forced a cry from her lips and she fell to her knees. Horrified, she stared at the ground as a fresh trickle of blood dripped from the bridge of her nose to the dirt below. She pushed herself backwards with her one usable hand, then struggled to pull the tail of her tattered shirt from her pants. Bunching the damp material up into her fist, she held it gingerly to her forehead. She tried to put pressure on the wound to stop the bleeding but the pain was too intense.

A bandage was what she needed, something to wrap around her head. Her cold fingers worked at the knot holding the bandanna around her neck. It wouldn't budge. Kenny crawled back to the edge of the stream, searched for and found her knife among the rocks. When she raised the sharp blade to cut away the bandanna, her hand shook so badly she was afraid of cutting her own throat. Finally, she thought of her breast band. One-handed, she fumbled with the buttons and managed to open her shirt. The band was fastened on the left side and it took several frustrating minutes to unhook the pins. Kenny gave a sigh of relief as she unwound the soft, white cloth and freed her breasts. Then the impossibility of her situation finally hit her.

There was no help for her. Kenny could not let anyone attend her wounds without their learning of her true sex. She had sworn to die before ever being forced to live again as a woman. Despair gripped her heart. And for the first time in years, for the first time since Kenny's mother left her to the brutal care of her father, she allowed herself to cry.

*T*he telegraph clerk brought the dispatch to the Stockton sheriff's office just before dark. Sheriff Cooper, a patient, older man, showed no outward response to the clerk's excitement. Without rising from his chair, he took the paper from the man's trembling hand and nodded. When the clerk showed no intention of leaving, he softly encouraged him to head back to the telegraph office to "keep an ear out for any further wires." Shaking his head at the retreating figure, the sheriff rearranged piles of wanted posters and old telegrams that cluttered his desk. He leaned over the newest telegram and studied it carefully. "Another damn stagecoach robbery." Frustrated, Sheriff Cooper slid his chair back over the worn wooden floor boards and stood. He rummaged through a desk drawer for some matches, and proceeded to light two of the carbon-stained oil lamps on the nearest walls.

He sat back down at his desk and made a few notes with a stub of a pencil. He returned his attention to the telegram. No amount of study changed the hastily written words. The sheriff puffed a disgusted breath out through his thick mustache and tilted back his chair. He slowly glanced around his dirty office, his gaze traveling over the low bench along the wall, the cabinet that held four dusty rifles and one spotlessly clean. The small potbellied stove needed some stoking to take the chill out of the air. The sheriff leaned back in his chair, rubbed his forehead, and eyed the windowless cell, thankful it was empty for the time being.

Tonight's telegraph could be a copy of the one he had received a month ago from Placerville. Or the one three months back from Leadville. Not quite a year back, the same words had come from the sheriff in Durango asking for his help.

Cooper scratched his lean belly through a thin cotton shirt. A burning feeling was rising up in him and he no longer had the self-control to hold it down.

"God damn it!" he yelled, swinging his arm across the desk and scattering papers across the floor. "Them bastards are making a fool of me."

He sprang from his chair and kicked his way across the room and back, scuffing and tearing papers as he went. The sound was small satisfaction to his frustration. He pounded his fists on his thighs as he paced.

"I know who you are, you sons of bitches," he ground the words through his teeth. "And when I get just one shred of proof, I'm gonna hang all of you myself."

Stockton's last two sheriffs had met their deaths without leaving much useful information. As far as Cooper was concerned, two men, both fool enough to get their heads blown off, one at the dinner table and the other at a poker table, could not have given him very good advice. He'd investigated locations and questioned ranchers and other locals that he doubted the other lawmen had considered. After months of this, the sheriff was just about convinced he knew who was behind the holdups and murders.

When Cooper drew a line on the map connecting each holdup site, he was left with a rough circle whose center lay between Stockton and Jackson. It was beyond coincidence that any lawless drifters would cast such a circle. No, Sheriff Cooper was convinced the bandits had ties to the area. He had patiently picked his way through the possibilities until he had narrowed them down to one.

Trouble was the proof. Pinning a crime on a drifter or some cowhand was an easy thing to do; people never cared enough to ask a lot of questions. On the other hand, blaming a crime on men the townspeople believed were upstanding land owners was another matter. Being an outsider didn't give the sheriff a big handful of power, and he would have to watch his step to keep both the badge and his life.

His fury left him as quickly as it had come. He looked shamefaced at the mess on the floor and was glad that there were no witnesses to his tantrum. In the street, he maintained an image of cool deliberation.

Cooper ignored the creaking of his knees as he bent down and picked up the papers one by one. Mostly he just added them to the growing pile on the corner of his desk, but when he came to the latest telegraph from Jackson, he carefully folded it and put it in his shirt pocket. The next piece of paper he picked up caught his eye. He read it again and remembered it from the mail about a month back.

The letter was a request for information about a missing girl. The sheriff shook his head and sighed. He'd seen a few of these situations and had even been the one to find a few of the bodies. Women without the protection of their fathers, brothers, or husbands never came to a good end. No reason to believe that this Nelson girl would be any different. His stomach churned and he hoped that this girl had at least gotten beyond his jurisdiction before meeting her end. He crumpled the paper and tossed it into the stove. He stoked the embers and watched the paper ignite, the flames quickly consuming the name of the missing girl.

Sheriff Cooper straightened and went to the cabinet that held his rifle. The weight of the gun felt good to his hands. It helped take his mind from the black rut it had fallen into. He stepped out the door, adjusted his gun belt, and looked out into the sunset. The early evening April sky was clear, the air cooling with the setting of the sun. He pulled the door closed behind him and strode off toward the stables. It had been too long since he had last ridden up toward Jackson.

The darkness of the night surrounded Kenny Smith. Nothing was clear to her. She alternated between periods of awareness and dreaming, but no matter the state of her mind, she continued to walk. During a few moments of lucidity, Kenny realized that she had wandered too far away from the course of the stream.

She stopped and tried to quiet her ragged breath. She closed her eyes and concentrated, listening for the sound of running water. The night carried no sound except her breath and the pounding of her heart.

Kenny had no way of knowing how far she had traveled
from the stream, nor in which direction. There was no
landmark to be seen on the moonless night — for all she knew
she could have gotten turned around and was now heading
back toward the mountains. Befuddled, she stood stone still for
a moment, shrugged her healthy shoulder, and struggled on.

When the horizon had just begun to turn the ugly gray
of false dawn, Kenny's progress was abruptly stopped short. A
sudden flash of pain ripped across her stomach and down both
thighs causing her to cry out. Hours ago, she had inured herself
to the agony of the bullet wound in her shoulder and the
laceration across her forehead. Kenny tried to step back and
look down at her body but something had a hold on her. With
her right hand, she reached up to push herself away. "Damn
it," she yelled, as she punctured the palm of her hand on a
metal barb. "Ain't nothing going right."

As the sky began to lighten, she could see the wires and
their barbs. The wire connected to the rough-hewn fence posts
ran out in both directions from her, continuing as far as she
could see in the dim light. With a quiet tearing sound, she
pulled away from the barbs that had snagged her clothing.

Judging by the faint glow in the east, the fence line ran
north and south. There was no reason to go north; the flatlands
in that direction were empty for miles. If she followed the fence
line to the south she hoped she would ultimately cross the creek
that would lead her back into town. Not that she knew what
she would do when, or if, she made it to town.

She turned south and walked along the fence line. Her
progress was easier now that the sky was beginning to brighten.
Kenny managed to maneuver easily around obstacles in her
path instead of just falling over them as she had during the
night. The light also made it easier for her to concentrate, in
spite of her thirst and pain. Kenny focused on the fence line
and putting one foot in front of the other.

When the sun had finally risen enough to begin to
warm the left side of her face, Kenny noticed what appeared to

be a small cabin about a half mile ahead. It was perched below a small rise above the flatlands, and just before the mass of the forest which covered the horizon. Kenny walked to the next fence post and clung to it exhausted.

Patiently, she studied the line shack, waiting to catch sight of some movement or a wisp of smoke rising from the chimney. Nothing moved. There was nothing to be seen, and in her present condition, Kenny was too easily able to convince herself that the shack was abandoned. She shoved herself away from the fence post and stumbled forward. Her fatigue was almost unbearable now that an end was in sight.

As she approached the yard, she realized that she had been mistaken. The shack was not abandoned. The well-swept front porch and the hoofprints of at least one horse proved the shack was lived in. For a brief moment, she thought of continuing on, but she could go no farther without rest and water.

With cautious steps, Kenny stepped uneasily onto the porch. The ancient floorboards creaked loudly under her weight and suddenly she was afraid that the house might not be empty after all. Frozen in place, she waited, knowing that if the door were to suddenly swing open, she would not be able to run away.

A minute passed and nothing happened, but Kenny's fear did not diminish. She had to get into the shack and clean her wounds as best she could, find some food and water, and then get the hell out. If she took too much time the owners of the house might return and catch her. There was no way she could accept help without someone learning she was a woman, and no way to explain her injuries without giving away the fact that she was the Jackson stage driver. Through sheer determination, she tried to shake off her fatigue and clear the fear from her mind. If only she didn't have to hide what she really was — a woman.

Kenny slowly pulled the door open and leaned on the doorjamb. The whole interior of the shack could be seen in one glance. No one was home.

She left the door open behind her and entered the dimly lit room. She placed her hand on the top of the cookstove and estimated that the people who lived here had not been home since at least yesterday. A battered coffee pot sat on the back corner of the stove. Kenny gave it a shake; it was half full. She drank the coffee quickly from the spout, not waiting to take the lid off. It was cold and bitter, and the best thing she had ever tasted. Without pausing to breathe, she drank until she had drained the pot.

Her hand was unsteady as she returned the pot to the stove top. Suddenly, a wave of dizziness overcame her and the biting aftertaste of regurgitated coffee stung her throat. Her knees threatened to buckle. She stepped backwards carefully, and collapsed on the bench behind her.

She did not know how much time passed while she sat with her head held in her one good hand, but she knew the light-headedness would not go away quickly this time. As it was, her grasp of reality was tenuous and she was losing track of the reasons why she could not just lie down on one of those bunks and sleep.

Kenny eyed the closest bunk; it looked so comfortable and warm. She had been cold all through the night, surely it would do no harm to rest until she got warm...

Before she realized what she was doing, Kenny stumbled over to the nearest bunk and began pulling back the rough, gray wool blanket. "Don't do that," she said aloud. The sound of her own voice surprised her and helped to clear her head.

"You can't stay," she told herself firmly. "You gotta find food and go." Allowing herself to pull the blanket off the bunk, she struggled to wrap it around her shoulders.

A loaf of bread wrapped in a tea towel sat on the corner of the table. A wooden box in the corner yielded a handful of dried beef and several wrinkled potatoes. She stacked the food on the table, then looked for something she could use to carry water.

One of the window ledges held a small bouquet of

dried weeds stuck down into the narrow top of an old whiskey bottle. Kenny carefully removed the brittle stalks, and placed them on the ledge. She limped out to the front yard, trailing the blanket in the dirt behind her. She found the well around the other side of the shack, but after trying to haul up a bucketful, found that she did not have the strength in her good arm. The only other source of water was a half-empty horse trough. Knowing that she could not afford to be finicky, she filled the bottle from just below the surface of the murky water.

By the time she returned to the shack her breathing had become labored and a fierce fire continued to burn in her shoulder and throughout her body. She knew that she should check out the wound and make some attempt to clean it. Her coarse cotton shirt was stuck to the dried blood on her chest and back. Kenny was grateful that the bullet had passed through her shoulder. The wound had not bled for several hours and she didn't want to risk doing anything that would cause it to bleed again.

Kenny stumbled to the bench next to the table and sat down. She waited for some relief from the pain to no avail. Her heart beat rapidly and her temples pounded. Slowly, she tore off a hunk of the bread and broke it into small pieces. Chewing was painful; her jaw struggled with every bite. Her head ached mercilessly, but she could not swallow well enough to eat without chewing. She stared at the bread as her despair returned.

"I'm gonna die..." she said in a feverish whisper.

The meaning of the words did not bother her. The thought of being found here, dead or alive, no longer bothered her either. She put her head down on the table, and with a weary sigh, let all of her pain and fear fade away.

Seven

All Sophie wanted to do when she awoke the next morning was to get out of Jackson. She had spent an uncomfortable and anxious night in her hotel room. Nightmares and the unfamiliar noises of town had taken turns disturbing her sleep. Tired and cranky, she wanted no more of the drama that seemed to surround the lives of other people.

After dressing with shaking hands, she did her best to tame her long, tangled hair. She doubted that the result would be considered presentable, but she could not find the will to care.

Sophie walked to the window and peeked out through a crack in the curtains. It was not yet six o'clock and the streets were already noisy. Yesterday's excitement had evidently not calmed. People thronged the sidewalks, chattering and pointing and waving their arms. Looking down on them in disgust, she imagined the smell of their sweating bodies, the reek of tobacco and wood smoke that never seemed to wash away. Sophie dreaded walking in their midst and wondered, without much hope, if she could have Twitch brought to her from the stable. She dropped the curtain and turned away to stand in indecision, trapped by her desire to escape and the anxiety of entering that stream of people. But this small, dreary room with its cheap, faded wallpaper could not hold her any longer.

Out in the hall, she noticed for the first time the dirtiness of the hotel. The walls and ceiling were black with soot from the oil lamps that punctuated the line of doorways. Dusty gray spiderwebs clung to the corners. She pulled her arms tight to her sides and wished for a bath to clean away the physical insult of this town.

When she reached the bottom of the stairs that led into the lobby, she paused. The smell of food drifted out from the restaurant, the odor of bacon fat and eggs almost turning her stomach. The hotel clerk looked at her curiously from behind his counter. Sophie concentrated on the faded flower pattern of the dusty carpet as she walked toward the counter.

"Can I do somethin' for you?" the clerk asked, his voice surly with suspicion.

"I was wondering if I could have my horse brought around." Sophie spoke hesitantly, addressing her words to an unshaven spot on his chin. Despite her civility, the clerk did not respond.

Her unsettled emotions suddenly focused and became fury. She turned her darkest glare full upon his face and was fiercely satisfied as he almost stepped back in surprise. Stepping closer, she leaned over the counter and spoke quietly in a manner that would not be denied.

"I want my horse. She is a brown mare named Twitch. She is boarded at the Jackson Stables." She paused, waiting to see the clerk's hurried nod. "I will be waiting."

Sophie turned and stalked across the lobby. She fanned out her skirts like a pair of giant wings and perched on the edge of an overstuffed couch. After she turned one last baleful eye toward the clerk, he rushed out into the street.

He was back in a moment and approached her respectfully. Glaring at him in appraisal, like an owl transfixing a field mouse, she waited for him to speak.

"Tyler'll be right here with your horse, ma'am," he squeaked.

Casually, Sophie dropped her attitude of annoyance and smiled sweetly, pretending that his actions were an unexpected favor. "Well, thank you very much."

The clerk was plainly baffled by her quick changes and the sincerity in her voice. He stammered some nonsense and escaped back behind his counter, where Sophie ignored him for the remainder of her wait.

She had hardly settled back into the plump cushions before a scruffy, towheaded boy in bib overalls banged past the screen door and trotted up to her. His appearance swept over her like a fresh breeze.

"You waitin' for the mare?" he asked through the gap of his missing front tooth.

Sophie smiled and nodded. The boy did not return her smile, but looked at her mournfully. He spun around and went to the door without looking back to see if she followed.

The smile did not leave Sophie's face as she trailed him out the door. Twitch was tied to the porch railing; her long ears swiveled with what Sophie took to be pleasure as she approached. The boy untied the reins and held them out to her. Sophie did not take them from him.

"You're awfully glum," she teased.

He continued to hold out the reins. His solemn face did not change.

"Would you like to earn a penny?"

A brief glimmer of interest shone in his eyes before he could hide it. Sophie took a copper piece from her purse and tucked it in the pocket of his bib. "Tyler, all you have to do is lead me out of town through this crowd of fools," she said in a conspiratorial whisper.

He studied her for a moment, then nodded. "Yeah, they're fools," he confided with surprising bitterness. "All of 'em!"

She mounted Twitch and Tyler pulled them forward into the street. He weaved his way through the crowd, pushing and shoving without concern for the occasional curses he received. As he walked, he glanced back at Sophie several times, his expression becoming friendlier with each look. Sophie just tried to relax and trust him to guide her through the mob.

"Wanna see somethin'?" Tyler asked her suddenly as they passed the general store.

The crowd had thinned and Sophie was feeling much more comfortable. She nodded and allowed herself to be led back behind the store and then several buildings farther down.

Tyler stopped them at a squat, ugly structure that seemed to draw itself inward, away from the other buildings. The boy motioned her to get down. Sliding off the horse, she followed him to a grimy window. He stood on his toes and peered through the glass. What he saw inside apparently satisfied him for he moved aside to let Sophie look. Her hair brushed the dusty glass as she bent down and pressed her nose to the same greasy spot Tyler's nose had left against the window pane.

Her eyes needed a few seconds to adjust to the dim light inside the room. Nausea returned as the adjustment was made. Frank's bullet-ridden body was stretched out on a long board directly beneath the window. She resisted the impulse to jerk her head away from the glass. Fighting her queasiness, she studied Frank's face. He looked like he had been a nice man, as best as she could judge from his present condition.

When she felt that Tyler would be content with her show of strength, she stepped back from the window. He was sitting in the dirt beside a rain barrel watching her and she thought he was impressed by her lack of squeamishness.

"Did you know him?" she asked as she crouched down beside his skinny body.

"Yup." His voice sounded matter-of-fact and very adult. "Knew Kenny, too."

"Ah..." Sophie now understood his resentful attitude.

"Them fools," he gestured angrily in the direction of the main street. "Them fools think Kenny robbed the stage and shot Frank."

"And you know better?" Sophie felt uncomfortable that the topic had yet again turned to that young man, Kenny Smith. Unreasonably, she felt like she could never get away from hearing about him. Uneasy wisps of her dreams tried to capture her attention. She pushed them away savagely.

Sounding defensive, Tyler stated, "Yeah, I know better. Kenny wouldn't do that. He was always nice to me. Even let me drive the stage once."

"And so you don't think he would kill anyone." Sophie had reservations about Tyler's logic, but she didn't want to hurt his feelings. In a kinder voice, she asked, "So where do you think he is? Why hasn't he come back?"

Tyler's eyes filled with tears, but he struggled to keep his voice calm. "I think he's dead. If he was alive, he'd a come back here, no matter what."

There was nothing to gain by voicing her doubt. Tyler very clearly believed in Kenny's innocence, and to continue to show her distrust would just make him think she was one of "them fools."

"Ya know what I think?" Tyler was suddenly excited and did not wait for her response. "I think the robbers killed Kenny and took his body and buried it in a mine shaft. No one'll find it for thirty years and then it'll just be bones and no one'll know who it is. But I'll know and I'll tell 'em and prove they was wrong." He stopped to take a breath and the excitement fell away from him as he remembered that the body he was talking about was that of his friend. His tears came again; this time he could not control them.

Sophie looked away, pretending not to notice. What could she say to Tyler? How could she comfort him, or act as if she shared his trust in Kenny?

"I didn't know Kenny," she finally confessed.

Tyler brusquely wiped his tears away with the sleeve of his shirt, and sniffed loudly. "Well, if you did, you'd know I'm right — 'n' you can ask anyone who knew him, they'll say the same thing."

"Who else knew him, besides Frank...?"

"Hannah and Belle and Lizabeth and Sadie." Tyler counted the names off on his fingers as he said them.

"I know who Hannah is, but I don't know the others."
Sophie was not at all surprised that the listed names were all
female.

"They're the ladies what work in the saloons. They just
love Kenny, they always ask me to tell him hello."

Sophie raised her eyebrows. The women were whores.
No common person looking for a witness to someone's
character would take much account of the words of a whore.

Her thoughts went back to her meeting with Kenny in
the general store. He had been very handsome, she had to
admit that, and the way he looked at her when he took her
hand...Sophie shook her head and tried to ignore the warmth
that caressed her body at the memory.

"When the sheriff comes today, I'm gonna tell him that
Kenny would never kill nobody." Tyler emphasized his words
with a small, shaking fist.

Studying his earnest expression, Sophie thought of the
corpse that lay on the other side of the wall, not ten feet from
them. This man Kenny had a loyal friend in Tyler. She
wondered if Frank had believed in Kenny's loyalty. Was Tyler's
faith in Kenny deserved, or would the man have been able to
kill the boy, too, if he had thought it necessary?

Sophie didn't know what to believe, but she knew that
the world was changing. Life was becoming more dangerous
every day. Since coming out West, she had discovered violence
and brutality that she could not have imagined in her beloved
Boston. She doubted that the West could ever be truly civilized.

Tyler's voice brought her out of her contemplation.

"Maybe you ought to stay and talk to the sheriff, too,"
the boy said hopefully. "If enough people stand up for Kenny
the sheriff'll have to believe us."

Sophie shook her head sadly. "I'm sorry, Tyler. But I
didn't know Kenny. I can't say that he wouldn't commit a crime
like this."

Tyler scowled and looked away from her face.

"Maybe if I'd known him like you did, he would have

been my friend, too." Sophie hoped that the words sounded believable to the boy, even if she herself had doubts. "But to me, he's just a stranger, and you never know what a stranger might do."

"That's true," Tyler admitted.

"Please don't be angry with me," Sophie spoke quietly, resting her hand on his skinny arm. "I know he was your friend, but I just can't speak for someone I never knew. I do know that I'd like to be your friend. Can't Kenny and I both be your friends?"

"Kenny's dead," Tyler stated flatly.

"I'm sorry." Sophie removed her hand and was silent, waiting for the boy to make the next move. The silence dragged on, but she remained patient.

Finally Tyler said, "I like your horse."

"She's very smart." Sophie took his speech as a willingness to accept her friendship and she was genuinely pleased.

"She's a McLaren horse," he said, pointing to the brand on Twitch's hip. "Are you a McLaren?"

"Yes, I guess I am. But I haven't been branded yet."

He laughed at her bad joke. She smiled and stood up, brushing the dust from her skirts.

"I'd better be getting home," she said.

Tyler jumped up and grabbed Twitch's reins. "Want me to lead ya the rest of the way out of town?"

"I think I can manage from here. You'd better go buy yourself some candy."

Tyler clapped his hand to his pocket, his expression showing that he had forgotten about the penny. He beamed once he found the coin was still securely in his possession. At the same instant, Sophie realized she had forgotten Robert's rifle at the stable.

"Tyler, did you see a rifle next to Twitch's stall?"

"Yeah, was it yours?" His voice sounded surprised at the thought of her carrying a gun.

She nodded as she thought of going back through the crowd to retrieve it.

"I'll run get it for ya," Tyler offered.

"I'm not very happy with needing to carry it," she thought aloud. "I wish I could just leave it."

Tyler shook his head. "My pa says it's not safe out there for a good woman to go riding alone. You'd better take the gun," he informed her gravely. Sophie could see a glimpse of the man he would become in the lines of his small face. "Those robbers are still out there, ya know."

Taking his advice seriously, Sophie nodded. Without another word, Tyler trotted off toward the stables.

While she waited for him to return, Sophie mounted Twitch, not bothering to make the pretense of riding sidesaddle. Her little friend probably wouldn't much care about her lack of propriety, especially since he seemed to be friends with at least half of the town's whores.

Tyler reappeared and handed the rifle up to her, not giving her position a second glance. He grinned at her, his tongue tip showing through the gap in his teeth. Laughing, she rode away with a friendly wave.

*J*ackson was dingier than Sheriff Cooper remembered. He rested his horse on the wagon track that led into the outskirts of town. Every building within his view was the pale, weathered gray of neglect. The only splashes of color seemed to be from the signs that advertised the saloons and whore houses. Most of the ten or twelve buildings that made up the town clung to the edges of the main street. There seemed to be no depth to Jackson. He shook his head at the short strip of tiny shacks that made up the red light district. Unlike Jackson, most modern towns had restricted whoring enough to keep it out of the sight of decent folks. He couldn't decide which was the better route. At least Jackson was up-front about the painted ladies' contribution to the town.

Cooper shifted his butt in the saddle. His horse took a nervous step to the side and he patted its shoulder absentmindedly. The smell of its sweat was comforting to him; he felt right at home in the saddle, even though fatigue seemed to catch him a little quicker now than it did in the old days.

He dug in his shirt pocket for his tobacco and papers. As he rolled himself a cigarette he contemplated what his next move should be. He had already ridden out to the mine, for what that was worth. Any clues to the robbers' identity or actions had been erased by the idiots of the self-elected posse. He never understood why these types of men just couldn't stay home and let others with a little sense deal with these kinds of problems. *If I just had two good men*, he told himself for the thousandth time.

Lighting the smoke, he inhaled deeply. The customary pain of the harsh tobacco was welcomed by his lungs; some bitter coffee would be a perfect companion. Mind made up, he clicked his tongue and, without needing any further encouragement, his horse started down the road to town.

*T*witch snorted and stopped short as Sophie rode her up to the side yard. Sophie struggled to keep from sliding down over the horse's neck; she had been daydreaming and hadn't even realized they were so close to home. She bumped her heels lightly against Twitch's sides to urge her forward, but Twitch laid her ears back and refused to move.

"What the hell is wrong with you?" Sophie asked sternly, but without anger. The horse's actions were confusing. The stubborn animal would not move past the lilac bush at the corner of the house. "If you think that this'll get you a bite of my lilacs, you are sorely mistaken."

Twitch swung her head around and gave Sophie a one-eyed glare.

Shrugging, Sophie slid off Twitch's back. The mare danced sideways, shoved hard against Sophie, and pushed her backwards.

"Stop it," Sophie commanded, but the horse continued to push at her with her head. Sophie reached up and released the strap holding Twitch's bridle. She pulled it down from over her ears, and took the bit from her mouth. "There you go, now leave me alone."

Twitch gave her one last shove then seemed to give up. Sophie pulled off the saddle blanket and awkwardly carried the blanket, bridle, and rifle in her arms as she rounded the edge of the house. She had almost stepped up onto the porch before realizing that the door was open.

Flinging down the horse's things, she held the rifle ready, mentally chiding herself for not paying attention to what Twitch had been trying to tell her. She listened for any sound that might be heard over her pounding heart, but the house and yard were silent. She silently stood for a moment not knowing what to do, listening to the wind that had just picked up.

The nearest help was the McLaren ranch about two miles across the flatlands. Grimacing, she thought of riding up to Robert and saying that she needed his help. She quickly decided it was better to face whatever was here alone.

The porch creaked softly as she put her foot down. There were no other sounds in the morning stillness. She had the sudden image of herself appearing very foolish and she wondered if Robert was hiding in the house or somewhere around the yard laughing at her. He would call her a coward and lecture her yet again on how she should not be here. Perhaps he had come back to teach her another of his lessons. But obviously she had learned from him, for she was prepared and carrying the rifle. Still, she was determined not to show him her fear. The gun would keep him away from her, and who else besides Robert or one of the ranch hands would come to this out-of-the-way line shack?

Sophie took a deep breath and lowered the rifle. Hopefully she had not been seen creeping up to her own house like a thief.

She stepped up to the door, then froze in fear. A single glance into the small room had shown her the man who sat at her table. He was dressed in the distinctive pants of a stagecoach driver and his fierce, green eyes burned directly into her own.

Eight

Sophie raised the rifle quickly as the driver lunged toward her. Stepping back, she fired a wild shot. A bottle on the table shattered, spraying liquid and shards of glass across the room. The man stumbled but continued to come toward her. She took several more steps backwards and struggled to cock the gun. As the bullet entered the chamber, the man was framed just inside the doorway. Sophie took quick aim and was ready to squeeze the trigger when he staggered to a stop, doubled over, then collapsed sideways onto the floor.

Holding her ground, Sophie's shaking hands kept the rifle aimed at Kenny Smith's body. She fought with herself about whether to shoot him anyway, although he seemed to be defenseless at this moment. It was a trick, a part of her mind cautioned her, the part that wanted to kill him and be done with it. He would show her no more mercy.

"Get up!" she demanded.

He did not move.

"I'll shoot you whether or not you get up," she warned. Still, he made no move. Sophie couldn't see any evidence that he continued to breathe.

She moved closer, careful to stay out of the man's reach. Looking at his face, she saw the path a bullet had taken across his forehead. It had narrowly missed the corner of his eye as it had ripped away part of his eyebrow. His shirt was torn and dirty; she recognized the rust color of dried blood on the left shoulder. Apparently Frank had gotten in a couple of shots before he was killed. She leaned as far forward as she could while keeping her balance, and watched his chest for movement. Finally, she saw the slow rise and fall of his shallow breathing.

The faintness of his breath convinced her that he was truly unconscious, and she doubted he would live for long without attention. She debated what to do next. Should she ride for help, or just stand back and let him die? There was still the option to just put a bullet into him and end both of their worries, but a small, nagging doubt had surfaced in her mind.

If Smith had been one of those who robbed the stage, why was he here? Surely the other outlaws would have taken care of him and seen that he received medical attention. Sophie was not naive. She had no confidence in the fellowship of thieves, but she thought that if his friends did not want to help him, they most likely would have killed him to keep him from talking if he were found.

But she felt there was more to this situation, and this man, than what the eye could see. She knelt down and looked at the lines of his pale, handsome face. The sound of his voice came clearly to her memory, the words he had spoken feeling like a caress against her skin. Reaching out, she touched his forehead; his brow appeared tense even in unconsciousness. He sighed softly as her fingers brushed his skin.

Sophie snatched her hand away and pushed herself frantically backwards, feeling as if she were fighting her way out of a trance. Her body trembled with fear. This man somehow had the power to influence her emotions in a way she had never before experienced. He was dangerous, too dangerous for her to deal with alone. She had to leave, to mount Twitch and ride for help. But he would be dead before she returned.

She backed away toward the door, her gaze never leaving him. Doubt and determination battled within her — she had no sense of what was the right thing to do. Mired in indecision, she stood immobile in the doorway.

Suddenly she could see Tyler's trusting little face, and she thought about his conviction of this man's goodness. A fool she might be, but she felt that, before he died, she had to learn the truth of what happened during the stagecoach robbery.

Her mind made up, Sophie rushed out of the house and ran to grab Twitch's bridle from the ground where she had dropped it. She leaned the rifle against the door frame safely out of the intruder's reach, and returned to his side. Quickly, she tied the reins tight around his wrists. She took a firm hold on the bridle and pulled his body closer to the table, surprised at how little he seemed to weigh. After she wrapped the bridle around the table leg, she knelt and secured it with the strap. The long reins would give his hands some mobility, but Sophie thought it was no threat, as weak as he appeared to be.

As she straightened up, she noticed that he wore a long knife on his belt. The moment was suddenly unreal, for she recognized it as the one from her dream. Thinking back to her meeting with him in the general store, she had not remembered actually seeing the knife. Grasping the wide handle, Sophie pulled it from his belt. It was heavy in her hand. Heavy, but comfortable. She went to her bunk and hid the long blade under her mattress.

With the rifle safely back in her hands, Sophie walked over to the rocking chair and sat down to wait. While she did not allow herself to look at his face, she kept a close eye out for any movement. The image of Frank's corpse came to her mind and she concentrated on that memory, using it to prevent any compassion from clouding her judgment. She held the rifle in firm hands and rocked steadily. The crunching of broken glass accompanied the impatient squeaking of the wobbly chair.

Kenny Smith was already tried and convicted. All that remained to be done was to find him and string him up from the nearest tree. People in Jackson had little patience for the sheriff's questions. After all, in their minds, the crime was solved. The sheriff was just wasting time with talk and allowing the robbers to get even farther away.

Cooper seldom offered his own opinion, nor did he express his belief that this was just another in the series of unsolved holdups. It didn't bother Cooper that all the previous robberies were clear-cut, shoot 'em up and grab the cash deals. It was something he couldn't put into words, but he had a deep gut feeling that he was dealing with the same gang. Still, it was never smart to get one's mind set too firmly before looking into matters. It was always possible that this stage holdup might not have had anything to do with the others. It might be that a whole new mess of outlaws had moved into the territory.

Cooper made his way through town, letting himself be seen in the saloons, the hotels, the restaurant, and even along the back street cribs. He listened to the stories, and it seemed that everyone had at least one story about Smith, but something just didn't sit right with him. For one thing, despite everyone being convinced that Kenny was the culprit, no one had much bad to say about him. Either the sheriff was dealing with a cold-blooded murderer who had been brilliant enough to set himself up with the identity of a generous, kindhearted man, or the town was seriously wrong in its distrust.

Before lunch, the sheriff dropped into the barbershop. There would be plenty of talk to hear there, and besides, he hadn't had a decent shave for the longest time. When he pushed through the door and into the narrow room, all talk stopped abruptly. Every eye in the place turned toward him. Along with a feeling of hostility, there was a sense of expectation in the room. Cooper nodded his head without a word and lowered himself down onto the small bench beside the door. Though he had his doubts, he hoped that they would accept his conclusion in the case, even if it didn't match their expectations.

The activity and talk resumed after a few more awkward seconds. Pushing his hat back from his forehead, the sheriff breathed deeply. The room was scented with the smell of

cigar smoke and shaving lather. There were two barbers
working the floor. They talked nonstop, sometimes borrowing
from each other's conversations as they worked side by side.
The men in their chairs were tilted back and listening, probably
none too eager to speak themselves while the straight razors
stroked so close to their throats.

Cooper realized that he was already bone-tired and his
work had just begun. The ride over the mountains had taken
more out of him than he cared to admit. He was getting too
old. It was a good time to consider getting out of this job while
he could still leave it alive. Life had taught him the lesson that
if you're slow, you're dead. And that didn't apply only to
drawing a gun.

"Sheriff."

Cooper looked up at the speaker. The barber was
offering him the first chair that had come open. Glancing over
to the three men that waited along the opposite wall, he said,
"I believe these men were here first."

"It don't matter. They ain't got work to do." The barber
laughed, but it didn't lessen the insult of his words. "'Sides,
they'll still be just sittin' in here when they're done."

The men nodded, their faces without expression.
Cooper shrugged his shoulders and stood with a grunt. He
took the offered chair and let himself be tilted back. The barber
draped a hot towel over the lower half of his face, then Cooper
could hear the razor being sharpened on the leather strop. The
heat soaking into his face and neck was relaxing.

"So, you mean to catch those coach robbers, don't
you?" The sentence didn't sound much like a question. More
like a challenge.

The sheriff nodded his head.

"I think the hombre you're dealin' with is a mighty
smart one." The barber spoke his words down the edge of the
razor he held up to the light. He eyed the sharpness and
nodded his approval.

Before he could start the shave, Cooper replied, "So you're sayin' he's smarter than me?"

The barber squirmed and cleared his throat. The sheriff heard a chuckle from one of the men along the wall.

"Well, no. I didn't say that. I just mean...well..." the man stumbled over his words. "I mean he's just clever. Had to be, to set it up the way he did."

"You think so? I wonder about that, seein' how the whole town is of the mind he did it. If he was smart, seems like he'd try to put the blame somewhere else."

The barber didn't answer for a moment and no one else in the room spoke either. There was a sudden increase of tension in the air. Cooper pinched his lips shut tight as the barber lathered his face up with the shaving soap. He was gratified to see that the barber's hand was steady. Before the man could lift the razor to his face, Cooper got in one more question.

"Did you ever shave him? What'd he talk about when he came in here?"

The barber stopped with his hand poised above the sheriff's chin. He shook his head. "Nope, I didn't. How 'bout you, Bob?"

His partner, the other barber, laughed a bit before answering. "No, I never did. Don't think the boy ever needed it."

The sheriff held his mouth still as the razor scraped along his jawbone. He was content to sit quiet and listen to the idle talk that began with his silence. When the shave was done, he flipped the barber two-bits. Rubbing his chin thoughtfully, he pushed out the door, and stepped into the street.

When at last Kenny opened her eyes, she could once again feel the cold water of the stream against her cheek and the hardness of rock against her side. There was no waking up from this nightmare. As her vision cleared, she saw that she was eye level with his boots. He was going to start kicking her again.

As she moved her lips, trying to work up the strength to speak, he stepped toward her. She wanted to beg now, but she didn't know if she should plead for life or death.

"Please, don't kill me," she whispered weakly.

"And why not?"

"I — I don't want to die." Kenny was confused: the voice sounded different and she could not hear the movement of water over the rocks. Something had changed, but her mind was not clear enough for her to figure it out.

"And do you think that the people you've killed wanted to die?" the voice continued unrelentingly.

Kenny managed to turn her head enough to see that the barrel of the gun was again pointed at her forehead. She tried to raise her hands to shield her face, but her wrists were bound together. The nightmare had changed and she was unable to comprehend what was happening to her.

Her tired brain told her that understanding was not worth the trouble and the pain; not when the blackness wrapping around her felt so peaceful. Kenny tried to let herself fade back into unconsciousness, but she slowly became aware that distantly someone was calling to her.

"Mr. Smith, if you don't want to die, you'd better try to wake up."

It took no effort at all to ignore the voice, although it did sound vaguely familiar. A woman's voice...but that made no sense at all. It must be her imagination.

"Kenny, open your eyes."

A light touch brushed against her jawbone as her head was turned carefully, and she felt the smooth metal of a cup against her lips. Automatically, she took a sip. It was clean, cold water. She struggled to gulp down more of the liquid, but the cup was pulled away from her mouth. With a groan of frustration, she opened her eyes.

A woman's face hovered over hers and blue-gray eyes

stared unsympathetically into her own. Even after she blinked several times, the image did not disappear.

"Where am I?" Kenny rasped.

"Next to death, I'd say," the woman answered, her voice as cold as her eyes.

"Is he gone?" Kenny asked, too weak to wonder why the woman seemed to have a great bitterness toward her.

"Is who gone?"

"The man who shot me...he robbed the stage." Kenny was surprised at the woman's ignorance. Who else could she mean?

"Well, since you are most likely the man who robbed the stage and the man who shot you is dead, I really don't know what to tell you."

Kenny was speechless. She had robbed the stage? The man was dead? The questions were too much. Exhausted, she lay her head back and let her eyes close again.

"No, you don't," the woman demanded, pulling Kenny's head up by her hair. "You're not dying until I hear you confess, and if you want me to help you, you'll tell me the truth. Did you rob the stage?"

From somewhere deep inside Kenny came a weak surge of anger, born of her pride in the job she had done. She glared into the woman's accusing eyes and grated, "I am the driver. I was robbed."

The woman silently returned her stare, her expression revealing nothing that would suggest she believed Kenny's words. But she carefully lifted Kenny's head a little higher and returned the cup to her lips.

Kenny drank long and loud. She had not had a good drink in ages. The water flowed cool down her burning throat and soothed the ache in her stomach. "Thank you," she whispered.

The woman eased Kenny's head back down, this time placing it gently on a folded corner of the blanket Kenny had tried to steal. She draped the rest of the cover over Kenny's wounded shoulder.

Kenny heard her walk away, but didn't have the will to follow the woman's movement with her eyes. The woman spoke to Kenny in a voice that did not ask for a response.

"I'm going to fix you some soup, it doesn't look like you've eaten in a while." Her words came clearly over the rattling of pots and pans. "We'll get you some strength, then you can tell me why I should believe you."

Cautiously, the woman reached over Kenny's body to take the dried beef from the table. Her movements showed her distrust and Kenny knew she was not going to be easily convinced of her innocence. Kenny could not blame her.

"I'll advise you not to sleep," she said in the same instant Kenny had closed her eyes. "You may not wake up again."

Kenny stared up at the ceiling as the scent of boiling beef filled the room. Her stomach told her she was starving and yet she was so very tired. It was a struggle to stay awake. She needed to be able to get up and move around. "Will you untie me, ma'am?"

Laughter rang through the cabin. "Not likely. After you've eaten, I'm going to check your wounds, then we'll see about tying you a little more comfortably."

"No!" Kenny objected wildly.

The woman turned on her, furious. "Whatever you may think, mister, I'm not stupid. I will not untie you, regardless of what you say about it."

"I don't want you touchin' me," Kenny shouted, using the last of her strength to sit up and struggle with her bonds. The leather holding her wrists would not budge. Leaning weakly against the leg of the table, she fought to keep from crying in frustration. "Just stay away from me," she pleaded.

With a rustle of skirts, the woman knelt down and looked at her, her expression strange. "Don't you realize you're going to die a fool if I don't help you?"

The certainty in her voice frightened Kenny. Of course, she didn't want to die, but how could she let this woman touch her and find out the truth?

"Drink this." The woman held out a bowl of steaming broth.

Kenny took it, lifting it to her mouth within the slack of the reins that tethered her to the table. Her hands shook so much that the liquid threatened to spill out. The woman cupped Kenny's hands in her own and together they held the bowl to her lips. Kenny drank all of the soup without lowering the dish. The woman silenced her expression of thanks.

"Save your voice for the questions I'm going to ask you," she advised.

Kenny nodded her head.

"How did you escape from the robbers?" she asked as she squatted down in front of Kenny.

"I didn't escape. They shot me and left me for dead."

"Or Frank Buckland shot you when he realized what you were." The woman's words were hard-edged and angry.

"He was my friend," Kenny whispered, turning her head away. The tone of the woman's voice left no doubt that Frank had been killed.

"If you didn't rob the stage, why have you been hiding?"

Her life might very well depend on the answer she gave to this question, and Kenny could think of no good reason why a person in this situation would hide if they were not guilty. She had to be realistic — what good was her secret now? Dead or alive, the woman would soon know that Kenny was not a man. Kenny decided that she would rather be alive during the discovery. She took a deep breath. "Because I am a woman."

*S*ophie burst out laughing. The force of her laughter rocked her back on her heels. Who could believe his gall?

Then Kenny sat silently, staring at the floor until Sophie's laughter subsided. Sophie wiped her teary eyes on the edge of her skirt and gazed at him, feeling a kind of silly admiration at his audacity.

When Sophie looked into Kenny's deep green eyes, she was shocked to see the tears. She watched in disbelief as his numb fingers struggled with the buttons of his shirt. When he pulled the cloth apart to reveal the small breasts, Sophie's breath left her in a rush.

"Oh my God," Sophie whispered. "But — it's not possible." She did not want to believe her eyes. When she looked anywhere but at his — her breasts, she could not see anything but a man. She had to clasp her hands tightly together to keep from reaching out to touch her chest. Kenny Smith was a woman!

"You understand why I gotta hide?"

The rough, masculine voice raised the hair on Sophie's arms. "All right, I believe you. Stop talking like that," Sophie demanded uneasily.

"I can't." Kenny's hands moved again, this time to pull away the dark bandanna to expose a deep scar crossing her throat.

"What happened to you?" Sophie cried.

Kenny looked at her as if the weight of the words needed to explain her life were too heavy to bear. Her handsome face was pale except for the bloodied gash across her forehead. The abuse her body had suffered showed painfully in her eyes. But Sophie could see that the weakness from her wounds was her only frailty. The strength of this woman was more than she could measure, more than she could possibly imagine.

Kenny swayed and Sophie quickly reached out to ease her body back down onto the floor. On an impulse, she untied Kenny's hands, and rubbed them until the circulation returned. She no longer had any doubts of Kenny's innocence.

Sophie looked down at Kenny's face and realized that she was crying without making a sound. Sophie touched her cheek lightly.

Nine

The sheriff sat with one hip on the narrow window sill and dragged slowly on his cigarette. Again, he let his eyes travel across the width of Kenny Smith's former residence. The room was small and featureless, the floor and walls nothing but bare wood; it was a place meant for the kind of folk who didn't mean to stay long. Smith had not left any clues to his life or personality in that room.

Cooper dropped the cigarette butt to the floor and ground it under his heel. He reconsidered his assumption. The lack of clues could be a clue in itself. The bed held the small pile of belongings that Kenny Smith had left behind. A pair of jeans, a couple of bandannas, two rolled-up pairs of socks, a week or so worth of receipts from the hotel restaurant, and a gap-toothed comb were the only possessions the sheriff had found. Either Smith had been starting from scratch and building a new life, or he had only brought along the bare necessities required for faking one.

From his questioning of townspeople, Cooper knew that no one had any idea where Smith had come from or why he had settled in Jackson. He had never carried a gun or started a fight; he wasn't known to be a drinker. On the other hand, he had been popular with the "ladies." Those women were the only residents of Jackson that Cooper had spoken to who insisted on Smith's innocence. He smiled as he wondered what kind of man could win the hearts of so many hardened whores.

Especially when none of them would admit to actually having lured the man into their beds.

Cooper had visited the stage office earlier that morning. The report was that Smith had been a conscientious worker, had never missed a shift, and had kept the stage running on time. Willing to fill in wherever needed, Smith had proven himself the best man for the job. Perhaps these facts had as much to do with the stage manager's fury as the fact that his shotgun man had been killed. It was hard to lose a good driver. The manager expressed his anger clearly.

"We won't stand for this," he shouted at Sheriff Cooper. "If this Smith feller gets away with this holdup, we're gonna have to look for every two-bit, lazy driver we got on our lines to try the same thing."

"Nobody's gonna get away," Cooper tried to reassure him.

"I listen to you talkin', but I don't see you doin' a whole hell of a lot to bring him in."

"Why don't you just calm down and let me do my job my way?"

"We can't wait. We're takin' our own action to make sure he's caught and hung. And we ain't gonna wait for no judge and jury." The manager took dirty bandanna from his pocket and wiped his brow.

The words gave Cooper a bad feeling. He had a good idea what was next. "What are you suggestin'?"

"We're offerin' a reward for Smith's body." With that, the manager lifted a sheet of paper bearing a quick sketch of a young, smooth-skinned man. "A five-thousand-dollar reward. And fifty bucks for any man ridin' with him."

"That ain't gonna do nothin' but make a lot of people trigger happy."

"Whatever it takes, Sheriff. We mean to get this varmint. And we don't mind if he doesn't live to be hanged."

"Don't it bother you that he won't live to be tried first?" the sheriff questioned.

The manager shook his head slowly. Sheriff Cooper had left in disgust, too angry to carry along one of the posters of Smith's face.

As he paced the short length of the room, the sheriff couldn't believe the effort Smith had put into this role. He'd never known an outlaw to work so hard and so well, no matter how high the expected take had been. Smith was a puzzle. And one that was not going to be easy to solve. Cooper sighed hard and walked to the bedside. He held the pair of jeans up to his hips. They were too small. The socks would do and he could always use the bandannas for handkerchiefs next fall. He stuffed the things in his pockets and left the rest to the hostess of the house.

*A*fter four long and worrisome days, Kenny still hovered somewhere between life and death. Sophie had bathed and tended the woman's wounds the best she knew how. There was not a lot she could do with her limited supplies and scant knowledge of gunshot wounds. She had to content herself with the belief that she had done all she could to help. The rest was up to Kenny and her will to survive.

After Sophie had managed to wrestle Kenny's limp body onto a bunk, Kenny had never fully regained consciousness. Several times she had awakened, but each time she didn't know where she was and was terrified when Sophie approached her. Worse yet were Kenny's nightmares — revealing how she was tormented by the memory of the man who had robbed and tried to murder her. Sophie could not imagine what horrifying things the man had done to her, but the sounds of Kenny's fear were contagious. Each time Kenny begged quietly and desperately for her life, a sense of dread and unreasoning terror filled Sophie's heart. The fear followed her throughout the days, and the nights were long with restless sleep.

Sophie took to carrying the gun with her every time she

left the house. One day, she spent several hours packing
firewood from the woodpile up to the side of the porch, and
hauling the remainder of Twitch's pile of hay closer to the
house. The horse wandered where she would and Sophie could
not find the heart to tie her, but she felt more secure knowing
that Twitch would be close to the house.

After several sleepless nights, Sophie's nerves were worn
to their limit. Her hands shook and her body jerked every time
a movement or sound from Kenny startled her. What she
needed was a way to give both of them some peaceful sleep.
Last night she had tea made from local herbs. The brew seemed
to soothe her own nerves slightly, but did nothing for Kenny.

In desperation, she dug through the small pile of
belongings that had been left in the line shack before she had
moved in. She had shoved the things in the corner under a
bunk without really looking to see what was there. In a cracked
and brittle old saddle bag, she found a half-full bottle of cheap
whiskey.

Uncorking it, she took a cautious sniff. The smell alone
made her eyes water, convincing her that the liquor was strong
enough to do what she needed.

Sophie boiled several cups of water, then melted in a
thick dollop of honey. She poured Kenny's cup half full of
whiskey and added the steaming water. Drinking her own cup
hot, with very little alcohol, she waited for Kenny's to cool.

The warmth of the whiskey soon eased some of the
tension in her shoulders and made her realize how bone tired
she was; she yearned for some decent sleep. With a soft sigh,
she took the other cup to the woman's bunk and sat down
beside her.

Kenny had been doing very well at taking the broth
and other liquids Sophie had given her, so although she was
sometimes feverish, Sophie was not afraid she would become
too weak to hold on. Now, Sophie raised Kenny's head and held
the cup to her lips. Kenny took several swallows, then suddenly
began to struggle.

Sophie almost dropped the cup when Kenny abruptly pulled her head away. She waited for a moment until Kenny seemed to calm, and lifted her head again. Once the liquid touched her tongue, Kenny tried to pull back, then swung her arm wildly and knocked the cup from Sophie's hand.

Sophie leapt to her feet as the whiskey and water soaked the front of her dress. She stood dripping and shaking with anger. The stress of the last few days finally peaked and Sophie lost her temper.

"What in the hell are you doing?" she yelled at the defenseless woman.

Kenny did not respond to the words, but the anger in Sophie's voice affected her strongly. She cowered, her hands raised to ward off expected blows. Her body trembled with fear. Sophie sat back down on the bunk and held the young woman's shaking hands.

"God, I'm sorry," she whispered with remorse. Lightly, she rubbed Kenny's temple next to the fresh, white bandage that covered her forehead. "Hush now. No one's going to hurt you."

Kenny opened her eyes and looked somewhere above Sophie's right shoulder. "Frank?" she asked to the darkness in the corner of the upper bunk.

"Frank is gone, Kenny."

"Frank! Where is Frank?" Kenny's voice became frantic and she fought to sit upright.

Sophie pushed her gently back down on the mattress and tried to hold her there by her uninjured shoulder. Her fingertips rested against Kenny's throat and she felt the rapid beat of Kenny's racing heart. Kenny's muscled shoulders strained against her hands, and Sophie had to lean her full body weight onto her arms to keep the woman from moving. She realized that if Kenny felt the need, she could easily overpower her. Sophie suddenly felt very weary.

"Please don't fight me, Kenny," she pleaded softly. "I want to help you."

Kenny stopped struggling and looked into Sophie's eyes. Her vision was not quite focused and Sophie wondered who she was seeing. Her lips moved soundlessly. Sophie leaned forward, but could not hear any words. Reaching up, Kenny awkwardly touched Sophie's hair.

Sophie fought her reflex to pull away from the contact. With an effort, she held still and allowed Kenny to fumble her rough fingers through her curls. Only when Kenny tried to pull Sophie's lips down to her own did she resist. Kenny did not fight her refusal. Sophie unwound the fingers from her hair and sat up. Kenny clutched at her arm.

"Stay with me," she whispered.

"I'll be right here," Sophie assured her while trying to release her arm from Kenny's strong grip. The movement made Kenny anxious.

"No, stay with me." Her voice was demanding and edged with fear. Her hold tightened until it was painful.

Sophie gritted her teeth against the hurt and as soon as she forced herself to relax, Kenny's grip immediately lightened.

"You need to rest," Sophie said, in a prim voice she hadn't heard herself use since her days of teaching.

Kenny did not respond.

Sophie kicked off her shoes and, without allowing herself to question her actions, quickly stripped off her sodden dress. Clad only in her slip and underclothing, she lay down next to Kenny on the narrow bunk.

Lying on her side, with her head resting on Kenny's right shoulder, she inhaled sharply at the feel of the bare skin, warm and smooth against her cheek. Kenny sighed and closed her eyes. Sophie carefully tugged a corner of the blanket over her lower body, and tried to pull it higher to cover Kenny's breasts. She fought with the blanket for a moment, then realized that it was tangled with Kenny's feet. After a few tries, she gave up on the struggle and let the blanket drop to cover what it would.

Sophie was uncomfortably aware of the length of

Kenny's body pressed against her own. She didn't know what to do with her hand; it would not stay perched on her own hip. Finally, she placed it softly on Kenny's belly well below her breasts. For the first time in days, Kenny's breathing seemed normal and Sophie tried to let its rise and fall relax her.

Kenny's body gave off a pleasing warmth which was answered by a growing heat from Sophie's own. She contemplated Kenny's features in the soft candlelight. She was handsome still, in neither a masculine nor a feminine way. Sophie had never met anyone like her; she was at a loss for words that could even describe this perplexing woman. Sophie was intrigued. And truthfully, the last four days of unanswered questions increased her fascination all the more.

Against her will, Sophie's eyes were drawn to Kenny's breasts. They were well formed, smaller than Sophie's own, and very nice to look at. Almost without awareness, Sophie's fingers rose to trace the dark skin surrounding Kenny's nipple. Sophie held her breath in surprise and delight as Kenny's body responded, the nipple hardening beneath her touch.

An unfamiliar wetness joined the warmth between Sophie's legs. She had the curious and compelling desire to lean her head down and put her mouth to Kenny's breast. There was a strange comfort in the fact that she was a woman, her body so different from the men Sophie had touched. The softness of her skin and the promise of things hidden created a need in Sophie she had never dreamed existed.

Her trembling hand reached down and pulled away the corner of the blanket that covered Kenny's lower body. Her fingers brushed the very edge of the tangle of dark hair. Dizzy with desire, fatigue, and the whiskey she had drunk, Sophie had to struggle with herself not to reach deeper. She could not do that without Kenny's conscious consent.

But would Kenny consent? Sophie doubted it. Even if Kenny did share these desires, she apparently had many women to choose from. Sophie had never overestimated her own attractiveness and, not for the first time, she felt she would be passed over for something better, someone prettier.

The thought made her angry, an unusual response to the situation. She had always been hard pressed to care what anyone thought of her. Yet suddenly, she cared. Suddenly, she found herself needing.

Her hand rested softly on Kenny's side as the revelation coursed through her. It came with a feeling almost of nausea. The emotion was frightening. She closed her eyes, her forehead creased with pain. As she lay there quietly, fear erased her earlier desire. Finally, she gave in to her fatigue and, despite her emotional turmoil, fell into a troubled sleep.

*K*enny awakened slowly, feeling the unaccustomed caress of a soft hand against her hip. The sensation blended with the fragments of a dream, and she had difficulty separating reality from fantasy. She finally came to the conclusion that the touch was real and opened her eyes.

After endless days of delirium, Kenny's mind was clear. She knew where she was and what had happened to bring her here. But she was frankly confused at finding herself naked in bed with another woman.

The faint light of a guttering candle illuminated the body next to her. Kenny bent her head down to see the woman's face. She remembered the slightly large nose, the serious brow, and the black hair of the woman from the general store. Kenny also had a vague memory of the woman finding and questioning her. She had revealed her secret. Life would certainly be different from now on.

The woman's hand moved down to Kenny's thigh and lightly stroked the inside of her leg. Kenny tensed; breathing quietly was suddenly difficult.

It was apparent that the woman was asleep and unaware of her actions. Kenny knew she should move the woman's hand, but she hesitated, not wanting to wake her, for she could see the lines of exhaustion on her face. Kenny recalled with a twinge of guilt her stepmother's accusation that she had never been a good patient. Of course, her stepmother had never given her this kind of care.

Kenny experimentally flexed the muscles of her left arm while trying to keep her shoulder relaxed. Her muscles were weak, but there was no numbness or pain. She guessed that the bullet had missed hitting any bone. Moving her left hand slowly downward, she caught the woman's hand as it moved up her leg. She held the long, delicate fingers still for a moment, then with care, placed the hand on the narrow strip of bed between their bodies.

The woman sighed. Her brow wrinkled. Kenny held very still, not daring to move a muscle. The woman did not awaken.

Kenny closed her eyes. Exhaustion washed over her and she wondered how long she had been here in this cabin. Until the woman awoke, she had no way of knowing the day. Quietly, she rested, wishing she could get up and test the rest of her body, but she made an uncharacteristic effort to be patient.

For the next couple of hours Kenny drifted in and out of sleep before a movement next to her fully awakened her. She opened her eyes and looked into the concerned face that looked down at her. The blue-gray eyes above her watched her with a guarded expression.

"Are you here?" she asked Kenny.

Kenny was bewildered by the question.

"Well, I can see by your expression that you're finally hearing me." Quickly, Sophie pushed the cover back and stood. "How are you feeling?"

"I feel all right." Carefully, Kenny pushed herself up to lean on her right arm. "I feel lucky."

"I guess you are, if your story is true. Though I must say, your evidence is pretty convincing." She nodded at Kenny's naked body.

Kenny felt herself blushing, but forced herself not to

make a move toward pulling up the blanket. The woman stared at her; Kenny did not look away from her eyes.

"I don't suppose it would do me any good to ask you why you pretended to be a man," Sophie said before turning away.

"You can ask. I ain't got anything left to hide."

Then Sophie laughed a quick, short burst. "I will," she promised. "But now I should concern myself with making you some solid food, while you're still able to eat it."

Kenny ignored the insinuation that she would not be conscious for long. "What's your name, ma'am?"

"Sophie. And I already know yours," Sophie smiled. "You like hotcakes?"

"Sure." From the bed, Kenny stared as Sophie pulled on a dress, then quickly gathered the ingredients she needed. A cloud of white dust rose as she dumped flour into a large bowl, then added some water from a cracked pitcher. Kenny continued to stare at Sophie's back as she briskly stirred the batter. Soon, the mouth-watering smell of hotcakes filled the tiny room.

An uneasy tension also began to fill the small cabin. Kenny found it impossible to reconcile this woman with the one who had just minutes ago touched her so intimately. There was a coldness about this woman that would push even the warmest person away. Nevertheless, Kenny's interest was provoked. She had, all her life, been irresistibly pulled in by the impossible.

Sophie was either unaware of Kenny's scrutiny or just didn't care that she was being watched. Kenny sat for another moment, admiring the woman's movements. Then she noticed her pants, clean and folded, at the foot of the bunk. She reached for them carefully, holding her left arm close to her body to avoid aggravating her injury. Pulling the pants toward her, she pushed her legs over the side of the bed.

"I wouldn't advise that," Sophie warned without turning around.

Kenny didn't answer. The movement had sparked a dizziness that threatened her consciousness. She tried to ride it out, but the darkness at the edges of her vision would not clear. The world stopped spinning only when she closed her eyes, and she kept them closed even as she felt a light touch against her cheek.

"Your body's not ready to be up yet," Sophie said, making a gentle effort to push Kenny back down onto the bed.

Kenny resisted the pressure and glared up at Sophie. "I want to put my pants on."

Sophie shrugged at Kenny's stubborn protest. Shaking her head, she stood back to watch Kenny's unsteady, one-handed struggle. Kenny fought with the pants for a full minute before she was forced to give up.

"Will you help me?"

"Will you stay in bed if I do?"

Kenny nodded, knowing there was no way she could stand up even if she wanted to. Sophie pulled the pants up over her legs. Kenny turned and lay down on her back, enduring the exhausting effort it took to raise her hips enough for the pants to slide on. Sophie buttoned her up with sharp tugs, then went back to the stove.

Kenny was glad to be left alone for a minute. Her weakness was frightening. She was almost gasping for air and the light-headedness had not left her. Still, she was determined to gain some control of this situation.

As soon as she could speak in a normal voice, she asked politely, "Where's my shirt?"

"It's ashes in the stove. Wasn't even worth washing to use for cleaning rags."

"You got a shirt I can borrow?"

"No."

Kenny clenched her jaw and instantly regretted the movement as a jolt of pain went through her forehead. "I had money in my pants pocket. I can pay for it."

Sophie seemed unimpressed by Kenny's anger. She set a

plate of hotcakes on the table before replying, "Everything that you had in your pockets is in a coffee can under the bunk. Your knife is there, too. But I can't let you borrow a shirt because I don't have one."

"I can't look like this all the damn day." Kenny gestured at her bare chest. "Don't you have something I could wear?"

"Yes, I have several dresses that would probably fit you."

Kenny struggled with the effort not to swear at Sophie's suggestion. "No, thank you," she said in a flat voice.

"I had a suspicion you wouldn't like that idea." Sophie pulled the stool up to Kenny's bunk and sat down, balancing the plate of hotcakes on her lap. She cut a small wedge with the side of her fork and held it out to Kenny.

Kenny stared up at the food, mildly insulted. "I s'pose I can feed myself."

Sophie did not move the fork. She returned Kenny's stare for a moment, then asked, "Do you have any idea of the things I have done for you and to you during the last four days?"

Kenny's face turned a bright red.

Sophie nodded meaningfully. "Now, if it pleases me to feed you, I think I should be allowed to do that."

Kenny silently opened her mouth and Sophie smiled as she fed her the small bite of hotcakes. Her mouth was dry and chewing was difficult. Slowly, she worked over the food, her eyes avoiding Sophie's. But her embarrassment was not only over her helplessness, she was ashamed that she had been so ungrateful.

Her eyes lit on Sophie's hands. Here was a safe place to look — she wouldn't have to read the expressions that crossed the other woman's face, while she'd still know when a bite was coming. Sophie's hands were fine-boned and delicate. Kenny imagined that, with an easy life, her hands would be considered elegant. She watched the grace with which Sophie held the fork and how cultured her movements were. And how out of place those hands looked in this rundown cabin.

Kenny's strength seemed to increase with each bite she took. She didn't know if it was the food or the sight of Sophie's hands that caused the warmth to rise up from her belly. Remembering the soft feel of Sophie's palm against her thigh brought the blush back to her face.

"Are you feeling all right?"

Kenny nodded, still refusing to look at Sophie's face.

"You just went all red and you're breathing kind of hard," Sophie said kindly as she put her finger under Kenny's chin and tried to raise it. "Are you sure...?"

Swallowing hard to down her last bite, Kenny hurried to reply, "No. I'm fine. Really."

"Maybe you should lie down."

"No. I don't need to lie down."

"You shouldn't push yourself." Sophie leaned to the side and carefully placed the plate on the floor. "We don't know what might be causing a reaction like that."

"I know what caused it." Kenny finally leveled her gaze at Sophie and answered with an honesty that surprised herself. "You did, Sophie."

Sophie's eyebrows rose. "I did? Oh, because I embarrassed you?" Her face became serious. She placed her hand on Kenny's knee. "I'm sorry. I didn't mean — "

"It ain't embarrassment." Kenny had to concentrate hard to keep her legs still. Sophie's touch had set them to trembling. "It's just— it's just you."

Sophie's look showed incomprehension. Kenny gently took Sophie's hand and lifted it off her knee. The skin was even softer than she remembered. She held it for a moment, then leaned forward enough to lower it to Sophie's lap. After releasing her hand, she leaned back reluctantly.

"I don't understand," Sophie said kindly, still expecting an explanation.

"I can't explain," Kenny answered. She felt courageous and she decided to let herself do this; she had restrained her desires long enough for one lifetime. "I can show you."

Sophie again raised her eyebrows and Kenny acted before the woman had a chance to pull her head away. She gripped Sophie's jawbone firmly with her right hand and quickly pressed her lips to Sophie's open mouth.

Sophie's entire body stiffened and she seemed frozen to the spot. Kenny took the opportunity to move her lips softly, pulling Sophie's lower lip into her mouth. Sophie didn't breathe; Kenny could see her eyes still opened wide. Gently releasing her grip on Sophie's face, Kenny allowed her the chance to move away if she wanted to. She didn't move.

Encouraged, Kenny slid her hand across Sophie's cheek and around the back of her neck. Sophie made a small sound deep in her throat and slowly closed her eyes. The incredible sensation of the moment made Kenny feel that she was going to pass out. There seemed to be no blood left in her head. Unwillingly, she broke the kiss and let Sophie go.

"That's what you do to me," she whispered. Suddenly feeling dizzy, and a little fearful, Kenny leaned back against the wall.

Sophie sat stock still. Her eyes had opened when Kenny moved away. She stared as if she could not believe what had just happened. Her fingers reached up and touched her lips lightly as if to convince herself that they were her own. The gesture shot another surge of desire through Kenny's body.

"I'd like to do that again," Kenny confided.

Sophie visibly came to her senses. She shook her head and stood up, knocking the stool over onto its side. "No. Don't ever do that again." She wiped the back of her hand across her mouth. "You're delirious. You're not thinking clearly."

Kenny laughed. "My mind ain't never been this clear before."

"No." Sophie seemed determined to deny the desire that had so obviously gripped the two of them. "You're tired, we're both tired. That's all."

The look she gave Kenny as she said these words was

almost pleading. Kenny sighed. "Yeah, maybe you're right." The words had no conviction, but Sophie accepted them anyway. "I guess I should lie down."

Sophie didn't hesitate to take Kenny's shoulders to help her ease herself down on the bunk, but Kenny watched as it was Sophie's turn to avoid her gaze. She closed her eyes to narrow slits, open just enough to see Sophie's profile as she stood uncertainly above her. Letting her breathing become slow and deep, she let Sophie believe that she was falling into sleep.

Sophie stood for another minute more, lit by the warm glow of the candle. Before she turned away, Kenny saw her once again reach up and put her fingers to her lips as if tracing the outline of Kenny's kiss. Kenny smiled and covertly licked her own lips, not wanting to waste a bit of that stolen kiss.

Ten

Kenny smiled from the shade of the front porch as she
watched Sophie grooming her horse. For the first time
in a week she didn't feel guilty for watching instead of
working. Today Sophie had let her help with the dishes and
stayed patiently supportive as Kenny did an awkward, one-
handed sweeping of the house.

Kenny was satisfied with her efforts, but admitted to
herself that she was a little embarrassed at how tired those small
tasks had left her. She had grown up trusting the strength of
her body, and until now it had never failed her. This near-death
experience had removed that trust. No matter how temporary
her injuries were, they had given Kenny a disturbing look at
her own mortality.

She shook her head at the thoughts. A sheepish grin
crossed her face as she thought of the pride she took in
sweeping Sophie's floor. Not long ago, she would have refused
in anger to do such work. I'm certainly changing, she confided
to herself. Nothing to do but accept that truth. Leaning against
the wall, she stretched her bare toes out to wiggle in the warm
sunlight.

She was dressed in her driver's pants, against Sophie's
warnings, and the top half of a worn slip that Sophie had
sacrificed to Kenny's stubbornness. Kenny never relented in her
refusal to wear a dress, although going topless for a couple of
days did have its embarrassing moments. But she was able to

outlast Sophie's determination to get her properly dressed in women's clothing. One day, Sophie walked up and tossed the full-length slip and a pair of scissors on Kenny's bunk. Kenny cut the undergarment to a good length and wordlessly tucked it into her jeans. The makeshift shirt left her arms and most of her shoulders bare. But it made checking her bandage easier and Kenny was secretly pleased at the look it afforded her muscles. Her pleasure increased tenfold when she caught Sophie's unguarded, admiring glance.

Kenny herself had seen plenty to admire in Sophie. She was amazed that she had ever thought this woman was plain-looking. Her face had a strength and character that could be overlooked only by the casual glance. And while Sophie never had much to say with words, her facial expressions always spoke her mind. Kenny was fascinated by the wordless conversations the woman seemed to have with herself when she thought Kenny was sleeping. Unfortunately, Kenny was able to read the serious misgivings Sophie had about her uninvited guest. That thought removed the smile from Kenny's face.

Though Kenny was recovering quickly, beyond Sophie's expectations, she suddenly felt that her progress was too slow. As she regained her strength, Sophie told her about the mood of the town, and that the general opinion was she had held up the stage and murdered her old friend. Kenny was hurt, but not surprised at the townspeople's convictions. She knew that every day she remained with Sophie increased her chances of being caught here. And if she was caught, she had no doubt that she would be hanged without a trial. Worse yet, if Sophie was found to be sheltering her, she too would most likely hang.

As Kenny pondered her options, she felt a slow burning begin in her stomach. Certainly, she had to leave, and there were a hundred towns no worse than Jackson that would shelter her, but when she looked at Sophie, she was filled with a strange reluctance to leave this place of comfort and safety. Leaving was the last thing on her mind as she watched Sophie's affectionate care of her horse.

Kenny didn't look away as Sophie turned from Twitch and walked toward her. Sophie's hair was loose and blowing in the light breeze, and Kenny wanted nothing more than to wrap her fingers in the full curls and feel their softness against her face.

Sophie had almost reached the porch before she realized that Kenny was staring. As she hesitated at the step, Kenny could read the exact moment when she succeeded in gathering her determination to ignore Kenny's boldness.

"How are you feeling?" she asked lightly.

"How? Or what?" Kenny bantered.

Sophie didn't bite. The flirting was either unnoticed or patiently ignored. She brushed past without another word and entered the house. Kenny heard her inside washing her face and hands.

"Damn," Kenny whispered. Flirting was much more successful when the woman thought she was a man. But when she was a man, she had to hide her true gender, so the flirting never led anywhere. Now that she had nothing to hide, her advances were ignored. Life was not fair.

Bracing herself on her good arm, she levered herself upright. Her body was still stiff, but most of the soreness was gone. She suffered a headache every evening, and the scar on her forehead plagued her with an unbearable itch. Her shoulder would be worthless for some time, but considering the extent of her wounds, she was healing rapidly.

She stopped in the doorway and waited for Sophie to finish drying her face. Sophie did not turn around. Standing with her back to Kenny, holding the wet towel, she was clearly waiting for something.

"I got to get out of here," Kenny said with an unintended abruptness.

Sophie stiffened and Kenny was surprised to realize that her words were not at all what Sophie had expected.

"I can't stay." Kenny softened the tone of her voice. "I'm a danger to you."

When Sophie turned to face her, she had control of whatever emotion she had felt at Kenny's words. "You're not strong enough to go," she said simply.

Kenny knew that Sophie spoke the truth, but she had to consider the risks. Leaving now might well endanger her own life, but staying could cost both of them their lives.

"Anyway, you can't go," Sophie continued. "You owe me."

Again Kenny was surprised. Embarrassed, a guilty flush spread over her face as she realized she hadn't even considered repaying Sophie for her help. She reached into her pocket, took out the little money she had, and put it on the table.

"It's not much, but it's all I have. I can send — "

"That's not what I meant," Sophie interrupted, pushing the money back across to Kenny. "You owe me a story. You haven't told me why you are pretending to be a man."

The words made Kenny pause. With a sigh, she ran her right hand through her short hair. Kenny knew an explanation would be expected and she had given it some thought over the past few days of recuperation. But she knew nothing she could say would convey the frustration and desperation that she'd felt all her life. The sense of never belonging, the feeling of being alone even in her family's crowded house. Kenny believed these things could not be expressed. Perhaps Sophie would not understand; maybe no woman could ever empathize with her.

The floor squeaked rhythmically as Kenny paced the short room, trying to organize her thoughts. She didn't hear Sophie's approach and flinched when she felt the unexpected touch on her arm.

Sophie frowned. She was annoyed at herself for touching without speaking first. Kenny smiled forgiveness.

"Come, sit down. I don't expect this will be easy for you," Sophie urged, steering Kenny toward the table. Her expression was open and kind. She hurried to the stove and pushed the coffee pot over the fire, then returned to sit at Kenny's side.

Kenny sat on the hard bench and looked at the tabletop, avoiding Sophie's eyes.

Pausing briefly, she began. "Well, my mother disappeared when I was seven. I guess she got her fill of my father." Kenny grimaced. Now that she'd begun her story, the words and the sadness poured out of her with ease. "And I guess that meant she had enough of us kids, too, since she didn't invite any of us to come along. We'd been livin' in Utah for about a year and my father'd joined up with that religion there, the Mormons. Do you know it?"

Sophie nodded, attempting to keep her face empty of any judgment, but not succeeding.

"He wanted all of us to belong, he wanted a second wife. My mother didn't agree to either of his wants. Those days were the first times I remember him hittin' her. He'd always been mean and quick to punish me and my sisters, but I never saw him hurt her until then."

"I'd always been boyish and it just got worse after she left. My father let me act that way since he didn't have no sons and needed help around the farm. It was never a problem until about four years ago." Kenny paused and took a sip of cold coffee that had been sitting on the table since lunch time.

"What changed?" Sophie asked.

"His third — no, his fourth wife had given him a son. The boy finally grew old enough to do the chores I'd been doin' all those years. You probably won't understand, but I just couldn't go back to doin' women's work. I tried, but I just couldn't make myself fit. I was always too loud, too strong, too restless for my sisters and his wives. They all hated me for reasons I never understood."

"I think I can understand why," Sophie said without explanation. She motioned for Kenny to continue.

"I fought being a woman 'til this happened." Kenny pulled down her ever present bandanna to show the scar on her throat. "I got this for talking back to the old man my father wanted me to marry."

Sophie's face darkened, and although it was obvious that she wanted to speak, she kept her lips pressed tightly together.

"The old bastard had about ten wives already. Everybody said the older he got, the younger his wives had to be. I figured it wouldn't be long before he'd be following pregnant women around, waiting to see if they would drop a girl. I asked him, didn't he think I was a little too old for him?" Kenny smiled, remembering the look of outrage and insult on the old man's face.

"'Cause of my bad luck, my father heard what I said and his quick temper flared. It was an accident mostly, he didn't mean to do nothin' like this. I was sittin' on the fence when he struck me. I hadn't expected it, since I'd been pretty much free to speak my mind 'til then. Anyway, the blow knocked me kind of sideways off the fence and I landed on the edge of the plow." Kenny absentmindedly rubbed the long scar running across her throat as she spoke. "It did keep me from worryin' about marriage for a couple a years. I didn't recover too quick. They all thought I was mute, and I'm not sure why, but I never told 'em any different."

"I stayed quiet for a couple years and I played along at being a woman while I made my plans to high tail it. I don't know why I waited so long to run away — guess I was scared. But I took bein' a woman as long as I could. When that old bastard decided he still wanted me for a wife and started comin' back around, I finally had the courage to leave. But I'll tell ya, it wasn't easy to go without gettin' some kind of revenge against my father."

Sophie waited a few moments before saying anything. Obviously, she was trying to keep herself from speaking her mind. "I think it shows that you're a better person than he is."

Kenny imagined that vengeance would feel more satisfying than the knowledge that she was a good person, but it still pleased her to hear the words. "You said you understand why they hated me..." she began, then was suddenly filled with fear at what Sophie might have meant. Was she so strange that women just couldn't like her?

Sophie laughed softly at Kenny's expression. "I suppose they hated you out of envy. Almost every woman dreams of the freedom that you must've had. Of course they would resent you and try to force you back into being like them. If they couldn't escape that life, why should you be able to?"

"You don't like bein' a woman?" Kenny asked, disbelief raising the pitch of her low voice.

"I am happy being a woman, especially now that I don't have to worry about what any particular man thinks of me. But I've never known any woman to be completely happy with the life she was expected to lead." Sophie's voice revealed that her thoughts were somewhere far from the room they shared. "There's always a desire for leaving life, one way or another."

Kenny thought about that, what it meant that most women were unhappy. She had always thought it to be some shortcoming in herself, but if so many women felt that way, it had to be natural. But why did they accept those roles if they were not happy? And if her feelings of being trapped were so common, what about her sexual interests? Were those feelings also common?

Kenny looked up at Sophie and considered the possibility. She had strong suspicions about Sophie's interest in her, but how could she approach that subject? Not having the words to express the way she herself felt, how could she speak of it to another woman? She remembered the way Sophie had touched her in her sleep, and how she'd responded to her kiss. As those unsettling memories flooded her mind, Kenny struggled to keep her expression blank.

Sophie seemed unaware of the turn Kenny's thoughts had taken. She was silent, apparently musing over the sad story she'd been told. Kenny was surprised to notice that the room was becoming dark. The sun had almost gone down during their conversation.

Wordlessly, Kenny lit the lantern, and Sophie smiled at

her as she got up to prepare their dinner. She did not ask for help, but Kenny, with her new awareness of Sophie's feelings toward women's work, was willing to offer what help she could.

Nothing more was said about leaving.

*A*s she busied herself preparing supper, Sophie was surprised to notice that her hands were shaking. She stirred the frying potatoes with a briskness she hoped would conceal the tremors from Kenny's too observant eyes. Although the young woman's story had upset her, she knew it was not the reason her body was so affected. She was reacting to Kenny's closeness.

Over the aroma of the sizzling food, Sophie could smell the fresh scent of Kenny's clean skin. They touched, fingers and bodies, as Kenny stood beside her and handed her ingredients. Sophie stirred faster.

When they sat down to eat, Sophie could not make herself look away from Kenny's face. She watched her eat the food they had prepared together, almost forgetting her own portion growing cold on her plate. Kenny ate slowly, politely, and Sophie was fascinated by the movements of her lips and mouth. The idea of those lips on her skin made Sophie's heart beat loud enough to be heard over the crackling of the fire in the small room.

Kenny finished eating, and with a contented sigh, pushed away her plate. She leaned back and stretched, the points of her breasts pressed against the thin cloth of the slip she wore for a shirt. Sophie held her breath. Her food had lost all of its flavor. She, too, pushed her plate aside.

"You didn't eat much," Kenny noted. "You feelin' okay?"

"Yes, I'm fine." Sophie tried to sound hearty and assuring, but she was learning that Kenny was a hard person to fool.

"You look kind of flushed."

"Do I? It must be the heat...from cooking," Sophie explained. She was not surprised that her skin was flushed. A fiery heat was spreading through her, a heat that had nothing to do with the coals burning in the cookstove.

Kenny contemplated her for a long moment; Sophie tried not to squirm or look uncomfortable under her gaze. She smiled with what she hoped seemed innocence; her effort was rewarded by a wide grin from Kenny.

"Guess we'd better clean up," Kenny said as she rose from the table.

Sophie reached over and took the plate from her hand. "These dishes will still be here tomorrow. Let's have some coffee out on the porch instead."

"That's a wonderful idea."

Sophie suppressed a shiver, loving the sound of Kenny's voice. It suggested that there were even more wonderful ideas in store. She pushed down the thought and stood. Kenny came around the table and took hold of her arm.

Suddenly, Sophie was frightened. Sexual desire this compelling was a new experience. She had to be losing her mind to even contemplate making love with a woman. And to consider it with this woman was madness. Sophie realized she was taking Kenny solely on faith. What did she really know about her?

Sophie looked into Kenny's eyes and saw nothing but kindness.

"Let me get the coffee," Kenny suggested. "It's time I did some waitin' on you."

"You don't have to..."

"I want to."

"But your shoulder..."

"Go. Sit down," Kenny insisted, giving Sophie a little push on the back. "I can do this, really."

Still Sophie hesitated, feeling irrationally uncomfortable being pushed out of her role as caretaker. "The cups are on the..."

Kenny interrupted her again with a voice that said this was the last time. "I know where the cups are."

Sophie knew she was being ungracious. Letting her resistance fall, she managed a smile. Kenny responded by giving her another gentle push that set Sophie walking to the door.

The evening was turning cool. The sun had already disappeared behind a massive bank of thunderclouds advancing from the west. Sophie sat down on the step and breathed in the dusty smell of the approaching rain. Behind her, she heard the quiet clinking of a teaspoon against a cup as Kenny stirred honey into her coffee. She leaned her head back and looked up to the darkening sky. The waxing moon, grown well beyond its half, was directly above her.

A woman could get comfortable...she allowed herself the forbidden thought, but only for a brief moment.

"No honey, right?"

"Right." Sophie reached back and took both of the coffee cups from Kenny. She had carried them out one-handed, hooking her finger through the handles. "How much did you spill?" Sophie teased.

"No coffee. But if I was you, I'd be careful where I sat on the bench. You might stick down." Kenny held her hand out in front of her and pretended to pry her fingers apart from the stickiness of spilled honey.

"That's the last time I let you in my kitchen," Sophie vowed.

Kenny sat down next to her on the narrow step. Their shoulders touched and Sophie resisted pulling away. The contact became a point of heat that spread across her chest and down through her body. Out of the corner of her eye, she watched Kenny's movements.

Kenny leaned her face over her coffee cup, letting the thick curls of steam warm her skin. Her eyes were closed, her forehead relaxed, and Sophie was reminded that Kenny was still so young. The harshness of her life had not yet done much to affect the lines of her face.

"How old are you?" Kenny asked without opening her eyes.

Sophie's grip tightened on her coffee cup as Kenny again seemed to be able to read her thoughts. With an effort, she dismissed the fear as nonsense and answered, "Thirty-two."

"Thirty-two," Kenny repeated, her voice toneless.

"Does that sound ancient to you?"

"No." Kenny turned toward her and lifted a hand to her hair. "But I see you have some gray. And these lines..."

Sophie blinked her eyes as Kenny touched the faint wrinkles above her cheekbone. "Crow's feet," she silently named them.

"I get the feelin' that you didn't get 'em from smiling," Kenny continued. "But you haven't told me nothin' about your life."

"I don't like to talk about it," Sophie whispered. "Not because it's been a bad life. It just hasn't been much of a life at all."

"I'm not sure I believe that," Kenny responded, after a moment of quiet between them.

Sophie shrugged. "You're welcome to believe what you will. But I can promise you that you are the most interesting person that I have ever met in my entire life."

Kenny laughed out loud. "Now, that's sad," she said.

"Do you think so?" Sophie asked earnestly. "I think this situation is actually quite remarkable."

Kenny looked at her with a puzzled expression.

"Think about it," Sophie said. "You've lived the lives of a boy, a man, and a woman. You've had respect and a paying job. You've been robbed, beaten, and barely escaped being murdered. You crawled over miles of wilderness to find help and here you sit, acting like you've never been hurt, wearing pants, and laughing at me when I say that you're interesting."

Before she finished speaking, they were both shaking with laughter. Kenny sloshed coffee over her foot as she tried to put down her cup. She leaned back and let the laughter flow.

Sophie wiped tears from her eyes as she watched Kenny. Humor was just the release she needed after the last few stressful weeks. She sighed with satisfaction as her laughter faded.

"Now, don't ask me about my life," she commanded.

"Yes, ma'am," Kenny said with mock soberness, as soon as she could speak.

Sophie bravely reached out and put her hand over Kenny's. She did not pull away, but Sophie had not expected her to. Perhaps some of Kenny's daring attitude toward life was rubbing off on Sophie. Maybe wanting something was the only justification needed for taking a chance. Sophie looked at Kenny's profile. A hint of a smile still lingered at her lips. The memory of those lips pressed against her own was strong. She recalled the power of Kenny's hand on the back of her neck, pulling her even closer into that kiss. A week's worth of desire had only increased the seductiveness of that moment.

But she had told Kenny never to do that again and Kenny had respected her wish. Strange as it seemed, Sophie's conviction about the wrongness of their desire had faded away even before her lips had stopped tingling from the touch. Now, she regretted her words, but it was impossible to take them back. It was also impossible for Sophie to even conceive of taking the first step back to that passion.

Suppressing a sigh of disappointment, Sophie turned her head away from Kenny and looked out into the night. She slowly removed her hand from Kenny's and held it tightly between her knees. Her laughter was gone. Suddenly, she felt like crying. She had never imagined that desire could be so frightening.

Eleven

He found himself at the edge of the clearing again. For almost two weeks he had managed to stay away, forcing himself to ride the endless miles of McLaren fence line, avoiding any company until his desires got so strong he had to ride to town and buy a whore. In his most clear-minded moments, he knew his lust was not Sophie's fault, but it was sure easier to blame her than to accept what he considered his weakness.

As he rode the lines, he thought often of the time he'd attacked her in the shack. He couldn't get rid of the feel of her pressed up hard between his body and the wall. It was the first time he'd ever touched her. Robert shook his head to release himself from the powerful memory. She shouldn't have shown her fear. That was something he could not resist. He was addicted to the feeling of making people fear him. Knowing that she hated him made the feeling even stronger.

If she hadn't brought up Allen's name, he would have satisfied himself with her and the whole thing would be over. He was sure he needed her just one time to break the spell she had over him. What he had to do was find a way to reconcile his needs with the obligation of respecting his brother's memory. When he figured that out, she would no longer be able to use his brother's name against him.

So here he was, at the clearing's edge, with no idea of how to master her. But he couldn't leave her alone. He just needed to test her, to see if she'd learned anything, or if there was anything he could learn from her.

*K*enny nuzzled her lips and nose into the sweet smell of Sophie's hair. Sophie pressed her back against Kenny's breasts and pulled Kenny's arm tighter around her. Kenny's palm brushed the soft skin over Sophie's collarbones. The feeling was incredible, the softness divine. Kenny sighed in deep contentment at the warmth generated by the contact of their bodies.

Seconds later, her body stiffened and her eyes flew open. She was shocked awake with the realization that Sophie was, for some reason, in her bed. The intimacy of their touch was disturbing, the way their bodies fit together was impossibly familiar. She tried to move her arm from around Sophie's body, but the woman made a quiet noise of protest at the movement and clenched her fingers into Kenny's forearm. Kenny held still, afraid to move, but afraid not to.

The warm haze of sunlight coming through the paper windows lit the room too brightly for her sleepy eyes. They had stayed up late into the night talking. Sophie had asked her countless questions about her childhood and about her brief life as a man and Kenny told her many things she thought she would never speak of again in her life. In return, Kenny had kept her promise and asked Sophie no more questions about her own past. Some of their conversation was not too clear to her now. But, regardless of what had been spoken or how tired she'd become, she clearly remembered going to bed alone.

Sophie stirred in her sleep, pressing even closer to Kenny. Kenny started to sweat. Her back was against the wall; she could not move away from the body that rested so temptingly against her own.

"Wake up, Sophie," Kenny whispered, hoping that she could wake the woman before she was unable to control her desire.

When Sophie did not respond, Kenny leaned her lips

close to her ear and whispered again. A strand of Sophie's hair tickled her cheek, but there was no other movement. Almost before she was aware of what she was doing, Kenny touched Sophie's earlobe with a light kiss. It wasn't enough...She then took the soft skin into her mouth and nibbled gently.

Sophie murmured and turned her head toward Kenny's mouth, exposing the smooth length of the side of her neck. Kenny's kisses traveled downward. Her chin pushed away Sophie's nightgown as she slowly kissed her way to Sophie's shoulder. Kenny did not allow herself to think; if she did, she knew she would stop and maybe never have this opportunity again. She was hot, hotter than she'd ever imagined she could be and she did not want to stop. Again, she bit into Sophie's skin, harder this time.

The touch finally penetrated Sophie's slumber. She breathed in quickly, almost gasping, and turned to Kenny before opening her eyes. Her surprise was evident in her face, but Kenny stared at her with determination.

"What are you doing?" Sophie whispered the question. Kenny could hear a faint edge of fear in her voice.

Not allowing herself to become defensive, Kenny spoke roughly, "Why are you in my bed?"

"You had a nightmare."

Kenny read the lie as clearly as if Sophie had confessed her words were not true. "You're not a good liar," Kenny said in a softer tone. "Your face gives you away."

Anger flashed on Sophie's features and she pulled away. Kenny grabbed her shoulder and stopped her from leaving the bed. Even with her left hand she had the strength to hold Sophie against the mattress. She leaned down close to her face.

Sophie's anger grew, but she kept her voice low. "Let me go," she warned.

"You're not leavin' this bed 'til you tell me why you were sleepin' with me." Kenny spoke with her lips so close to Sophie's that they were almost touching.

Sophie's eyes burned up into hers, but Kenny thought

that her anger was subsiding. For once, she was wrong about Sophie's expression. With a move too quick for Kenny to defend herself against, Sophie slammed her fist into Kenny's left shoulder.

Pain exploded in blinding showers of light. Her head was filled with a bright red haze and the breath left her in a rush. The pain was too intense to even allow her to cry out. She fell face down onto the bunk. Sophie was gone.

Hot tears pressed against Kenny's eyelids and she did not fight them. The agony that radiated from her shoulder was immobilizing. But what felt absolutely the worst was the knowledge that she had deserved this.

Slowly, through her misery and pain, she became aware that Sophie was trying to turn her onto her back. Ashamed of her actions, she buried her face into the pillow and resisted the pull. Sophie stopped, resting one of her hands in the short hair at the back of Kenny's neck. She stroked lightly and Kenny finally felt her struggle for breath beginning to ease.

"I need to look at your shoulder," Sophie said in a voice tight with emotion. "Please turn over."

Kenny obeyed, but kept her eyes closed so she would not have to see the look of betrayal that was sure to be on Sophie's face. She lay silently as Sophie removed the bandages. An occasional tear squeezed out of the corners of her eyes and trickled down into the hair above her temples.

"You're not bleeding, that's good. How does it feel inside?" Sophie gently probed the skin around the bullet wound. "Can you move your arm?"

Kenny did not move or answer. The sharp pain in her shoulder had dulled, but the ache of her guilt increased with Sophie's caring touch.

"Please look at me, Kenny," Sophie urged.

Kenny could not. She pressed her eyelids tighter together as a fresh wave of tears demanded release.

Sophie was silent, her fingers tenderly rubbing the muscles around Kenny's shoulder. After several minutes Sophie spoke again, in a voice that made Kenny finally open her eyes.

"I'm sorry," she whispered. Her voice sounded distant and anguished. "I'm sorry, I'm sorry..."

Kenny was startled to feel the splash of tears falling on her chest. Sophie's head was bent low, her face close. Kenny reached up and touched her wet cheek.

"No," Kenny protested. "It ain't your fault."

Sophie shook her head hard, denying Kenny's assurances. "I got in bed with you. And I — I touched you," Sophie confessed, her voice ragged with sobs. "I wanted you...I still want you."

Kenny's muscles tensed and her heart beat fast. She could hardly believe the words, or their impact on her. Her body raged with instant desire.

"It's hard, it's just so hard," Sophie continued, unaware of Kenny's reaction. "I've never wanted anyone like this. I've never wanted..."

Kenny stopped Sophie's words with a fingertip pressed to her lips. Sophie sighed and looked bravely into Kenny's eyes. Kenny tried to reassure her with a smile. Opening her lips, she kissed Kenny's fingertip, then turned her face enough to remove it from her mouth.

"I imagine this is easy for you. But it has never been easy for me." Sophie directed the whispered words to the wall as if she could not look at Kenny. "I can't imagine doing this with a woman."

"I can imagine it," Kenny affirmed. "I've imagined it all my life, but I ain't never done it. Man or woman."

"You are a virgin?"

Kenny laughed with embarrassment at Sophie's delighted outburst. All of her pain faded out of perception in the light of Sophie's smile.

"You sure don't act like a virgin," Sophie said.

"That's just it, I'm an actor," Kenny admitted with a touch of pride. "Had you convinced that I was a man, didn't I?"

"Mm..." Sophie nodded. "And I wanted you then, too."

"More than now?"

"No." Sophie leaned back and looked down the length of Kenny's body. "Definitely not more than now."

The words and the look were like a physical touch on Kenny's hot skin. Tentatively, she reached out and put her hand on Sophie's thigh. Her skin also felt hot — it burned through the sheer cloth of Sophie's nightgown. Kenny rubbed lightly, moving her hand in small circles, moving her hand higher up Sophie's thigh.

Sophie looked down at her. Her lips were parted slightly and her breath was quickening. Abruptly, she leaned down and kissed Kenny on the collarbone. Her hair cascaded over Kenny's face and Kenny inhaled deeply the scent of that dark curtain.

Sophie's kisses began slow and hesitant, but soon increased to match Kenny's desire. Kenny shivered as Sophie's mouth moved down to her breast. Kenny pressed her body upward, instinctively urging Sophie to take her into her mouth. When the soft lips and searching tongue closed around her nipple, Kenny could not suppress her moan of pleasure.

Sophie was kneeling over her on the narrow bunk. Kenny wanted to feel their bodies full together, but she did not want to stop Sophie from kissing her breasts. Her fingers tangled with the long folds of Sophie's nightgown until her hand broke free and she felt bare skin. She slid her hand up until she touched the edge of Sophie's underwear. The cloth was hot and wet and Kenny knew just what that wetness was. And she knew that she shared the feeling.

Sophie trembled at Kenny's explorations and tried to open her legs for Kenny's touch, but her position on the small bed was too cramped. She pulled her head away from Kenny's chest as Kenny guided her body to lie beside her.

They looked silently into each other's eyes for a moment, each tense with desire. Finally, Kenny could wait no longer and crushed her lips against Sophie's willing mouth. Sophie's hand slid along Kenny's side, her skin slick with a light cover of sweat.

Kenny struggled to remove her right hand from under Sophie's body. Sophie did not move to let it go. Kenny's left hand was practically useless after the blow she had received, but she managed to maneuver it up to Sophie's head and to entangle her fingers in the thick hair.

Sophie's hand nudged the waistband of the pants Kenny had been too sleepy to remove last night. She regretted her laziness until Sophie effortlessly unbuttoned them and reached inside. Kenny had no regrets from the moment Sophie slipped her fingers across her wetness and then deep inside her body.

The feeling was unbelievable. Kenny was dazed and dizzy at the insistence of Sophie's touch and her own body's need. She forgot to breathe, she forgot to kiss Sophie's open and slightly smiling mouth.

Sophie moved her fingers rhythmically, never withdrawing them from Kenny's body. The side of her thumb pressed hard against the point of Kenny's desire as Kenny relentlessly pushed against Sophie's strong hand, her breath coming in gasps. Her orgasm was quick and violent.

The release did nothing to diminish Kenny's passion. Before Sophie had even removed her hand, Kenny was trying to push her back onto the bed, trying to reach her incapable left hand down to touch Sophie, desperate to give Sophie what she herself had been given.

Sophie's laughter was gentle as she took Kenny's hand. "Be patient," she whispered. "We have time."

Kenny did not argue, but wondered if the statement would prove true. Reluctantly, she allowed Sophie to get out of the bed and stand before her. Sophie took the hem of her nightgown and then gracefully pulled it off over her head. Kenny's body went weak — then, as suddenly, surged with power at the sight of Sophie's nearly naked body. She sat up in the bed and let Sophie crawl past her to the back of the bunk.

Kenny gingerly lay down on her left side facing Sophie. Her shoulder troubled her, but even the pain felt good to her heightened senses. Momentarily, she fought with her impatience, her desire to devour Sophie whole, but it was a battle she could not win.

They kissed deeply, their tongues moving with familiarity into each other's mouths. Kenny loved the hard press of Sophie's long nose against her cheekbone. She loved their kisses, but she longed to move her mouth lower, to Sophie's breasts, then lower still.

Suddenly, Sophie pulled her head back and Kenny took it as an invitation to shift her body downward and to move her lips across Sophie's chest.

"Stop!" Sophie demanded, her voice wild with fright. Kenny stopped instantly. "What did I do?" she cried.

"Be quiet!" Sophie whispered. "I hear a horse."

Kenny closed her eyes and tried to listen over her heavy breathing. She couldn't hear anything. "It was just Twitch."

"No, I know Twitch's hoofbeats. It's not her..." Sophie listened again, then shoved Kenny away from her in her haste to get out of the bed. "Oh my God, I think it's Robert!"

Kenny scrambled out of the bunk and made a frenzied search for the shirt she'd forgotten she no longer owned. "Who the hell is Robert?" she yelled.

"My husband's brother." Sophie's voice was muffled by the thick layers of a yellow dress she had pulled over her head.

"Your husband's brother?" Kenny stopped in her tracks, shocked into immobility. "You have a husband?"

"No, of course not," Sophie snapped at her as if Kenny were a feebleminded fool.

"What do you mean — "

"Oh God," Sophie interrupted. "We have to hide you."

"Don't change the subject," Kenny shouted. "Do you have a husband or not?"

"Jesus, Kenny. He's been dead forever!" Sophie grabbed Kenny's boots and shoved them at her. She looked frantically around the room, searching for any other evidence of Kenny's presence.

Kenny thought of hiding under the table, but there was no cloth to hang down to hide her. She could fit behind the cookstove but it was still too warm from last night's banking of coals. Her only chance of escape would be to tear out a window and try to sneak away while Sophie kept the man occupied.

Sophie had a different idea. "Get up on the top bunk," she instructed, pushing Kenny toward the bed above the one she'd slept in for the last two weeks. She quickly stripped the blankets off Kenny's bed.

Kenny threw her boots onto the bunk and awkwardly tried to boost herself up. Her shoulder was too weak and Sophie had to put her own shoulder under Kenny's butt and give her a lift. Kenny squeezed tight into the corner with her face against the wall and Sophie piled the blankets up over her.

Kenny tried to quiet her breath and lie still as Sophie rushed out of the cabin. She could only hope that Sophie had completely hidden her with the blankets. She listened to the muffled sound of voices from outside, and tried to make herself small.

Sophie smoothed down her wild hair and cursed under her breath as she watched Robert and his horse prance into her yard. Why had the man chosen this day, this time to show up? She'd prayed that she would never have to see him again, all the while knowing that hope was futile. Whatever brought him here today, she was sure she wouldn't like it. As she crossed the doorway, she remembered to pick up the rifle and carry it out in the crook of her arm.

Sophie stepped off the porch and walked out into the yard. It would be best to keep him as far from the house as she could and not give him any reason to want to enter it.

Robert rode the horse so close to her that it was insulting, practically inviting it to hit her with its shoulder. She stood her ground as he stopped with his stirrup just below her breast. He scowled down at her as she stubbornly waited for him to speak first.

"I guess you been stayin' out of trouble." Robert spoke without emotion. "Least I ain't heard any rumors from town yet. I gotta admit I'm surprised."

Sophie found nothing in his words worth responding to as she stared up at him silently.

"Where's that horse I lent you?"

"She's around back," Sophie lied. She really had no idea where Twitch might have wandered, but then she never considered it any of her business. Twitch would come when she was called and that was good enough for Sophie.

"I didn't see it when I rode up."

Sophie shrugged. If he couldn't find her, he couldn't take her back. "What do you need here, Robert?" she asked rudely, feeling somewhat reckless.

He almost smiled at her insolence. "To tell the truth, I came here as a favor. You know the stage was robbed a while back?" He waited for her nod, then continued. "The robbers are still loose. People think they might come back and hit it again. You're awful close to that kind of action out here."

"I'm no closer to the mines than I am to town," Sophie pointed out.

"You're not likely to see anyone that bloodthirsty in town. These men are murderers and cutthroats. I'd hate to think what they might do to a woman found alone." The sharp curve of his smile told her that he was anything but repulsed by the images he imagined.

Sophie went cold and wondered how long she would be safe from this man. Trying to ignore his attempts at intimidation, she looked for the real reason for his visit. Most likely he was just trying to frighten her out of his useless shack.

"I still have the rifle you gave me," she said, patting the smooth wooden stock and trying to instill some gratitude into her voice. Robert's horse shifted its weight; its movement shoved the toe of his boot into her breastbone. She stumbled back a step, trying not to show that it had hurt.

Robert pulled the horse's head cruelly to the side. The

horse blew hard and stepped sideways. Robert did not apologize
to her, but spoke spitefully, "You'd best keep track of the gun.
This is not a safe place for women."

"Yes, Robert. I agree with you."

He looked at her as if trying to find a meaning hidden
behind her words. Just because he didn't find one didn't mean
there wasn't one there. Suddenly he seemed impatient to be
going.

"Before I go, I better warn you not to go to town for a
while. If they find the driver of that stage, there's gonna be a
lynchin'." He raised his bushy eyebrows at her. "'Less of course,
that's a show you'd like to see."

She suppressed a shudder at the frightening image of
Kenny hanging from the end of a rope. "Do you really think
the driver did it?" she asked in a thin voice.

He spat over the side of his horse. "Don't know who
else it could've been. He was the only stranger that stayed
around town lately."

Sophie had a hundred questions and a thousand denials
threatening to pour from her lips, but she closed her mouth
tightly against the desire to stand up for Kenny's innocence.

Robert gathered his reins, and before Sophie knew what
she was doing, she had reached out to grasp his stirrup. His
surprised and annoyed expression made her speak in a rush of
words.

"Robert, you know that I didn't take anything of Allen's
when I left your house. Now I don't have anything to
remember him by."

A dark scowl hardened Robert's face as Sophie paused
for breath.

"I don't want much, Robert. Maybe just a hat or some
clothes of his? Maybe some of the shirts I sewed for him?"

Grudgingly, Robert consented, clearly relieved that she
had not asked for anything of value. Allen's clothes would never
fit his broad frame anyway. "I'll be back at the ranch in a
couple of days. You can ride down then and get 'em."

Sophie thanked him with genuine appreciation. A smile crossed her face as he rode away less than happy with the results of his attempted intimidation.

Kenny was sitting with her feet dangling over the edge of the bunk when Sophie reentered the cabin. Sophie sat down at the table without speaking and Kenny respected her silence, but Sophie could feel her watching. She put her face in her hands and closed her eyes in an attempt to distance herself from everything that had happened in the last few days, but the smell of Kenny still clung to her fingers, reminding her of the problems she would have to face.

"You're right," she admitted after a few minutes of thought. She spoke the words softly, without looking at Kenny.

"What do you mean?"

Sophie sighed. "You can't stay here." Her voice sounded too harsh even to herself.

Kenny didn't make a sound until Sophie heard her bare feet hit the floor. The thump was followed by a short grunt of pain. Kenny padded over to the table and sat down across from Sophie. Her eyes looked everywhere but at Sophie as she pulled on her socks and boots.

Sophie bit her lip and wished she could take back the sound of her words. Kenny's profile did not reveal her thoughts or emotions, but Sophie imagined that she must be angry.

"I said you can't stay here — "

"I heard what you said!" Kenny snapped the words like a whip at Sophie's face.

"Please, let me finish." Sophie softened the tone of her voice, her words faded into almost a whisper as she confessed, "You can't stay...but I don't want you to go."

The meaning of Sophie's words seemed to take a moment to sink in. Kenny looked at her in puzzlement, then her eyes widened. Apparently, she became aware of the expression on her face at the same time Sophie did. Her eyes narrowed and she smiled a smile that could have meant anything. The thick line of the healing scar on her forehead gave her face a resolute appearance as she nodded her head with determination.

Without knowing why, Sophie found herself worried by that look. "What are you thinking?" she asked guardedly.

"I'm goin' to find a way to prove I'm innocent," Kenny declared.

Sophie was horrified. "You can't be serious. Everyone believes you're guilty."

"But I'm not," Kenny pointed out. "And there's gotta be a way to prove that."

"How are you going to learn anything? You can't even show your face around here — you'll be shot or hanged on sight."

"You're wrong about that," Kenny said with a smug little grin. "No one's lookin' for me, they're all lookin' for that handsome young man who drove the stage."

Sophie felt the corners of her eyes crinkling as a broad smile of understanding spread across her face.

As Sheriff Cooper passed the false front of the general store a figure suddenly burst out, slamming the screen door against the wall in his hurry. The sheriff's palm slapped around the butt of his gun and he had it half out of the holster before he realized the man was no threat.

"Sheriff! I been meanin' to catch you." He was a tall, lanky man, wearing a clerk's cap and a mustache so thin it looked like a line of dirt on his upper lip. Cooper had never talked to him before. "I want to know if you're on to the job of catchin' this Smith."

"I'm on the job," Cooper drawled, irritated by the unspoken implication that he was not. "And unless you got somethin' I need to know, you're just wastin' — "

"Name's Abe Black. You need to know that I believe, stage robbery aside, there ain't a woman safe in these parts until that man is caught."

"And what gives you that idea?"

"I saw the way he looked at women. It wasn't natural. He was always seemin' to be sizin' them up," the clerk's lip curled as he spoke the words. "He always looked hungry or somethin'. That don't mean good."

"I'll keep that in mind." Cooper nodded and tried to walk past. Abe stepped up quickly to block his path.

"And don't you be fooled that he didn't wear a gun, I happen to know that he's right familiar with 'em."

The sheriff tried to hold a look of patient interest on his face; he was moderately successful. "And where did you get this information?"

"I saw him in the store, talkin' to Sophie McLaren about rifles. He knew about different calibers and ammunition. He's familiar with 'em," Abe repeated.

"Who's Sophie McLaren?"

"Allen McLaren's widow. And that there's another reason I don't think the women folk are safe. Why, if you'd seen how he looked at her." Abe shook his head, his expression suggesting dire consequences. "And he followed her all through the store, just watchin' her with that look of his."

"Did they know each other?" Cooper tried to make the question seem offhand, but he felt there was a good possibility that there was something more to this relationship.

"No, I don't believe so. Mrs. McLaren didn't seem to recognize him and I never seen them together before or after. But I do believe she is in real danger from him, livin' out there alone like she does."

"She's alone?" Cooper was surprised. "Don't she live at the McLaren spread?"

Abe's disgust made him sputter for a moment before he could reply. "No, that Robert McLaren kicked her out hardly before his brother Allen's body was cold. He's dumped her out in one of their line shacks."

"Anywhere near Leeland's Glory mine?"

"It ain't too far."

"Anybody seen her since the holdup?"

"Oh, yeah. She was here in town when word of it came. She hung around for awhile, but I s'pose she's back out there now. She don't cotton much to company."

"You don't say." He patted the clerk on the shoulder as if to thank him for the information and slipped around him. Before he walked away, he said, "Reckon I should be payin' Mrs. McLaren a visit."

"That's a good idea, Sheriff. Maybe you can put some sense into her, tell her to come back to town and stay 'til you catch that Smith feller. She ain't safe no other way."

Twelve

Sophie studied the appearance of her cousin Anne, who had just recently arrived from Topeka. The shy, retiring young woman wore her bonnet pulled low over her forehead; she walked with her head bent and rarely looked up from the ground at her feet. The poor dear was mute, which was surely a blessing. She would likely die of mortification if she had the capacity to speak and was asked to say a few words.

One's first impression of Anne would be that the girl was pathetically ugly, with a total lack of personality. But if something within her limited range of vision chanced to catch her interest, a quick intelligence and a commanding expression would flash across her face.

"Don't look up like that," Sophie said for the fifth time. "You ruin the whole effect with that look. You're looking around at things like you own them, like you have the right to. Ladies don't do that."

"I'm never going to pass as a lady." Anne stood up straight and glared. The illusion was instantly destroyed and Kenny was left standing insolently, looking a little foolish and very uncomfortable in Sophie's yellow dress.

"Well, we can hardly dress you as a saloon girl; that would get you far too much attention." Sophie tugged and adjusted and arranged Kenny's outfit as she spoke.

"I wish I could wear a different dress," Kenny complained as she kicked at her skirts. "I don't like yellow; I've never looked good in yellow."

Sophie ducked her head to hide her amused smile at Kenny's vanity. "You're not supposed to look good. Now, come, Anne, show me how you walk."

Kenny shuffled off the porch with the dejection of a dog kicked once too often. Her brown, bare toes scuffed up the dust.

"Can't you look uglier? Or maybe addled?"

"How am I s'posed to look addled?"

"I don't know, just keep your face vacant. Wipe your nose on your sleeve every now and then."

"Sophie — " Kenny tried to protest.

"We don't want anyone to show any interest in you. You've got to be a little repulsive."

"If I get any more repulsive someone's going to kidnap me and sell me to the freak show," Kenny yelled. "That's not why I dressed this way."

Sophie laughed despite Kenny's real anger. She rubbed Kenny's cheek soothingly with the back of her hand and pressed their noses together. Kenny finally smiled.

"I'm sorry," Sophie apologized. "Perhaps I'm getting too carried away. I just don't want anyone to recognize you."

"They won't," Kenny assured her.

The sound of her voice still sent shivers down Sophie's back. She reached up and tried to tug the bonnet farther down over Kenny's forehead. "I don't like that eyebrow showing, but this bonnet won't cover it, and I don't know what else to do," Sophie fretted.

Kenny took her hand away and held it. "It don't matter. No one's gonna connect that scar to the stage driver."

"No one but the man who shot you." Sophie regretted her words the moment they were spoken. The color immediately drained from Kenny's face and the bravado she had shown since her decision to go into town dissolved. Pulling away from Sophie, she looked somewhere deep into the forest that bordered their clearing.

"But he's probably long gone." Sophie tried to sound convinced, but Kenny did not respond.

Sophie waited in silence for the moment to pass. It seemed that it would not, so she spoke again. "Do you still want to try this? I can understand if you've changed your mind, if you just want to run away..."

Roughly, Kenny jerked the bonnet off her head, then held it out like she'd never seen it before. When she spoke, her voice was so low that Sophie doubted the words were meant for her to hear.

"And if I run away, who's to say he won't be wherever I run to?"

The desperation in her voice caused a pain in Sophie's chest, but she forced herself to speak with an assurance she did not feel. "I'm sure we can learn something helpful in town. The robbery is probably still the only thing people are talking about. There has to be someone who knows more than just gossip."

The words sounded flat even to herself. Kenny strode past her and out of the yard.

"Kenny," Sophie called after her, wanting but not daring to follow. "Please, at least tell me what you're going to do."

Kenny kept walking, but her voice traveled back to Sophie. "I'm gonna bridle Twitch."

"Wait."

Frustrated, Kenny stopped and turned around slowly, her face showing her irritation. Sophie steeled her nerves and paced off the distance between them. She walked right up to Kenny.

"I admit that I don't really know you, Kenny, but I know you're innocent. I don't care what anyone else thinks of you." Sophie paused for a breath, then added, "And I don't think I would care what anyone thinks of us."

"Of us?" Kenny's expression was unreadable. "What are you saying?"

Sophie suddenly lost her resolve. She felt she had been stepping blindly out of bounds since she first met Kenny. And now, she had taken it one step too far. How could she say the words that would tie herself to this woman without knowing more about Kenny's feelings?

At last she said softly, "I want you to make love to me." Her words surprised even herself. Kenny was clearly stunned. But any hesitation Kenny felt was short-lived. She reached out gentle hands and cupped Sophie's cheeks, drawing her face forward until their lips met in a searing kiss.

Sophie's legs went instantly weak and she leaned her body against Kenny's strength. Kenny breathed into Sophie's mouth and Sophie drew the warm air into her lungs. The power of that simple exchange of breath made Sophie dizzy and she silently begged Kenny to take her into the house and lay her down. But Kenny had other plans. She pulled her body away from Sophie, then took her hand and led her to the forest's edge.

"I don't want to be interrupted again," Kenny explained softly as they walked farther into the cover of the woods.

Sophie let herself be guided through the trees. Her feet sank deeply into the thick layer of pine needles that blanketed the forest floor. She wished her feet were bare like Kenny's so she could feel the soft spring on the soles of her feet.

In a short time Kenny found the spot that satisfied her. After leaning Sophie against a tall tree, she stepped back. Sophie watched her pull the yellow dress off over her head. Underneath, she wore the half slip and her driver's pants rolled up to her knees.

"Kenny! What are you doing with those pants on?" Sophie couldn't believe the woman's stubborn foolishness.

Kenny just laughed as she rolled down the pants legs. She spread the yellow dress out over the pine needles and gestured for Sophie to lie down.

Sophie shook her head, not willing to let go of her indignation at Kenny's decision to endanger herself by wearing those pants. Kenny continued to smile as she walked slowly up to Sophie. She stopped, rested her chest against Sophie's, and pressed her thigh hard between Sophie's legs. Moving her hips seductively, she breathed lightly in Sophie's ear.

Sophie stopped breathing as Kenny took her hands and pushed them back against the tree trunk behind her. Her resistance melted.

"Do you want to take off your dress, or should I work around it?" Kenny asked with a grin.

Sophie struggled to find her voice. "I'll take it off," she whispered.

Kenny moved away and sat on the ground next to the yellow dress. She leaned back and stared with patient desire as Sophie's nervous fingers fumbled with her buttons.

"Are you just going to stare at me?" she asked, feeling a little embarrassed, a little defensive.

"Yup," Kenny said with satisfaction. "'Less you need help, that is."

Sophie didn't answer. She set her jaw and released the last of the buttons from their loops. At last, lifting her head defiantly, she slid the dress from her shoulders. Her bravery was rewarded by the look of pleasure that crossed Kenny's face. The sheer undergarments Sophie wore did little to hide her body from Kenny's eyes. The sunlight that slashed down through the trees silhouetted her curves and shadowed the dark hair between her legs.

Kenny swallowed hard and again motioned for Sophie to lie down. Sophie went to the dress and sat down cross-legged before Kenny. Her hands found the folds of cloth that gathered at her lap and bunched them into her fists. Kenny moved quietly, positioning herself to kneel in front of Sophie.

"Are you afraid?" she whispered.

Sophie nodded. Her breath caught as Kenny gently, but insistently, pushed her backwards. She looked up through the

tree branches to the patch of blue sky above her. Kenny
stretched her body out to cover Sophie's, her weight holding
Sophie down to the earth. Sophie pressed her hands to the
ground at her sides.

Kenny kissed her temple and whispered, "I ain't gonna
hurt you."

"I know, I know that," Sophie breathed. "It just feels so
different with you. I feel so...so present. Do you understand?"

"No. I'm sorry." Kenny spoke slowly, her words coming
between soft kisses. "But you got to remember, I'm new at
this."

"Are you afraid?"

"Oh, yes," Kenny assured her, laughing quietly at her
own honesty. "But I'm not going to let it stop me."

"Then neither will I," Sophie decided, though the
words sent a fresh wave of fear through her heart. She lifted her
hands to Kenny's back and held tightly to her.

Kenny patiently waited for Sophie to return her kisses
before she grew bolder. Sophie opened her lips to Kenny's
tongue and sucked it in deeper, holding it gently with her
teeth. The feeling seemed to explode Kenny's desire and Sophie
felt almost washed away by the force of passion that tensed
Kenny's body above her. The weight lifted as Kenny fought to
push Sophie's slip above her hips.

Sophie grabbed her hand. "Let me take it off," she said.

Kenny moved to one side and watched Sophie remove
the rest of her clothing. Sophie's pale skin gleamed where there
was no tan, the dark circles around her hardened nipples
contrasted with the white skin of her breasts. Kenny did not
hesitate, but leaned forward and eagerly took Sophie's nipple
into her mouth.

Sophie breathed in quickly, deeply. Kenny's lips and
tongue were moving, teasing, drawing desire from the depths of
Sophie's being; she felt disoriented, as if her nakedness were
exposed to the world, and the universe itself rippled with her
need.

Kenny was above her again. She had removed her own slip and her bare skin brushed softly across Sophie's breasts. Kenny used her knee to pressure Sophie's legs apart, then lowered her body, the soft wool of her pants tickling the insides of Sophie's thighs.

Sophie's need had become a craving. She was aching to be touched, to be filled by Kenny's fingers. Moving her hips beneath Kenny, she urged her to satisfy her uncontrollable desire.

Kenny shared this hunger. She kissed Sophie's lips, her neck, her earlobes, the hot touches sparking deeper fires. Sophie was surprised to hear herself moan. She took hold of Kenny's head and turned it so that her lips touched Kenny's ear.

"I want you," she whispered, her voice vibrating deeply. "I want you now."

Kenny seemed turned to stone in Sophie's arms. Sophie pulled her head back to look at Kenny's profile. Her jaw was clenched tight and her forehead creased.

"What's wrong?" Sophie asked, a sinking dismay clutching at her stomach.

Kenny shook her head. "Nothing. Nothing is wrong," she said, panting. "I'm just trying to do this slowly. I want to be gentle, but you're pushing me so hard."

Sophie laughed, the sound of it was wild to her ears. "Kenny, I'm not the virgin. I'm ready for you, for whatever you want."

"Whatever I want..." Kenny repeated, then moved quickly, making her decision before Sophie could take back her words.

"Oh God," Sophie whispered, her body tensing as Kenny kissed a line of fire down her belly and over her mound of soft hair.

Kenny slid her hands under Sophie's legs and lifted them until Sophie's knees bent and her feet were drawn in to touch Kenny's sides. She rubbed her lips against Sophie's inner thighs.

Sophie reached down and grabbed Kenny's hair, trying to move her head away. "Kenny, no," she protested.

"You said whatever I want. This is all that I want."

The words tickled her hair and blew cool against her wetness. "But, I've never..."

It was Kenny's turn to laugh. "And you told me you're not a virgin."

"Kenny..."

Sophie's words were cut short by her sudden intake of breath. Kenny's fingertip had gently parted the tangle of dark hair that hid Sophie from her. Her tongue followed the same path, sliding smoothly over Sophie's burning skin. Her thumbs spread Sophie's outer lips and held her open. Sophie felt herself being examined, explored, first by Kenny's eyes, then by her mouth. Sophie took her hands away from Kenny's head to cover her face.

"You are so beautiful," Kenny whispered without moving her mouth from Sophie. "Thank you. Thank you."

Sophie's body was rigid with a delicious tension. The embarrassment of having Kenny's face at her most intimate center faded in the presence of so much pleasure. She had never felt such softness, such strength. The insistent touch of Kenny's tongue, now inside her, now brushing the hardness of her clitoris, was a torment she hoped would never cease.

But her body could not withstand. Too soon Sophie felt the pressuring of what had to be an orgasm. She reached wildly for Kenny. Kenny took her hand and held it with a fierce grip. Her other hand moved insistently between Sophie's legs.

"Kenny, Kenny," Sophie whispered, the name becoming a chant that removed awareness of anything but her lover from her mind.

Kenny's mouth settled on Sophie's clit. Sucking the hardness firmly between her lips, she tongued her forcefully. Her fingers slid into Sophie, opening her wide and plunging in as deeply as they could reach into that sweet treasure.

Sophie's legs clamped down on Kenny's shoulders; her hips raised to open herself further to Kenny's touch. Her body shook, then shuddered. Kenny stayed with her, never losing contact, pushing her closer and closer to that fall. With a shuddering gasp, Sophie let herself go, and the force of her coming rocked both women into a stunned silence.

Sophie's body dropped down to the yielding, pine-scented ground. She reached for Kenny, who was already moving, sliding up to rest on top of her. Kenny's face was shining with wonder...and the slickness of Sophie's wetness. Sophie reached for the slip crumpled on the ground beside her, and used the hem to gently wipe Kenny's face.

Kenny's body was now heavy with relaxation. Sophie could not feel any of the tension that was normally present in her strong shoulders and back. As Sophie rubbed her bare skin with light fingertips, she felt Kenny drift into a deep sleep.

Now that they were quiet, the sounds and activities of the forest life resumed. The rush of wings filled the sky from somewhere beyond Sophie's sight; the movement through the trees and up into the sky seemed to reflect the feeling of release that filled her heart. Closer by, a squirrel chattered loudly, probably scolding Sophie for disturbing the day's earlier tranquility. Sophie let the sounds and the sharp smell of sunlight on pine needles become a part of her calm. She had never in her life been in such a vulnerable position, nor felt so safe and protected. With a smile, she realized that the contradictions Kenny brought to her life were no longer something she feared. As long as she could hold Kenny like this...

Sleep gradually tangled Sophie's thoughts; she did not struggle to stay awake. The day was softly slipping away and Sophie let it go. Tomorrow was soon enough for the plans they had made.

A tall man with a brown Stetson pulled low over his

eyes stood in the alley shadows between the hotel and the post office. His body seemed relaxed as he leaned casually against the boards, his right foot crossed over his left. But the lack of visible tension was deceptive — the man was fully alert. The red glow of his cigarette was bright in the dim light. Smoking, he waited for the jangled approach of his partner's spurred boots.

"Diamond." Though he spoke in a soft voice, it carried out to the man who had almost passed him in the alley.

"Hey, I got notice you wanted to see me." Diamond matched his pose to the other man's. He accepted the already rolled cigarette the man offered him. Lighting up, he spoke through the smoke between them. "But I don't know why we gotta meet like this. Thought we'd have a couple of shots of whiskey together."

"We will, but not just now. I wanted to talk to you where no one else would be listenin'."

"You got another job set up for us already?"

"I got a job for you, Diamond. An easy one. Just involves talkin'." The man flipped away his cigarette butt and continued, "Thought you'd be the perfect man for it."

Diamond laughed without taking any offense from the words. He knew he had the reputation of being a talker; he also knew that the man next to him trusted him to never say the wrong thing. The trust was well deserved. Diamond could keep secrets.

"I need you to stir up some action, get people riled." He handed Diamond a five-dollar gold piece. "Do some drinkin', some talkin' — we want a vigilante group formed."

"And what or who do you want this group to be chasin'?" Diamond snickered.

"Kenny Smith."

Diamond laughed. "Ridin' to hell, are we?"

The man also laughed, but the laughter never reached his cold, gray eyes. "Close enough. I want you to head them out to the old mine shack by the Eullabelle."

Diamond turned his head quickly to look into the man's eyes. Nothing could be read there. "But that's where Martin's holed up. That bullet he took from the shotgun man — "

"Martin's done for. He's cashin' in anyway. Let them find him and think they're on the right track. I already left behind a few of Smith's meal receipts that were in the stage bag."

"But what if Martin talks?"

"That's why you're ridin' along. To make sure he doesn't," he said impatiently.

Diamond scratched his chin thoughtfully. He was up to the job, but he still had a sense of honor. "You sure Martin's done for?"

"I'm sure. His guts are rottin' out. You'll be doin' him a favor."

"All right." He took a long draw from the smoke. He wouldn't question the plan any further. "Where you gonna be?"

"I've got to ride out to the creek and make sure Smith's body won't be found. It'd kinda foul up our story if someone was to stumble onto him."

"How soon you want this done?"

"Start it now. I want them out to the old mine shack tomorrow mornin'."

"Tomorrow?"

"Yeah. You be sure that sheriff goes with you. I got a bad feelin' about him. I'm gonna find out what kind of questions he's been askin'."

"You think I can get them stirred up so quick?"

"No doubt. They been on edge for two weeks. They're all ready to kill somethin'." The man turned and walked away down the alley. He called back over his shoulder, "Just don't let it be you."

Diamond laughed again. He stomped his boots on the hard-packed dirt and set his spurs to jingling. This was going to be fun.

"Sheriff! Sheriff, you'd better wake up!"

Cooper sat up in his bed, his hands scrabbling across the blankets in search of his pistol. He whipped the gun from its holster and leaped from the bed in the same instant. Crouching to one side of the door, he called out over the wild pounding.

"What the hell's goin' on?"

"Sheriff, there's a mob formin' up. They say they know where Smith is and they're bound to go fetch him back."

A faint gray light came through the shuttered window. Cooper estimated the time to be at least an hour before dawn. For any lynch mob to be roused up this early meant they'd probably spent the whole night whetting their courage with whiskey.

"Shit." Cooper took hold of the door knob and twisted it open quickly. He caught the surprised look on the night clerk's face as he almost fell forward through the door. "Where are they now?"

"Down at the stables picking mounts."

Cooper started out the door.

"Sheriff," the clerk's voice stopped him in the hall. "I reckon you'd better put your trousers on."

Cooper's face turned as red as his long johns. He was back inside the room in two steps and pulled his pants and shirt on quickly. He gave the clerk a dark scowl as he hauled his boots on. "You better not tell a soul about this."

"No, sir," the man sputtered. "No, I won't."

A quick count in the predawn darkness showed the mob consisting of about fifteen men. Less than half were mounted as the sheriff approached; the others staggered around their horses struggling to get them saddled.

"What the hell do you men think you're doin'?" Cooper barked loudly.

They all turned to face him. One of the mounted men deliberately spat on the ground near Cooper's feet. "We're doin' something you should'a done a week ago. We're going to string up a robber and a murderer."

"You ain't goin' nowhere. None of you know the least thing about catchin' outlaws."

"We know at least as much as you do, then," another man replied. The others laughed.

"And at least we got the balls to go and try," another spoke up. Cooper didn't recognize anyone.

"You boys've been drinkin'. If you did stumble across one of them outlaws, half the lot of you would be killed before you even knew what happened." Cooper tried to keep his voice calm. Responding to their insults would only worsen the situation. "And what makes you think you know where to find 'em?"

"They been spotted holed up in an old mine shack out by the Eullabelle. A feller saw Smith there with his own eyes. That's enough for me." A shout of agreement went up from the vigilantes as their horses began prancing.

The first man that spoke leaned down to the sheriff and offered a challenge. "You can either come with us...or stay and make sure the town folks are protected."

The laughter caused by his taunt was short-lived as the sheriff answered calmly, "I suspect it's you all that'll need protectin'. I'll ride with you." He walked through the suddenly quiet group and went to the stall where he'd left his horse.

A gap-toothed boy stood shivering by the gate. His eyes were filled with both sleep and excitement. He looked up, wordlessly searching the sheriff's eyes.

Cooper pulled his saddle from its peg on the wall and turned his back to the boy. "What is it you want, boy?" he asked as he cinched the straps tight on the buckskin.

"I want you to stop them," the boy whispered.

"And why is that?" Cooper didn't find it hard to believe that this kid would show more sense than the liquored-up men outside.

"'Cause I don't want nobody to kill him."

"Who?" The sheriff squatted down to the boy's eye level. "Who don't you want killed?"

"Kenny! Kenny Smith. I tell you, he didn't do it." The boy straightened his back and gave the words as much conviction as he possessed. "I swear it to you."

"What's your name, boy?"

"Tyler, sir. My pa owns the stables."

"Well, Tyler, what makes you so sure of this Kenny?"

Tyler balled his fists up tight and held them tense at his sides. "He was a good man, Sheriff. I just know he wouldn't kill Frank for no money!"

"Well, then. Why ain't he here, tellin' us just that?"

Tears came to the boy's eyes. Cooper regretted asking the question so coldly.

"I don't know," Tyler whispered. "I just know he didn't do it. Don't let them kill him, please."

Cooper put his hand on the boy's shoulder and stood slowly before answering. "I'll do my best, Tyler. I'll do my best to bring him back here alive, so he can answer all our questions."

Despite his words, Cooper knew the chances of bringing Smith back alive were next to nil. If he were a betting man, he'd fold his hand right now.

Thirteen

The town of Jackson looked distinctly different from Kenny's new viewpoint. The streets seemed to stretch out to the flatlands beyond; they were narrower, more crowded. And the numerous little alleys between the buildings they passed held an ominous air, even in the bright light of morning. Every man lounging by a hitching post or sauntering along the boardwalk seemed to be a threat; the wide brims of their hats leaving their faces obscured by shadows, their hands dangerously close to their guns. One man stopped in the middle of tightening his horse's cinch strap to stare after them as they passed down the boardwalk. Kenny could feel his eyes on her back and fought the desire to run. She had never in her life felt so threatened.

When she and Sophie walked under the shadow of the boarding house she had called home, Kenny could not resist lifting her head to look up to the window of her old room. Someone stood there; a man leaning against the frame flipped the ashes from his cigarette onto the boardwalk below. Suddenly she was overwhelmed by unexpected grief at the loss of her life as Kenny Smith. That person was dead, but still, she lived on. Kenny felt abandoned, as if she had been buried and forgotten before she'd, in fact, stopped breathing. Her chest was tight and constricted, although the clothing that she now wore was actually less binding than her breast band had been.

"Anne," Sophie cautioned, taking Kenny's elbow with a firm hand. "It is not polite to stare."

Kenny bowed her head and stumbled on, unsteady on her feet. She was grateful for Sophie's lingering hold on her arm. Her body was shaking out of control and sweat sprang out on her forehead and upper lip. Hopefully, the emotion helped to make her appear more addled. With a firm hand, Sophie led her across the rutted, hard-packed street and up the steps to the general store. The biting smell of pickled vegetables and peppered jerky hung about the building. The odors were familiar, but no longer brought Kenny any sense of comfort.

"I must stop at the store," Sophie said in a clear voice. More quietly, she added, "Don't look at anyone, even if you recognize their voices, and especially if they were friends of yours."

Kenny nodded dumbly and stepped aside to allow Sophie to enter the store ahead of her. As Sophie pulled open the screen door a friendly voice carried out of the shadows between the aisles.

"Well, hello, Mrs. McLaren."

Remembering how the clerk had recognized her from a single meeting in the past, Sophie almost knocked Kenny backwards into the street as she jumped back and let the screen door slam shut. She grabbed Kenny and turned her toward the alley.

"You can't go in there; that clerk never forgets a face." Sophie peered over Kenny's shoulder, glaring at the place the sound had come from. "Seems like he could find something better to do with his brain."

Kenny was surprised at how her heart raced. She went deeper into the shadow of the alley, feeling truly like a fugitive.

"This was a damn stupid idea," she hissed quietly.

Sophie leaned against the wall and nodded. "I should have come alone. There's really nothing you can do, and we're just putting you in danger."

"I can't just let this go," Kenny countered sharply,

swatting the folds of yellow cloth that confined her stride. "It's this damned dress. I can't even walk, how am I s'posed to — "

"Don't even think you can come here dressed like a man," Sophie interrupted, her voice low and her fingers digging into Kenny's arm. Footsteps rang on the boardwalk, accompanied by the jingle of spurs. Sophie stepped in front of Kenny and shielded her from view. The steps hesitated at the opening of the alley, then continued on.

"I'm making this harder for you," Kenny admitted. "I guess I should just hide somewhere while you look around." The thought galled Kenny; she had already had too much inactivity.

Sophie patted her hand. "I think you should just go to the cemetery."

Kenny sighed heavily and looked away from Sophie. Her resolve to visit Frank's grave had dwindled in the light of day. She missed him — he had been the first true friend she'd had in her life — and she dreaded seeing the indisputable proof that he was dead. Her last memory of him, and the only one she could reliably bring to mind, was the shocked look on his face the instant the bullet had driven into her shoulder and knocked her from the stagecoach. Although she did want to erase that final memory, she wasn't sure whether it was wise to replace it with the sight of his freshly turned grave.

Kenny looked at the ground between them as she damned the tears she had steeled herself against, but was unable to control. She had gone so long without ever crying — now it seemed the tears flowed out of her with the slightest provocation. To her disgust, she was weakening, becoming a simpering woman, and she cursed herself for that. Where was the strength she had prided herself on, the tough face she showed the world? She had to get it back.

She looked down at the sleeve of the yellow dress she wore, then managed a thin smile as she threatened to wipe her nose on the cloth. Sophie grabbed her arm and made a quiet sound of dismay. Kenny chuckled as she took the handkerchief

Sophie quickly produced from her bag.

"All right," Kenny said decisively. "I'll meet you at the cemetery when you're finished."

"Good. Good." Sophie spoke with obvious relief. "I really don't think you're safe on the streets."

Kenny nodded, then impulsively hugged Sophie close to her. Sophie returned the embrace without hesitation. Kenny was grateful for Sophie's willing contact — the touch lent her strength.

Kenny released her and stepped back. Nodding encouragement, Sophie pointed toward the other end of the alley.

"Don't be long, please," Kenny whispered, desperation turning her voice even rougher than normal.

"I'll hurry," Sophie promised.

Kenny took a deep breath and began walking down the alley.

The cemetery was on a low-rising hill at the southern outskirts of town. Kenny's reluctant steps headed her toward the weathered fence that surrounded the collection of grave sites. She squinted her eyes as the sunlight glinted painfully off the occasional polished marble headstone. Most of the markers were made of wood, many splintered and streaked with age; weathered names and dates were impossible to decipher. Over it all hung a solemn stillness, interrupted by the soft cooing of a mourning dove.

The bright yellow glow of fresh wood caught her attention before she noticed the dark mound of earth that covered Frank's grave. Her steps became even more hesitant, but she managed to force her feet up to the very edge of the grave. Frank's final resting place was shadowed by a pompously huge block of granite marking the home of one Elijah Quince. Kenny gratefully folded her trembling legs and sat down, her back supported by Elijah's monument.

Her eyes once again filled with tears. This time Kenny let the sadness flow from her without restraint, her face buried in Sophie's handkerchief.

"I was right, Frank," she whispered between her sobs. "I'm sorry, but I was right. I wish you'd listened to me."

When the weeping had passed Kenny felt drained, her body heavy and listless. But somehow, she felt lighter in spirit than she could ever recall feeling. On impulse, she took off her borrowed shoes and dug her toes into the soft dirt, then leaned forward to read Frank's inscription.

His name was followed by a single date, so she was not the only one with no idea of how old Frank had been. The words that came after that date threatened to bring back the grief she thought she had relieved. The marker read, in accusing capital letters: MURDERED BY THE HAND OF A FRIEND.

Kenny fell back and buried her face in her hands. With her knees drawn up tight to her chest, she rocked against the cold stone behind her. Racking gasps shook her body, but she no longer had any tears to cry. She clung to the hope that Frank had known better than what was written there, that he would be just as insulted as she was by the words.

The slow clopping of a horse's hooves brought her back to awareness of the world around her and the danger she still faced at being here. She pulled the long folds of her dress in around her and cautiously peered around the sheltering block of granite.

A large man in a dusty brown slicker stopped his horse near the fence at the far end of the cemetery. He faced the west, his head turned away from Kenny. It was clear he was impatiently waiting for something, for as he sat there, he repeatedly flicked the end of his reins sharply on the right shoulder of his horse. The animal flinched each time, but managed to keep its movements restrained.

Kenny half stood, wondering if she should try to hide here until the man left, or if it would be wiser to escape now while he was looking away from her. She had told Sophie that she would wait here, but now she believed she would be safest hiding in the stable where Twitch was waiting. Her decision was delayed by the arrival of another man who galloped in from the west. His agitation was apparent as they spoke; he waved his arms and gestured in an attempt to convince the first man of some fact.

Kenny did not wait, but took advantage of the distraction to scoot out of the cemetery and head back to town at a quick pace. She had come within a hundred yards of the first buildings before the sound that she had dreaded came rushing to her ears. Stepping off the edge of the track, she hunched her shoulders, trying to make herself look small and unimportant. The sound and breeze of the horses brushed by her, but her relief was short-lived. One of the horses jerked to a stop just ahead of her on the trail.

As the man roughly pulled his horse around to face her, Kenny attempted the vacant expression she had perfected earlier that day. Putting her eyes slightly out of focus, she relaxed her features and looked up.

Here, haloed by the glare of the morning sun, was the face that had haunted her dreams since the day of the robbery.

Sophie struggled with herself not to follow Kenny down the alley and to the graveyard. She hated to let her go alone into the grief that the sight of Frank's grave was sure to awaken. But she turned her head away and closed her ears to the sound of Kenny's footsteps. No one could help Kenny with this. Sophie could only be there to offer support afterwards.

There was a tightness in her chest and Sophie knew exactly what that feeling was all about. Although the emotion was new to her, she was certain that she had fallen in love. What surprised her was how calmly she was able to accept that knowledge. That Kenny was a woman was amazingly insignificant.

Sophie left the shelter of the building and stood for a moment on the boardwalk. The strength she had felt at walking down the street with Kenny was gone now that she was alone.

Suddenly, she doubted the usefulness of her mission. What could she possibly learn that would clear Kenny's name when the majority of the townspeople had already pronounced her guilty?

Her indecision was pointless. Sophie straightened her back and pushed through the door of the general store. The clerk — she remembered his first name was Abe — still stood between the aisles. He watched her as she walked past him. Without taking the time to study her purchases, Sophie quickly collected and paid for the supplies they needed. Just when she thought she would be finished and gone before he tried to talk to her, she saw the clerk walking up beside her.

"Mrs. McLaren." His words were not quite a question.

Sophie turned to face him. She didn't speak, but raised her eyebrow and waited for him to continue.

A deep red blush started at his neck and spread to the tips of his ears. He licked his lips before speaking. "I'm glad to see you're all right. I mean, some of us have been worried 'bout you. All by yourself out there."

Sophie debated bringing up the presence of her "cousin," but quickly ruled it out. She didn't need the questions that would come of it.

"You do know 'bout the robbery, don't you?"

"Yes, of course."

"If you'd feel better to stay in town 'til he's caught, I'm sure my sister could put you up — "

"That's not necessary. I'm sure those robbers have no interest in me. But I do thank you."

"I'm afraid you might be wrong, ma'am. I seen how that Smith feller looked at you."

Sophie felt a rush of fear. She had no idea where the man's suspicions were coming from. "I don't even know that man."

"He saw you in here, Mrs. McLaren. I watched him followin' you."

"I'm sure you're mistaken. I've never met him." Sophie

tried to make her words cold enough to signal that she was finished with the conversation. Abe didn't give up that easily. He pulled a large square of paper from the wall behind them and held it before her. She took a deep, involuntary breath as she saw Kenny's face staring at her from the wanted poster.

"You remember now, don't you?" Abe's voice carried a satisfied tone.

After her response to the drawing, Sophie couldn't lie. She nodded her head. Five thousand dollars. She read the words in disbelief.

"I think he saw somethin' in you, Mrs. McLaren."

Sophie shook her head. "I'm afraid you're wrong, Mr., uh, Abe." Sophie struggled to make her voice sound cheerful and unconcerned. "I appreciate your worry, but I think I'm safe where I am. Robert looks after me," Sophie lied.

Abe's lip curled at the sound of that name. "He'd better."

"Do you mind if I take that?" Sophie reached out for the paper as she asked. Abe let her take it from his hand.

"Sure, I got a batch more. I'm handin' one out to everyone that comes in."

Sophie's heart sank. With Kenny's likeness on that paper and a reward of five thousand dollars, there was no way she could hope that Kenny could stay with her in this part of the country. Her only hope was to find out who had really robbed the stage. Without another word, she brushed past Abe and left the building. A burst of fear-induced energy propelled her toward the nearest saloon, where she hoped to find the whore named Belle.

The barkeeper reluctantly directed Sophie to the row of small, ramshackle houses behind the buildings of the main street. After leaving her bag of provisions at the stable with Twitch, Sophie walked the narrow back street, feeling as if a thousand eyes followed her every step. The roadway was littered with broken glass and pocked with the deep imprints of boot heels. Sophie clasped her hands together and held them at her stomach as a door swung open in the crib directly ahead of her. A man backed out of the darkened room, laughing, his shirt untucked and half open, his hat pushed back from his forehead. Spotting Sophie, his laughter died. He ducked his head and pulled his hat down to cover his face, then awkwardly loped down the road past her. Ignoring the stare of the prostitute leaning in the still open doorway, Sophie continued down the street and found the crib marked with a large red four. She rapped firmly on the door.

"Hold your horses," came the command from inside the tiny shack. "You got any idea what time it is?"

The woman sounded tired and irritated; her harsh voice did not suggest a promising interview. Regardless, Sophie stood her ground and waited for the door to open.

Belle's eyes widened, then batted in confusion as she looked out on her visitor. Her mouth opened to speak, but no sound came out.

Sophie spoke quickly to cover the awkwardness of the situation. "Belle?" she asked, then continued at the plump woman's nod. "My name is Sophie McLaren, I was wondering if I could have a little of your time."

Belle's eyes batted again with a renewed vigor, but she was quick to regain a businesslike composure. "I suppose so, hon. I guess it won't be the strangest thing I've done." Belle gave Sophie's body a quick appraisal as she considered what she thought Sophie was asking. "But I can't guarantee I'll know just what to do with you."

"Oh — oh no, you misunderstand me," Sophie rushed to explain, nervous laughter threatening to spill from her lips. "I just want to talk to you."

Belle breathed an exaggerated sigh of relief that Sophie thought was mixed with just a twinge of regret. "Well, come on in, then," she offered, swinging the door open wide.

Sophie looked past Belle into the dimly lit room. Besides the gaudy curtains and a shelf of trinkets, the only furnishing the room held was a large rumpled bed. A corset of tattered lace hung from the bedpost.

"Perhaps we could talk outside, over there, in the shade," Sophie suggested, pointing at a patch of shadows between two lanky cottonwood trees.

Belle smiled without taking offense and walked Sophie to the cool shade. "I don't think I been out of doors this early in the day for a long time," Belle bantered.

Sophie could feel that her mettle was being tested, but she was not worried. She could stand up to this woman's teasing. And as far as Belle's occupation went, as long as Belle herself was satisfied with what she was doing, Sophie could not fault her for it. Believing it best not to judge another, Sophie kept her voice pleasant, knowing that she herself was hardly the wholesome lady she appeared to be.

"It wouldn't seem that you've been missing much," Sophie said, gesturing at the dirty buildings and the hot glare of the sun with one sweep of her arm.

Belle smiled again, her face open and accepting. "Now just what do you think I can do for you?" she asked.

"I was hoping that I could ask you about the recent stage robbery." Sophie tried to maintain the lightness of her voice as she spoke.

Belle shrugged and looked puzzled. "What makes you think I'd know anything about that?"

"Well, I just thought that maybe you have been in the position to hear things..." Sophie's voice trailed off as she became aware of her poor choice of words. "I mean, I've heard that you did know the man who is accused of the robbery."

A dark scowl covered Belle's pleasant face. She glared at Sophie for a moment, then spoke harshly, "If you're one of them people tryin' to see that he hangs, I ain't speakin' to you no more. I happen to believe that he didn't do it."

"I agree with you," Sophie blurted out.

"You knew Kenny?" Belle asked.

"Yes...well, no," Sophie stammered, her face burning. She'd gotten in over her head and wasn't sure how to swim out.

Belle put a soft, friendly hand on Sophie's arm. "Don't you worry, dear. He made plenty of women feel the way you do."

Sophie let Belle believe that her confusion was caused by love sickness. In a way, she guessed it was true. She poured out her heart, careful to use the correct pronouns. "I just can't rest knowing that he is being blamed for this terrible thing. I've got to find out the truth." She allowed a quaver to enter her voice.

Belle shook her head sadly. "I wish I could help you, I truly do. But there's nothin' — "

Belle was interrupted by a streak of yellow that pushed between her and Sophie. Belle gasped and Sophie was stunned to see Kenny's frightened face pressed close to hers as the woman's strong grip crushed into the flesh of her upper arm. Reaching up quickly, Sophie put her hand over Kenny's mouth before she could speak.

"My cousin, Anne," Sophie explained apologetically as she hastily dragged Kenny to the side. "Excuse me...she's not all here," Sophie confided in a stage whisper before they disappeared behind a building. They left Belle staring after them in confusion.

"What the hell are you doing here?" Sophie's anger flashed out roughly.

Kenny had no response to the anger; her fear was too great. Sophie's heart sank as she anticipated Kenny's words.

"I saw the man — I saw him." Kenny was on the verge of hysteria. Sophie held her arms tightly and shook her.

"Did he recognize you? Does he know who you are?"

Kenny shook her head. "No, no, I don't think so. He just stopped and looked at me. I was too scared to even run. I couldn't move or yell or nothing," Kenny babbled. Sophie didn't try to stop her.

"I swear, it felt like he looked at me for an hour, I don't know how he couldn't have recognized me. But he just turned his horse around and rode off without saying anything. Oh God, I thought I was dead."

"Did he come into town?"

"No, he turned just before town and headed northwest."

"We've got to get Twitch and get out of here."

Kenny nodded, her face white and drawn. Sophie pulled Kenny into her arms and held her close. Kenny's fear made her own heart pound wildly. She had been a fool to agree to this plan, a fool to think that the two of them had any choice but to get away from this town and all of the people that had ever known a man named Kenny Smith.

*T*here was a faint light coming from inside the cabin. The sun was well up over the ridge and a hint of wood smoke was in the air. The sheriff positioned himself behind a small outcropping of rock facing the door, with the sun at his back. The other men had spread out silently, every one of them suddenly sober. Boasting talk in town was one thing. Standing up to a gang of killers was another.

Cooper had convinced them to just settle in and wait for the occupants of the cabin to come out and show themselves. There was no way of knowing how many men were in the house. They had not been able to locate where the men had tied their horses.

The man the others called Diamond had been all for storming the place. Cooper squinted his eyes and tried to make out where the man had hidden himself in the bushes. After a moment he thought he saw a brief flash of sunlight glinting off the man's rifle. Just by looking at him Cooper could tell that he was not like the other men making up this now less-than-enthusiastic mob. He was not afraid of killing or of being killed. Cooper wished that he had stuck closer to Diamond. He was not to be trusted.

The wait continued. Cooper found himself growing sleepy from the sunlight warming his back. It was difficult for him to keep his concentration on the cabin and the men inside.

His thoughts would drift and most of the time he spent trying to imagine how the men from town felt to be in this situation. Deep inside, he knew he wasn't right for this job anymore, but he didn't know what else to do with the rest of his life.

A sudden gunshot broke the stillness of the morning. Cooper jerked his head up in time to see a man stumble out from the doorway and fall over the porch railing. A belated shower of bullets followed from the men surrounding the cabin. Cooper raised his rifle but didn't fire. He cursed the rashness of the idiots he had aligned himself with. Diamond was standing, shooting his rifle without aiming and shouting to encourage the others.

After a moment the gunfire died down. There was nothing to be heard from inside the cabin, no shooting and no movement, as far as Cooper could tell. The man Diamond shot had not moved again. Cooper knew he was dead. Time seemed to be suspended along with the haze of gunsmoke that slowly settled over the clearing. The rusty hinges of the open door grated loudly. It came to a stop, full open, and Cooper could see the whole interior of the place. There was no one else within.

Cooper stood and walked slowly up to the dead man. He was unarmed. A dirty, bloodstained bandage was wrapped across his stomach.

"Is he dead?" a frightened voice called out to the sheriff. "You'd better shoot him again to be sure."

Cooper looked with disgust at the man who still cowered in the bushes. "Yeah, he's dead. If you greenhorns would've given him another ten minutes, he'd a probably died on his own. Guess he ain't gonna tell us much now."

Diamond walked up and pushed at the man with the toe of his boot. "Sorry, Sheriff. I guess I was a little trigger happy."

The words were light and did not match the expression on Diamond's face. Cooper leveled his gaze at him and waited for Diamond to look away. He held the stare longer than

Cooper expected. Other men came up to join them, completely unaware of the tension between the two.

"Like I said, Sheriff, I'm sorry." Diamond offered the words with the feeling that he didn't care if they were accepted or not. "Guess the waitin' just got to me."

Cooper nodded and let Diamond walk away. The man was too cool. Cooper doubted that much would get to him.

"Sheriff! Look at this!"

The voice came from within the cabin. Cooper made it to the steps before one of the posse came flying out, carrying a leather bag marked with the coach company's insignia, and waving a handful of papers. An excited chatter started up around him. Cooper took one of the papers and read it silently.

"It's a meal receipt from the stage company."

"I see what it is," Cooper responded, fighting with himself not to crumple the receipt in his fist.

"Look at the signature," Diamond suggested.

"Kenny Smith." Cooper handed the paper back. "It don't mean a thing."

"What are you talkin' about? It's proof he's been here."

"No, it ain't. It was probably just in the bag — "

"Sheriff, I'm startin' to wonder whose side you're on here." Diamond gave a long, cool look to the men that circled them. Anger and suspicion hardened every face.

"We got evidence here."

"No you don't. You got a piece of paper that has every right to be in that bag."

"We got everything we need."

The burning ache in Cooper's belly increased. He could no longer stomach their idea of justice. Vigilante justice was no justice at all. It was definitely time for him to find another line of work. He turned and walked away from the group.

"Where are you going, Sheriff?" One of the men called out to him.

"To get my horse. Nothin' to stay here for."

"Well, what do we do now?"

Cooper turned back to face them. "The stage company has a fifty-dollar reward for any man in Smith's gang. I suggest you load him up and get him back to town before he starts stinkin'."

"Fifty bucks!" A round of cheers went up. Cooper suspected some bartender would have the most of that fifty before the day was through.

"What are you going to do, Sheriff?" Diamond demanded.

"I got a thing or two to check out. You wantin' to ride with me?"

The words were a challenge. Diamond stood still and studied the sheriff's face. Long moments passed before Diamond looked away. "Reckon I'll stick with the posse and get my share of the reward."

"You do that," Cooper said curtly, turned on his heel and strode away.

*R*un away!

The words echoed in Kenny's head, repeating and repeating until she could hardly hear Sophie's voice from across the table. Running was impossible, running was what got her in this situation in the first place. If she'd just kept her head and closed her mind to the thought that there could be a different life for her, she'd be safe in her father's house. If she'd only kept quiet and stayed in her place...

No. There was just no way she could've lived that life. I'd rather be dead, she thought, another mental echo she'd heard many times. Now that death seemed to be crowding down upon her, her belief in those words faltered. Before, she had nothing to live for. Now...she glanced up from under her lowered brows and stared at Sophie's back as she cooked their dinner without Kenny's asking. Now, she had a taste of a life worth living. How could she let that go? How could she allow one evil man to snatch it from her?

Sophie was a miracle. A good, kind, beautiful woman, and more than Kenny could have ever expected to grace her life. What good thing had she ever done to deserve someone like Sophie? And what bad thing had Sophie done to deserve someone like her? All she'd brought Sophie was trouble and danger — all she'd shown her was weakness and fear.

Run away! Kenny almost whispered the words aloud. Folding her arms on the table, she put her head down and bit her lip to keep her mouth closed. But she should do it. It would be a kindness, just to slip out of here in the dark of night, to run away and leave Sophie her peace and safety. She wished for the bravery to stand up at that moment and announce she was leaving, and then walk out into the night alone. Trouble was, she couldn't even stir up enough energy to picture herself walking out that door. All the plans she should be making, all the decisions pressing in on her were like a weight that dragged her down into an emotional numbness. She didn't even have the strength to cry.

Kenny wanted nothing but to sleep, and wake tomorrow in a different life. There would be nothing to run from, and nothing would be the way it was now. Nothing, except Sophie.

She would sleep, and wake up in Sophie's arms.

Sophie watched Kenny with concern. They had come home without another word to Belle or anyone. Kenny had stripped out of the yellow dress practically before she was through the door, and had pulled on her pants and boots. But since that flurry of activity, she had hardly moved. The thin cloth undershirt revealed the tension of her well-developed muscles as she sat at the long table, her head in her hands, stone silent.

Sophie respected her silence and bustled about making dinner. Kenny didn't offer to help; Sophie expected that she was too upset to think about it. They ate dinner, still in silence, and

Sophie chewed slowly as she watched Kenny push the food around on her plate.

Worry gnawed at Sophie for the rest of the evening. Kenny surrounded herself in silence, neither crying nor sharing her fears. And as she withdrew deeper and deeper into her thoughts, Sophie could almost see a wall being built between them. Not knowing how to break it down, she wondered if she should even try. She suspected this was how Kenny's body dealt with emotional distress, and doubted it was caused in any way by Kenny's quickly healing injuries. Later, when Kenny fell asleep at the table, dumping her cup of tea and honey on her pants, Sophie knew she had guessed right. Kenny's mind and body were shutting down in self-protection.

Gently, Sophie helped her undress and get into the bed, where Kenny fell back asleep almost instantly. Sophie sat on the side of the bed for a few minutes and watched the strain ease from her sleeping face. Perhaps tomorrow Kenny would be recovered enough to discuss what they should do.

Neither sleep nor relaxation would come soon for Sophie as she paced restlessly around the long table, her mind grasping and discarding reckless plans. After an hour, she forced herself to quit the desperate search for ideas. Taking the last of the tepid tea, she went out to the front porch and watched the sun go down.

Gradually, her nervousness eased as darkness fell around her. To her surprise, as the darkness enveloped her, she realized that her mind had reached out several times to feel for Kenny's presence. Though Kenny had only been with her for two weeks, Sophie already felt that she belonged there. The routine had taken hold of her comfortably. She wanted to wake up every morning knowing that if Kenny was not in the same bed with her, she was at least there in her house.

Sophie leaned her chair back and listened to the quiet calls of night birds. The sound of Twitch grazing from somewhere beyond the lilac bush was comforting. She sighed in satisfaction and a little regret, for change was an unwelcome challenge to Sophie. She was at home here in this broken-down shack, at home as she had never felt in her life. But she knew she could not stay. If the cause for leaving was not Kenny, it would soon be Robert. Even knowing she would be forced to leave, she had dreaded deciding where to go — in fact, she had refused to think of it until this evening. But now that she had someone to love, maybe going would not be so hard.

Twitch rounded the corner of the house and stretched her neck over the flimsy porch rail. She nudged Sophie's shoulder with her head, begging for a treat. Sophie put out her empty hand and Twitch tested it with her fuzzy lips. She blew out in disgust at finding nothing but hand and Sophie laughed.

"You are spoiled rotten," she accused, fondly.

Twitch flicked her ear in the equivalent of a shrug.

"Do you think I can take you with me when we go?" Sophie seriously doubted that possibility. If Robert knew she was fond of the mare, he would take her back now. "Will you run away and join me later?"

Twitch stood motionless, without so much as a twitch or a wriggle or a swish of her tail. Sophie wasn't sure how to interpret the immobility; she'd never seen the horse stand so still while she was talking to her.

"Does that mean no?" Sophie asked lightly, trying to ignore the irrational sadness she felt at Twitch's imagined refusal.

Twitch turned away and ambled over to the water trough. And at last, the tension and fatigue of the day settled in on Sophie. She was so tired, making the trek to her bunk felt like too much work. But the thought of sleeping in her chair on the porch was not attractive enough to keep her from rising and sluggishly preparing herself for sleep.

After lying down in her bunk across the room from Kenny, she forced herself to stay awake for a few minutes. Listening to the soft, comforting sound of Kenny's breath, she let the tranquility of the night soothe her into sleep. Her last thought was the memory of their feverish lovemaking in the forest, of Kenny's body on hers, and the comforting weight holding her securely down to earth. How could she carry on if that mooring failed her?

Fourteen

The morning was tense. Kenny started the day angry because she couldn't wear her pants until the honey was washed out. Sophie, after offering to wash them and getting yelled at, stayed as far from Kenny as she could while still remaining in the small house and yard. Kenny had again donned the hated yellow dress and Sophie sympathetically watched her fight with the long skirts as she hauled water to heat for the laundry.

Sophie wished they could talk about seeing the man, about leaving, but Kenny was not in the mood for that kind of conversation. In fact, she didn't seem to want to talk at all. Sophie was determined to wait, maybe until Kenny approached her on her own.

By the time noon arrived, Kenny was still irate and unresponsive. Sophie, not wanting to make matters worse, decided to get away for awhile. The days seemed to run together in her mind, but she believed this was the third day since Robert had last come to the shack. If her memory was right, he should be home now, and maybe it would be a good day to collect some of Allen's things. Perhaps Kenny would cheer up when Sophie brought her some of Allen's clothes. She would surely appreciate having a choice of what to wear that didn't include dresses.

"I'm going to Robert's," she said after she bridled Twitch and was ready to leave. Kenny must have noticed her preparing to ride, but hadn't said anything about it. "I'll be back in about three hours."

Kenny nodded.

"I'm leaving the rifle with you."

Kenny didn't respond. The decision had been a hard one for Sophie. She knew Robert would be angry if he saw her without the rifle. Hopefully, some cowhands would be close by. He wasn't likely to make trouble with his hired hands around.

"Please be careful." Sophie was suddenly fearful. What was Kenny thinking? Was she planning to leave alone? Sophie hesitated. Sitting astride Twitch, she looked down at Kenny and bit her lip. She wanted Kenny to say something that would convince her that she would still be there when Sophie returned. Kenny did not speak, did not seem to be aware of Sophie's fears.

"Well, good-bye," Sophie stalled.

Kenny finally noticed Sophie's discomfort. Squinting in the sunlight, she shaded her eyes with her hand and looked up at her. Sophie could not read Kenny's thoughts and tried to smile cheerfully, but her expression was strained. Kenny took her hand and kissed the palm softly.

Sophie blinked back her tears of relief at the small gesture. Without another word, she turned Twitch away and rode off at a gallop. Not even the unpleasant prospect of seeing Robert could take away the deep feeling of love she carried for Kenny.

Sophie deliberately forced herself to ride up to the ranch as if she owned it. A small group of men stood by the barn watching as a farrier hammered a new shoe on a mare. It pleased her to see the foreman wave as she passed the corrals; the smile on his face was genuine. With much relief, Sophie realized that Robert was nowhere in sight. She let herself into the large ranch house, familiar with the place that used to be her home. It had never felt like hers, although Allen had said it was; the large echoing rooms and the bulky furniture had never welcomed her. With effort, she pushed away the feeling of being an intruder; she had the right, or at least the permission, to be here today.

She went to the bedroom at the top of the stairs. It had been Allen's and then theirs; now it was apparently Allen's again. Nothing had changed since the day she had packed her things and left the house at Robert's insistence. Sophie ran her finger along the dust layering the bureau, then impulsively wrote her name toward the back where it would not be found and erased. The action felt somewhat spiteful and satisfying.

Quickly, she gathered together several shirts and pairs of pants. She remembered to take some socks, but could not find a hat or coat. And though a part of her wanted to, Sophie could not force herself to stay in the house long enough to make a better search. It was not too important; Kenny would be able to find a coat somewhere before winter.

Impatient to be away from this brooding house, Sophie ran down the stairs and into the hallway. She paused at the door as she caught sight of the hat rack. Several old and battered Stetsons hung there; probably one of them had been Allen's. She grabbed a dark brown one — the oldest and dirtiest — and hoped Robert wouldn't even miss it if it was his.

Just as Sophie pulled the front door open and stepped out, she came face to face with Robert. Both froze in their steps, surprised by the other's presence.

"What the hell are you doin'?" Robert asked, his voice gruff with suspicion.

"I came to get the things I asked you for," Sophie explained without apology.

"Let me see," he demanded.

Sophie opened her bag. She took out the hat, then the shirts, draping them over the porch rail.

"That hat is mine."

"Oh, I'm sorry. I thought I remembered Allen wearing it." Sophie held it out to him.

"Just keep it," Robert said grudgingly. "I guess I don't have any use for it. What else you got in there?"

"Oh, yes..." Sophie pretended that she had forgotten there was anything else in her bag. "Just a pair of jeans. They are torn badly, but I thought they would make good rags for scrubbing the floor. Unless you have a mop you could lend..."

"No, no just take 'em. I hope you don't expect to come back here again."

"I wouldn't dream of it, Robert." Sophie stuffed the things back into her bag and stepped around him. To her dismay, Robert reached out and took her arm. His grip was unexpectedly light.

"I see that you're not carrying that rifle," Robert said, for once the contempt gone from his voice. "I hope that doesn't mean you've lost it somewhere, or sold it."

"No, Robert. It's at home. I felt I would be safe since I was coming to your place."

"What do you mean by that?" he asked quickly.

"Only that I think no one would be willing to cross you by coming onto your land," Sophie lied.

The notion went straight to Robert's head. He almost smiled. "Yes. Guess you're right about that." He fondly patted the pistol at his side.

Her compliment had completely changed Robert's demeanor. Sophie suffered his hand on her arm a moment longer, then casually tried to move beyond his reach.

His hold tightened. "Come inside."

"I really must be going." She tried to smile as she spoke. Anything not to offend him.

Robert reached out and pushed the door open. He pulled on her arm with a steady force. She was pulled forward, off balance. As her body moved closer to his, he turned to step behind her, then pushed her through the doorway.

"Listen. I don't want to hurt you." He released her enough to allow her to lean against the wall beside the door.

Sophie looked up into his eyes and was astonished to see that his expression made the words sincere. "Then don't do this," she said quietly.

"I got to. I can't stand it anymore." His voice was strained, his jaws clenched. "I can't stand the sight of you anymore."

"Let me go and I'll leave. I'll never come back here," Sophie pleaded. "You'll never see me again, I promise."

Robert slid his hands down her arms and took her by the wrists. He held them crossed between their bodies. "I don't want that. I want you to move back — to this house."

"I can't, Robert." The dark look in his eyes frightened her.

"You will." The coldness returned to his voice. He dropped one of her hands and gripped her throat with a wide palm. He pressed his mouth against hers in a savage kiss.

Sophie held very still, not breathing as she suffered his lips on her skin. His mouth was hard, pressing her lips painfully against her teeth. Robert breathed a long breath deeply through his nose and, with an unexpected slow movement, his kiss grew tender. He released her throat and let his hand slide down to her shoulder. She was astonished at the softness of his touch.

After another moment, he let her pull her face away from his. They both breathed heavily in the quiet room. Robert seemed unable to look her in the eye, but he didn't let her move away from the wall.

"Sophie, I've never felt this way," he tried to explain. "One minute it seems I hate you, and the next...I just don't know."

Sophie knew. She knew exactly what he was feeling and the knowledge frightened her more than his cruelty ever had. "Robert, you've got to let me go."

Robert shook his head and finally looked at her face. "No. I can't."

"You can't keep me here — "

His anger flared. "I can do anything I want. There's no one in this whole world who gives a damn about you, Sophie. No one but me."

Tears came to Sophie's eyes. Not long ago, his words would have been the truth. But things had changed. "That's not true," she whispered.

"Is that right?" He took her wrists again, all the tenderness gone from him. "You tell me who cares for you."

"I don't have to tell you anything."

He slammed her hands against the wall and leaned into her face. "You tell me," he warned, his voice a low growl. "Have you been seein' some man?"

She shook her head in denial. The gesture seemed to increase his anger. "Don't you lie to me," he warned.

Sophie struggled against his hold, but her strength was useless against his. "I'm not lying."

Robert raised his hand, his fury pushing him to smack her.

Suddenly, the door swung open. A large shadow filled the doorway. Robert jumped away from her and drew his gun. The motion was a blur.

"McLaren!" the man in the doorway shouted and stumbled backward against the railing, his hands raised defensively. "It's me, don't..."

Sophie and Robert recognized the man in the same instant — it was the foreman. Not allowing herself to think of the consequences, Sophie took advantage of the confusion and bolted out the door and grabbed her bundle. In a tangle of petticoats, she flew up onto Twitch's back. Her heart was pounding as she turned the horse's head in the direction of the line shack. She prayed that Robert would not follow. But the sound of a horse's hooves galloping behind her denied any hope she had. Twitch galloped at a breakneck pace, urged on by both Sophie's fear and the sound of the horse steadily gaining ground on them. But Twitch's small frame could not hold out long against the heavy-muscled steeds Robert liked to ride. Robert would catch up to her by the time she reached the clearing. And if Kenny was outside the shack when they arrived, Sophie was certain they were both doomed.

*K*enny cursed steadily as she hauled the last bucket of hot water out to the wash tub. All her work and all her plans and she was still wearing women's clothes, doing women's work. She stuffed her pants, socks, and one of Sophie's dark-colored dresses into the sudsy water, then reached in to stir them around, cursing again as the water burned her hand. With difficulty, she stopped herself from angrily kicking the tub with her bare toes.

Frustrated, she dropped down next to the tub and shook her stinging hand in the air. She had the choice of dragging over a bucket of cold water or allowing the water to cool on its own. Glaring up at the already hot, cloudless sky, she decided to wait on the water. The clothes probably needed to soak anyway. Kenny scooted herself over to the thin bar of shade that angled from the clothesline pole.

Wishing she had a decent hat, Kenny squinted in the glaring sunlight. Sophie's bonnet was still stuffed into the little pocket on the front of the yellow dress. Though she despised it, her head was beginning to ache from the eye strain. She sighed heavily and took it out of her pocket. At least Sophie was not here to see her in it.

As she waited for the water to cool, Kenny almost dozed off. She had no idea what was wrong with her, but she was finding it hard to keep her mind clear of sleep. The future was something she should be thinking about, but it was just too much of a bother. She leaned her head back and looked toward the cool shade of the forest and let her mind wander.

The sound of a galloping horse jerked her attention back to the clearing. Sophie was home already and Kenny was glad. She had been rude to Sophie all morning and knew it was past time to apologize for her brusqueness. She pushed herself up from the spot of shade and looked to the east. To her horror, the rider was not Sophie, but a tall man on a buckskin horse.

Kenny restrained her impulse to run. The man carried his rifle ready, and he did not look like the kind that would hesitate to use it. Her heart raced with fear, then nearly stopped when she saw the glint of a polished silver star on his chest.

He rode the horse into the yard and stopped a short distance from her in a cloud of dust. Kenny realized with a chill that the rifle was deliberately pointed at her chest.

"Are you Sophie McLaren?" he barked without introduction.

Kenny shook her head. He narrowed his eyes.

"Who are you?"

Kenny pointed to the ground, then knelt down slowly, keeping her hands visible. In the dust she wrote: Cusin Anne. She was careful to misspell the word. She looked up at him and pointed to the name, then to herself.

"Can't speak, huh?" he asked kindly, his attitude changing.

She shook her head again and pointed to him with a questioning expression.

"Me? I'm the sheriff from Stockton. Name's Cooper." He did not tell her his first name. "Came here to ask Mrs. McLaren a few questions. Will she be back soon?"

Kenny was relieved to see that he no longer aimed the rifle at her. Although she suspected that Sophie would be home within the hour, she didn't relish the idea of entertaining this man until she arrived. Yet again, she shook her head.

"Well, I guess I could come back another time," he drawled.

Kenny nodded her head eagerly. That was a wonderful idea. Suppressing a sigh of relief was difficult as he reached for his reins. But he was not to leave that easily.

"I thought that Mrs. McLaren lived here alone. How long have you been here with her?" he asked while casually glancing around the yard and house.

Kenny held up one finger.

"One day? One week?"

Kenny nodded at the second.

"How did you arrive? Did you come by stagecoach?"

Kenny thought that this questioning could lead to nothing but trouble. She batted her eyes and did her best to look confused at the query.

"Did your family bring you here?"

Kenny quivered her bottom lip at the mention of family. With a timid nod, she looked down at the ground.

"I think I understand," he said, in a voice so gentle that Kenny felt guilty for fooling him this way. "I'll talk to Mrs. McLaren. You tell her I'll come back tomorrow. Can you remember that?"

Kenny nodded earnestly and placed her hand over her heart. He smiled and tipped his hat at her.

"I'll let you get back to your washin'," he said as he turned his horse around.

Kenny watched his back as he rode slowly away, forcing herself to stand there on her shaking legs until he had disappeared over a rise. When she could see him no more, she sank down next to the washtub. Only then did she notice the gray and black striped pant leg that draped conspicuously over the side of the tub.

Blind panic coursed through her and, without thinking that the sheriff could be watching, she ran to the shack. Sophie's rifle was lying on one of the spare bunks. Kenny grabbed it up and checked to be sure it was loaded. In her haste to fill her pockets with extra bullets, she dumped the box over, spilling them across the bed. In a frenzy, she dug through the papers and old clothes that cluttered the bed, grabbing for the shells. A sheet of paper dropped to the floor. Kenny leaned to pick it up and stared down into a drawing of her own face.

For a moment she could not move. She read the words written there several times before she fully comprehended what they meant. A hot pain began to burn in the pit of her stomach. Five thousand dollars reward...she couldn't even dream of all the things that much money would buy.

Straightening slowly, she thought of Sophie. How long had she known of this reward? And why hadn't she said anything about it? Fear spread like ice through her veins. She had to get away.

*T*witch was lathered and breathing hard as Sophie pulled her roughly to a stop just outside the clearing. Anxiously, Sophie's eyes searched for Kenny, but she was nowhere to be seen. Sophie hoped she had the sense to stay out of sight. Within seconds Robert pounded into view. Gathering every bit of her courage, Sophie waited for him to approach. He stopped his horse a few yards from her and studied her carefully.

"Sophie," he said her name quietly. "I'm so sorry."

The words took her by surprise. She was confused by his rapidly changing emotions, and had no idea how to respond. He was willing to speak until she could.

"I didn't mean to do that. I didn't want it to be that way." As he spoke his hand clenched the hard leather of his holster tightly. "I just can't seem to handle myself around you."

Sophie imagined herself back in that grip to steel herself against whatever he might say.

"I can give you anything you ever want, Sophie. I'm gonna be a rich man. I can give things that Allen never could."

Sophie lifted her chin abruptly. He had given her the words she needed. "I think I understand how you feel, Robert. But I wish you could understand my feelings."

"I — I want to. What are your feelings?" he asked, stepping neatly into her trap.

"It's just too soon. I'm still thinking of Allen." She dropped her gaze to pretend a deep emotion. "I can't look at you, because I see his face. I still think of him every day."

The stiffness of his body made his horse prance nervously and, for once, he didn't discipline it harshly. He waited for her to continue. Deliberately, she allowed Twitch to step closer before she spoke again.

"I think, with a little time..." Sophie let her words trail off suggestively.

*K*enny hid at the edge of the forest, clutching Sophie's

rifle and thinking that her day could not get any worse. She was wrong.

Squinting her eyes, Kenny saw Sophie running Twitch toward the house, but she was not alone. A man, his body too large to be the sheriff Kenny had just met, was riding hard behind her. Kenny felt the hair on her arms and neck rising as the two figures drew closer to her. Her worst fears came rushing back to her as the two of them pulled their horses to a stop. Nausea washed over her as she immediately recognized the man who had robbed the stage and terrorized her. And now, to compound her horror, Sophie was involved. Had he somehow taken her prisoner?

He sat arrogantly tall in his saddle, his hand resting dangerously on the long pistol at his hip. His eyes did not leave Sophie and his expression and the words he was saying were obviously disturbing her. Even from this distance, Kenny could see that Sophie's face was drawn and pale.

Kenny aimed the rifle with care and estimated the distance the bullet would have to travel. She waited for a clear shot, not wanting to miss and hit Sophie, but the woman moved into her line of fire. Kenny's hands trembled and sweat made them slip against the smooth metal of the rifle. If he would just ride a little bit closer...

The two riders lingered just outside of the clearing. They looked to be discussing something quite seriously; Sophie shook her head repeatedly and pointed away from the shack. At last, she reached out and touched his cheek, letting her fingers trace the line of his jaw. When Sophie again pointed away, Kenny was stunned that the man obediently tugged at his reins and rode off without argument.

Kenny's mind reeled. Sophie was *not* his prisoner; she had ridden with him willingly. She had actually told him to leave, and he had listened. Incredibly, the man Kenny believed to possess all the power in the world minded the words of Sophie McLaren.

Kenny struggled to make sense of what she had just

witnessed. It was almost too much for her to believe that
Sophie had connections to the bandit. What did she know? She
could not be ignorant of who he was, so why was she making
the pretense of protecting and trying to help Kenny prove her
innocence? Were they keeping her hidden so they could commit
more crimes that she would be blamed for? The thought of her
face plastered on the wanted poster came to mind. A reward
that size might convince a woman to do almost anything.

Kenny suddenly had the clear and unnerving image of
herself hanging for those crimes. Of dying, carrying the blame
for Frank's death. Rage burned in her limbs like wildfire. Before
she could think, she swung the rifle to point at Sophie's head
and braced herself for the shot.

But she could not pull the trigger.

The gun wavered in her hands and her arms suddenly
lost their strength. Lowering the gun slowly, she leaned back
against the rough bark of a pine tree. Though she was most
probably a fool, she could not judge Sophie until she found out
what connection she had with the robber. It would be
dangerously stupid to come right out and ask. She decided to
pretend she didn't recognize him or suspect Sophie in any way.
Impatiently, she waited in the cover of forest until Sophie
entered the house.

Sophie swung around abruptly as Kenny stepped into
the doorway. Kenny nearly raised the rifle in reflex to the quick
motion.

"Thank God," Sophie exclaimed. "I thought you'd
gone."

Kenny walked past her and sat down on her bunk,
nonchalantly leaning the gun against the edge of the bed.
Sophie didn't miss the tension that Kenny could not erase from
her face.

"What's wrong?" She started to move toward Kenny,
then stopped herself. "What has happened?"

"The sheriff showed up here today," Kenny reported,
allowing the worry and fear of Sophie's betrayal to creep into

her voice. "Said he'll be back tomorrow."

Sophie gasped; her face whitened. "Does he suspect anything?"

"I don't think so. I was wearin' the dress." Kenny did not mention her fear that the sheriff had seen the incriminating pants. "And I didn't speak."

"I shouldn't have left you here alone," Sophie fretted, while thin lines of concern creased her forehead.

Kenny lay back on the narrow bed and studied Sophie's face. She had never yet been able to disguise her emotions and the distress she was showing certainly appeared genuine. But Kenny had to see how she reacted to the next question.

"Who was that man you rode up with?"

Sophie's face grew hard and she turned away. Kenny's heart skipped a painful beat as she clenched the blanket in her fists to keep from striking out.

"That was Robert McLaren, my brother-in-law."

"Your brother-in-law?" Kenny repeated, shocked. So he was not some stranger that had followed Sophie to the house or a suitor set to win her hand. Kenny was sickened to have her suspicions of Sophie's relationship to the bandit confirmed.

"That's right. And he's a bastard." Sophie spat the words. "I'm terrified of him, Kenny, and I need to get far away from him; you can't imagine how dangerous he is."

Kenny almost laughed at Sophie's understatement. Kenny believed Sophie was using her anger toward Robert McLaren to hide something. There was just something in Sophie's eyes that said she wasn't telling the whole truth and Kenny was determined not to tell Sophie that her brother-in-law was the stagecoach bandit. Silently, she agreed that McLaren was indeed a very dangerous man. And it seemed that Sophie was a very dangerous woman...

Fifteen

An hour before daybreak, Kenny slid out of bed and out the door noiselessly. Once outside, she led Twitch away from the cabin with soft words and a gentle hand. After one last look around, Kenny jumped on the horse's back, adjusted the old, battered Stetson on her head, and galloped away.

The sweet smell of wet grass filled her nostrils as she rode eastward. Though her insides were trembling with the knowledge of what she meant to do today, the rifle felt solid on her arm, the trousers comfortable on her body. Today was the day she would put a bullet through Robert McLaren's heart.

"A hell of way to repay the woman for saving your life," Kenny scolded herself, guilt crowding into her determination. But for now, she couldn't allow herself to feel any remorse or affection toward Sophie. Though it made her heart heavy, she suspected Sophie was involved in Robert's crimes, no matter how innocent Sophie tried to make their relationship appear. Kenny had made a quick judgment. It was possibly unfair, but under the circumstances it was the only judgment she could afford to make.

Last night had been horrible. Kenny had known that Sophie wanted to feel close again, wanted to make love, but she could not bring herself to touch Sophie or be touched by her. She tried to convince Sophie that the tension was caused by the emotional strain of the sheriff's visit, but Kenny was not sure how successful she'd been. Sophie had grown more despondent as the night wore on and hardly answered Kenny's attempts at conversation. But Kenny had managed to learn the basic layout of the ranch and the number of men Robert employed without Sophie becoming suspicious of her offhand questions.

The sun was barely lightening the horizon as Kenny approached the outbuildings of the McLaren ranch. She slid off Twitch's back and led her to a small stand of trees that was downwind of the barn and corrals, not wanting any other horse to catch the smell of her mount. She tied Twitch's reins securely to a tree branch and studied the spread of buildings below her.

The main house and the bunkhouse were easy to spot in the faint morning light. The windows of both buildings were dark. Avoiding a path that would allow her to be seen, Kenny ran swiftly and quietly to the shelter of the barn. She glanced at the three horses penned in the corral. According to Sophie, there should have been many more. Perhaps it was her good luck that Robert and his ranch hands were not here.

Kenny peered around the corner of the barn at the main house. A thin curl of smoke rising from the chimney renewed her hopes. All she had to do was find a vantage point that would give her a clear view of the front door. She would kill Robert without warning as he stepped out onto the porch.

What she was contemplating was the act of a coward. She knew that, but she also knew it was the only way she could kill him. He did not deserve a more honorable death at her hands.

Kenny looked over at the bunkhouse. No smoke came from the stovepipe, and still no light or movement could be seen through the windows. Gathering her courage, she darted over to the back wall of the long building. She crawled to a window and peeked through a dirty pane of glass. A double row of narrow bunks lined the walls. Kenny's eyes adjusted quickly and she could see that the beds held nothing but rumpled blankets. The squalid room was empty.

Kenny smiled wickedly and stood upright. If she could find a way up, the bunkhouse roof would be a perfect place to lie in a wait. Levering a shell into the chamber of the rifle, she stepped back from the window.

"What do you think you're doin' here?" A harsh voice almost stopped her heart.

Kenny spun around, knowing exactly who she would face. That voice was one she would never be able to forget. She turned, with the rifle held low, but ready.

Arrogantly, Robert leaned against the wall, not fifteen feet from where Kenny stood by the window. He sneered at her, not taking her threat seriously enough to raise his hands. A chill went up her spine from knowing that she had not heard a whisper of his approach, and she wondered how long he had been following her. Before she could speak, his face abruptly darkened with rage.

"Where'd you get those clothes?" His anger grew as he answered his own question. "That bitch Sophie gave them to you, didn't she? God damn that whore. Did she send you down here to steal from me?"

Kenny felt a cold fury at the insults to Sophie, but she didn't allow herself to be distracted. "She didn't send me, and I'm not here to steal." Slowly, she raised the rifle. "You're the damn thief and bushwhacker." Her forehead beaded with sweat.

Robert stared at her in astonished silence, recognition sinking in slowly at the sound of her voice. He stepped away from the wall, the arrogance suddenly gone from his face and posture.

"Do you remember me, McLaren?" She reached her hand up and pushed back her hat. The reddish scar was visible in the early light of dawn.

Robert laughed. "How in the hell...I was sure I'd killed you." He shook his head in disbelief. "I thought the animals got you — that was why they never found your body."

"Seems you were wrong."

Robert ignored the insult in her voice; his icy composure

had returned. "Shit, I couldn't believe how perfect it was that you were blamed. I was gonna do the same thing on my next job."

"There won't be a next job for you, McLaren," she told him, trying to instill a calm certainty in her voice. "I'm going to kill you. For what you did to me, you bastard, and for killing my partner, Frank."

Robert McLaren laughed heartily. "You're gonna kill me with my own gun, huh? You sure got guts, boy. But it ain't gonna happen that way, so you might as well stop aimin' that rifle at me."

Kenny responded by aiming the end of the barrel right between his eyes.

"Don't be stupid," he warned her, stabbing the air with his index finger for emphasis. "You put down that rifle and we can talk about you joinin' up with me. You're tough and determined, I can see that, and I could use somebody like you."

"I don't do your kind of work, mister, and I can't figure why you do. You got everything in the world here, what do you need all that money for?" Kenny shook her head.

A chilling smile returned to the bandit's face. "Ain't nothin' to do with the money, boy. I just like pointin' my gun at people and seeing the fear in their eyes. Guess you could say, I just like killin'." Robert's hands began to move away from his hips, out to the side.

Despite her determination, the words and the pleasure in his voice made her step back. Her hands were sweating against the cold metal of the barrel and her stomach felt tied in knots.

"You kill me, boy, and you'll see what it's like." As if he sensed her increasing fear, Robert took a step toward her to narrow the gap. She couldn't stop herself from backing away.

"It's power, plain and simple," he continued. "The strongest in the world. Nothin' compares to it, not drinkin', not being with a woman. You'll see. You kill me and you'll be just like me."

"No. I'll never be like you," Kenny spat vehemently.

He snickered. "Then put down that gun and we'll talk about what you are like."

"No." She shook her head slowly. "I came here for one thing, McLaren — justice. I'll see you dead for killing Frank and what you did to me."

Robert's lips tightened as he clenched his jaw. That tension was all the warning Kenny would get. Suddenly, the movement of his hand toward his holster was almost too fast to be seen. In a flash he drew the long pistol and jumped to the side, forcing Kenny to jerk the rifle to the right. Her sweat-slick finger slid down the short curve of the trigger and she fired. The bullet hit him high in the chest, too high. The force of the shot knocked him backwards, but he didn't fall. His cocky smile was plastered to his sun-beaten face and his pistol was still rising to meet Kenny's heart.

Frantic, her heart pounding out a melody of doom, Kenny struggled to lever another bullet into the rifle chamber, her eyes riveted on Robert McLaren's pistol. She felt as if she were moving in slow motion. She had been in this position before, lying on her back in a cold stream, staring at the messenger of death. There was no counting on luck this time. If she didn't kill Robert McLaren right now, she would die.

Quickly, Kenny cocked the rifle, and aimed lower, straight at his heart, aware that he had settled his aim on her as well. She stood her ground, no backstepping. Her muscles tensed, anticipating the recoil of her rifle, anticipating the shock of his bullet penetrating her flesh. But, before she could squeeze the trigger, a shot rang out from her left and the back side of Robert's head scattered in a spray of blood and bone. Confusion flooded over her as Robert's body slammed against the bunkhouse wall. His pistol fired, driving a slug into the ground at her feet. The rough wood of the wall held him upright for a moment, his knees buckling, his eyes questioning her even as the life drained from them. He opened his mouth to speak, then dropped to the ground at her feet.

Swinging her rifle around, Kenny crouched down against the wall. Robert's blood pumped out over her boots as she scanned the hillside for the shooter. The man who sat on the buckskin gelding lowered his rifle and urged the horse forward, ignoring the fact that Kenny's gun was pointed at him. Open-mouthed, Kenny watched Sheriff Cooper approaching, and could not decide if she should shoot him or not.

"You can let down that gun," the sheriff said pleasantly as he reined the horse up next to her. "I know who you are."

The offhand comment hit Kenny like a fist and fear surged through her body. The feeling was inconceivable — she'd thought she could not get any more frightened than she had been to find Robert McLaren standing behind her.

"I'm not goin' to let you hang me, Sheriff," Kenny stuttered bravely, but her words were empty and she knew it.

"You stay out of town and you're not gonna get hung. I figured I knew who was behind the robberies from the start." Cooper got down from his horse, turning his back to Kenny without hesitation. He shoved the toe of his boot under Robert's shoulder and pushed him over. Robert's lifeless eyes stared into the sky.

The sheriff quickly went through Robert's pockets. "I've been suspectin' this one since that robbery last year in Durango, him and his brother both. But I didn't have anything I could use to pin it on them. Men like this, you got to have more than a gut feelin'. The thing that slowed me up was not knowin' why. You got me the answer to that."

Kenny looked over at Robert. His hand had flung out to land next to her blood-soaked boot. She watched with horror as his fingers quivered and scraped at the dirt.

"Is he dead?" She whispered the question. A prickling hot sweat had broken out over her body.

"Yeah, he's dead." The sheriff took hold of Robert's sleeve and slung his arm over his motionless chest, away from Kenny.

Kenny took a deep breath. She sat down heavily and fought to keep from passing out. "I didn't kill Frank."

The sheriff squatted down and peered at her face. Slowly, he put his hand to the back of her head and pushed it forward gently until her forehead almost touched her knees. Holding her there for a few moments, he spoke in a soft voice. "I know that. I'll do my best to let everyone know that. You saved me some work and sniffing around here, not that I would'a found anything solid to pin on him and his men. I s'pose he was too smart to let any proof hang around. Then again, you never can tell."

Kenny felt the blackness in her head receding; the rifle was forgotten in her numb hands. As her breath came easier, the sheriff released her, but stayed close to her side.

"I don't know much about your life, son," he said slowly, emphasizing the word "son." "But I don't think you left anything so important in Jackson that you should go back for it. People are wonderin' who you are, and they ain't going to stop asking 'til they get an answer."

Kenny neither looked up nor responded to his comments. An ache was building in her chest.

"Here's what I'd like to do," the sheriff continued. "I'd like to go back to town and say that I found your body by the mine. Say that you fought it out, but McLaren killed you. Folks in town will probably make you a hero." He chuckled, then added in a serious voice, "But that's only if you promise not to go back there."

Kenny nodded. She had known since the holdup that she would never be able to regain her old life. But what was she to do? The ache became a hard fist that gripped her heart. She whispered, "Sophie..."

"Don't you worry none about Mrs. McLaren. I'm convinced she didn't know anything about these robberies. If she did, this jackass would'a killed her." The sheriff stood up and slapped the dust from his pants. "I guess this place will be hers now."

Surprised, Kenny raised her head and quickly looked around. She couldn't imagine Sophie living in a place this big, but had to admit to herself that she didn't know Sophie well enough to say what she would like. Maybe she would feel at home here. Kenny hoped so.

"I'm goin' back to town, and bringin' a posse back to wait for McLaren's men to return. No tellin' when they'll get back and it wouldn't do to get caught alone now. You'd better just clear on outta here."

The sheriff leaned over and struggled to hoist Robert's body onto the back of his horse. Kenny jumped to her feet and awkwardly helped to pull him over the horse's haunches. The sheriff nodded his thanks.

Kenny stood, still shaking, still hurting inside. "I don't know where to go," she said simply.

"Anywhere," he replied. "Take one of the McLaren horses. Just leave it in the first town you come to. Tell the stable master to wire me and hold it 'til I can bring it back here."

Sheriff Cooper mounted his horse and looked down at her sympathetically. Kenny knew she should be thanking him for all he was doing for her, but her pain made speech too difficult.

"Oh yeah," the sheriff said suddenly, digging into his pocket. "There was a reward for capturing anyone involved in the holdup. Fifty dollars. I think you deserve it, but I guess you won't be going into town to pick it up. Will this do you?" He held out his hand.

Kenny reached up and he put two twenty-dollar gold pieces in her palm.

"That and a few days hard riding northeast will get you set up in Denver." The sheriff took the reins and backed the horse away from her. "Don't dawdle around here son. This place is going to get mighty crowded in a little while."

"Thank you. Thanks for everything." Finally, Kenny was able to express her appreciation. But the sheriff just turned and rode away, raising one hand in a casual wave good-bye.

Kenny could not move for several minutes. She stood staring at the blood soaking into the dry ground, thinking that maybe her nightmare was truly over. At last she cried — tears of relief, and tears at the thought of leaving. She should have told Sophie good-bye in some way. A kiss, a note, something...

Still crying, she stumbled to the stand of trees where she had tied Twitch. She put her arms around the horse's neck and cried until she had no more tears. Twitch stood patiently, allowing Kenny to spend her grief, supported by the mare's strong body.

"I wish I could take you, but it wouldn't be fair," Kenny explained to Twitch when her voice returned. "Sophie loves you too much."

Twitch blew her soft breath warmly into the collar of Kenny's shirt. Kenny tied the reins together securely and looped them over the horse's neck, checking to be sure there was no way the long leather strips could come loose to trip Twitch. Patting her fondly on the hip, Kenny said quietly, "Go home."

Twitch took a few steps, then stopped and looked back at Kenny. She twitched her ear one last time. Kenny laughed and the horse tossed her head and took off for Sophie's at a run.

Kenny watched until the brown mare disappeared in the distance. Suddenly she realized she was dawdling, and she had no idea when Robert's men might return. She ran to the barn and picked out the strongest horse of the three. In the tack room, she found a bridle and, on second thought, a worn black saddle. She had had enough of riding bareback.

The horse was docile and Kenny was able to saddle him in a short time. Hunger was making itself felt in her belly, but she couldn't take the time to raid Robert's pantry. She mounted the tall horse and looked around one last time. Try as she might, she still could not imagine Sophie at home here.

Kenny rode past the main house; then, on an impulse, brought the horse back around and rode up to the porch. The weathered pine boards rang as she jumped off the horse and ran inside. She found what she was looking for on the kitchen table — paper and the stub of a yellow pencil. Quickly, but with care, she wrote: Sophie, I love you. K.

Kenny Smith rode away without ever looking back.

*N*ot long after, Sophie shaded her eyes and looked toward the sound of approaching hoofbeats. She held her breath, hoping. When Twitch came riderless over the ridge, a deep sigh left her chest in a wordless cry. It seemed that Kenny had decided to disappear as suddenly as she had once appeared.

"You're leaving your life again, aren't you?" Sophie asked, her eyes closed tight, trying to fix those beloved features in her memory. She thought about the words she hadn't had the time or the courage to say. She leaned her head back and spoke to the sky, wishing the words could somehow find their way to Kenny's ears. "I can understand why you have to go, Kenny. But why do you have to leave me here?"

Sixteen

The back of the hard wooden seat cut into Sophie's backbone as she sat, waiting for the stagecoach. She hardly felt the discomfort as her eyes wandered blankly over the dusty main street of Jackson. Occasionally a thought pushed its way into her consciousness, but she was done with thinking, long having lost control over the nature of her thoughts. Merely waiting was difficult enough.

The single black bag that rested at her feet held everything that Sophie was taking from this life into her next one. Inside were a few dresses, a hairbrush, all of her day-to-day things. Nothing unusual, except for a pair of men's pants, striped gray and black.

Sophie had no idea what her next life would be. She would wait and see, just as she'd been waiting for the last three weeks. Waiting for Kenny to return, for the ranch to sell, for the empty ache in her heart to fill and fade. And now she was waiting for the stage to come and take her away from the bittersweet memories. Even the thought of the stage itself prompted memories. She knew she would look to see, all the while knowing better, if a certain slender man would be holding the reins.

"Ma'am?"

Sophie ignored the small voice to the left of her. There was no one she wanted to talk to.

"Sophie," the voice came again, a little more insistent.

She sighed and looked over. It was Tyler, the boy from the stables, standing shyly in the shadow of the coach house. He hooked a bare toe into the dirt and gave her a tentative smile.

Sophie returned a weak grimace that the boy accepted as a smile. He plopped himself down next to her on the hard bench.

"I hear you're leavin' town," he said.

Sophie nodded and turned her head back to look vaguely at the street again.

"Hear you're sellin' the big McLaren ranch, too." Tyler didn't wait for her response. He continued to speak as he kicked his feet back and forth in excitement. "I wouldn't a done it. Those McLaren boys probably had treasure hidden all over the place."

"The new owners won't move in for a couple more weeks," she told him dryly. "You're welcome to look around until then."

"You mean it?" his voice squeaked with enthusiasm. Sophie was surprised that he managed to keep from jumping up that very instant and running off to start his search.

Sophie leaned her head back against the wall and closed her eyes. Tyler quieted, having finally noticed the seriousness of her mood. He was patient for almost two minutes, until his curiosity got the best of him.

"You're a McLaren, ain't you, Sophie?" he asked.

She nodded again.

"Well, why didn't you rob any of the stages?"

"I guess they didn't want me along," Sophie explained. "And besides, I just don't think I could kill anyone, Tyler."

"Oh yeah." His voice showed that he had forgotten the tragedies involved in the outlaw life. He dropped his head and pressed his bony knees together, then whispered sadly, "I still miss Kenny."

Sophie bit her lip to keep from admitting that she, too, missed Kenny. "Well, you were right about him," she offered as soon as she could speak without emotion coloring her voice.

"Yeah, but sometimes I wish he would'a been the robber. Then I'd know he was alive out there somewhere."

Sophie shook her head. "If Kenny was a bad man, he would never have been your friend. We have to accept that he's gone." Sophie could not bring herself to say that Kenny was dead. She couldn't tell Tyler the truth, but she couldn't lie to him either. "We'll just have to make new friends."

Tyler shrugged doubtfully. "You ever comin' back here?"

"No, I really don't think so."

"Then I guess I'm losin' another friend," he said with a sigh.

Sophie reached out and patted his leg. "I'm sorry, Tyler. But you'll probably be too busy digging for treasure to miss me for long."

Some of Tyler's earlier excitement returned. "Do you think maybe they hid the loot in the ranch house?"

Sophie smiled fondly at the distractibility of youth. "I don't know — I haven't been in the house since just before the sheriff caught Robert."

Tyler looked at her like he doubted her sanity. "You never even looked inside? There must have been money all over the place!"

"I couldn't spend that kind of money, Tyler." She didn't mention that the sale of the ranch would bring her more money than she could spend in a lifetime.

"I sure could." Tyler jumped off the bench and squatted in the dirt to persecute a beetle that had been innocently crawling by.

Sophie watched him, feeling the depression that had lifted a little during their conversation settling back around her like a heavy, black shawl. She didn't know where she was going, or what she was going to do with the rest of her life. The stage from Jackson only went two ways; east to Leadville, then to Denver beyond, and northwest to Price and on to Salt Lake.

Today's stage was the one headed into Utah, so that was the way she would go. When she arrived in Salt Lake she'd take some time to make plans before moving on.

"You takin' that horse?" Tyler asked, pointing to the brown mare that stood contented in the deep shadows of the coach house.

"Yes, she'll come along with the stage."

"You gonna tie her to the back?"

"No, Twitch doesn't care to be tied." Sophie saw the mare raise her head at the sound of her name. "She'll probably just run along with the rest of the horses."

Tyler stood up and walked over to stand in front of Sophie. He fidgeted, his face looking guilty about something. "Well, I'm s'posed to be cleaning the stalls," he confessed. "But I wanted to say good-bye to you."

"Thank you, Tyler. I'll write to you some time." Sophie reached out and gave him a quick hug. He accepted it graciously. "I hope you find treasure."

He broke into a gap-toothed grin. "I hope you do, too," he whispered, before turning and running off down the street.

The jangling of braces turned Sophie's head. The stage came into view, breaking out of the forest to the east of town, with the horses trotting. The driver must know that they are behind schedule, Sophie thought, wondering if Kenny had ever been so late.

The driver was a big man, his bulk turning to fat as the years advanced on him. The shotgun rider was also a large man — he held his rifle ready and looked as if he had not relaxed once during the long trip.

The driver pulled the coach past her bench, raising a thick cloud of dust that settled on Sophie's hair and dress. She took no notice. Standing up, she collected her bag and walked slowly over to the coach.

The shotgun man had jumped down from his seat. He watched her walk toward him, then said, "The stage won't be leaving for at least half an hour, ma'am." His voice was kind.

Sophie shrugged. What was another half hour in the context of her life? She put one hand out to the smooth wooden side of the coach and leaned against it.

"I'll take your bag," he said, and reached out. Sophie let him pull it from her hand without a word.

The weight of the coach shifted as the door swung open, narrowly missing Sophie's nose as it flew past. A man jumped out, then turned and offered his hand to the stage's other passengers. Sophie glared at his back. He was a gambler, she surmised, judging by the tailored cut of his black suit and the careful trim of his hair. He wore polished black boots and a wide-brimmed black hat pulled low over his forehead. He was unquestionably vain about his appearance.

Sophie watched as he helped down a pretty girl of about fifteen, her long brown braids twisted about her head in a clever way. She was thrilled at the man's gallantry. The next passenger was not so thrilled, although she received the same attention. Probably the girl's mother, Sophie thought, understanding why she glared at him so rudely. Never once looking at Sophie, he walked the women to the coach house.

The shotgun man tossed her bag on top of the coach. At her annoyed expression, he said defensively, "I'll make sure it's tied down when I get back up there."

"May I get in now?" she asked.

"Yes, but as I said — "

"I know, we're not leaving for a half an hour. Does it make a difference if I wait out here, or inside?"

"No, ma'am. Do as you please." His voice said he had given up on trying to please her. He held out his hand to help her step up.

Sophie knew that she was being unfairly rude to him. She tried to offer him a pleasant smile in return for his kindness as she reached out her hand.

Suddenly, the gambler was there, gripping her hand before the shotgun man could take it. He scowled and stepped back as the other man moved boldly between them.

Sophie wanted to pull her hand away, but he held it too firmly. His smile was bright under the slick hair of his black mustache. She allowed herself to be guided inside and chose a seat with her back to the front of the coach. A frown of displeasure crossed her face as she realized that the gambler had also entered the coach. He took the seat directly across from her. His hat cast a shadow across his eyes, but Sophie could feel him watching her.

Sophie knew that the trip would be never-ending if she allowed his behavior to continue unchecked. She did the one thing that she knew had unsettled every man she had ever used it on — she glared directly into his eyes and did not look away.

The idiot seemed pleased by her gaze. His smile grew wider and brighter. The curve of his lips, barely visible under his full mustache, suddenly gave Sophie the sense of an impossibly familiar kiss. He whispered, just loud enough to be heard across the width of the cramped but empty coach, "You have the most beautiful scowl I've ever seen."

Sophie gasped, "Kenny?" The name escaped her lips before she could stop it.

The gambler answered by getting up and moving to the seat beside her. Sophie let her hand be drawn up from her lap and kissed by the soft lips.

"Kenny," she whispered again. Her head was reeling, her body responding to Kenny's touch regardless of her mind's uncertainty. Kenny bowed her head and rested her forehead against the back of Sophie's hand.

"Oh God, I've missed you, my sweet Sophie," Kenny whispered.

Suddenly, Sophie dragged a scrap of anger from her depths and clung to the growing rage. "Then I guess it's lucky that I decided to take the stage today, of all days," she whispered, bitterly.

Kenny dropped her hand and leaned back. "Not so lucky for me."

Sophie felt the words like a slap in the face. Tears rushed to fill her eyes and a sob broke from her lips as she pulled away from Kenny. Kenny grabbed her arm with one hand and took her chin firmly in the other. Sophie struggled to keep her head from being turned to face Kenny. She squeezed her eyes shut tight, refusing to look into those eyes she'd loved.

"Is everything all right in there, ma'am?" the shotgun man's voice came from outside the coach.

"Say yes," Kenny hissed close to her ear.

Sophie shook her head. Kenny's grip tightened painfully on her jawbones. She looked into Kenny's eyes and was surprised to see fear.

"Please," Kenny whispered.

"Everything is fine," Sophie managed to say with a surprisingly strong, clear voice. She heard the man walk away. "Now, let go of me!"

"No, no," Kenny said flatly. "Not until you let me explain."

It was clear that Sophie could not escape without screaming for help and something inside her would not allow her to do that to Kenny. So she glared and refused to speak.

"The reason I said that your decision wasn't lucky for me is 'cause luck has nothing to do with my finding you today. You see Sophie, darlin', I've ridden this stage between Leadville and Price every day that it has run since I heard that the McLaren ranch was up for sale. And every day that you didn't get on made me afraid that you had ridden away on Twitch, that I'd missed you somehow." Kenny's soft voice was strained with emotion, but she did not pause. "I couldn't ask anyone if you'd gone or even if you were okay. Anyone who knew you would likely recognize my voice." Kenny's grip on Sophie's face loosened. "Sophie, I'm here because I love you and want to spend my life with you."

Sophie felt the coldness inside her beginning to melt. "But why?" she cried, "Why didn't you come back when you learned that Robert was dead? That he was the one — or didn't you know?"

"I knew, I was there when he died," Kenny admitted. "The day I left, I went to his ranch to kill him."

"You, Kenny? You killed Robert?"

"No, the sheriff from Stockton, Sheriff Cooper, shot him before I could. But do you understand that I could not let Robert McLaren live without tryin'..." Kenny's eyes searched Sophie's face for understanding. "I can never forgive what this man did to me. I never told you the whole story Sophie."

"Yes, I do understand. I hated him too, even before the sheriff told me he was the one responsible for a string of robbed stages, including yours."

"Sophie, you saying you really didn't know?" Kenny asked, surprise written all over her face.

"I didn't know. I had no idea, otherwise I would have killed Robert myself, given half a chance," Sophie swore, knowing that she would not have hesitated if she had had that knowledge. "But why didn't you come back to me, Kenny? I waited and prayed, even though I was confused. After you left my life had very little meaning; my heart was empty." Tears formed in the corners of Sophie's eyes.

"After the sheriff saved my life by shooting McLaren, he told me I had to get out of this part of the country. He knows about me, I'm sure." Kenny's hand softly caressed Sophie's cheek. "I thought he would explain to you why I had gone," Kenny said, as she pulled a white handkerchief from her breast pocket and tenderly dabbed at Sophie's tears.

Sophie could see that Kenny was uncomfortable that the sheriff suspected she was a woman. It could have been a very dangerous situation for her. "He didn't tell me; he never said a word."

"But surely when you read my note, you understood..." Kenny's voice trailed off at the blank expression on Sophie's face. "You didn't find the note I left in the ranch house?"

"I never went inside."

Kenny smiled and shook her head. "You never...Then I'll have to tell you what it said."

Sophie nodded, waiting and hoping.

"I wrote...I love you."

Sophie took a deep breath, pleasure coursing through her body like a crashing wave. She could barely speak to say, "And I love you, Kenny."

Kenny abruptly leaned forward and kissed Sophie with hungry lips. Sophie ignored the impropriety of their situation and willingly returned the kisses she had secretly longed for. The passion she thought she would never feel again flared deep inside her. Kenny finally pulled her face away and they stared at each other, both breathing with difficulty.

"We have about twenty minutes 'fore the stage leaves," Kenny whispered with a sinful glint in her eye. "I believe I can make love to you in that much time."

Sophie laughed out loud. "Not in this stagecoach, mister. And besides, my mother warned me about slick gamblers with furry mustaches."

Kenny grinned and reached up to stroke Sophie's hair fondly. "Do you like it?"

"No," Sophie said bluntly. "And I'm not sure I want to know where you got it."

"Oh, it's an interesting story," Kenny said, despite Sophie's words. "I met this actress in Denver — "

Sophie pressed her fingertips to Kenny's lips. "Stop right there."

Kenny removed Sophie's fingers from her lips and held her hand close to her chest. Sophie could feel the thick fabric beneath Kenny's dark vest. She held her mouth so close to Sophie's that their lips brushed when she spoke. The soft hair of the mustache tickled Sophie's nose. "I'll 'shave' it off when we get to Salt Lake, darlin' Sophie."

"And the eyebrows?" Sophie playfully bumped her head

against Kenny's. "Will you get rid of those bushy beasts?"

"They're going, too," she promised.

Sophie responded with a kiss.

Kenny wrapped Sophie in her strong arms and pulled her as close as she could. "I'm never going to leave you again, Sophie McLaren. No matter how I gotta live — as a man or a woman — I will be with you until the day I die."

Sophie closed her eyes, believing, but knowing that even forever would not be long enough for her.

The End

If You Liked This Book...

Authors seldom get to hear what readers like about their work. If you enjoyed this romance, *And Love Came Calling*, why not let the author know? We are sure she will be delighted to get your feedback. Simply write the author:

Beverly Shearer
c/o Rising Tide Press
3831 N. Oracle Rd.
Tucson, AZ 85705

About the Author

Beverly Shearer has spent all her life in the West. From helping to herd cattle on her father's ranch in Northern Idaho to being part of the herd in Denver, Colorado's rush hour, she has learned that the spirit of the West is eternal. The Western love of independence and freedom knows no gender and knows no age. The characters that people her books — the good guys and gals, and the bad guys — can still be found in the small towns and big cities from Washington to New Mexico, from Wyoming to Nevada.

When not writing, Ms. Shearer passes the time by working as a Sign Language Interpreter/Deaf Services Specialist, by studying for a degree in English, and by sculpting. She also has many spoiled, selfish and demanding pets.

Don't Miss This Exciting Mystery

Deadly Rendezvous: A Toni Underwood Mystery
Diane Davidson

Back in the lodge, Toni began wandering among the people gathered there, her eyes frantically searching for Megan. She had a frown on her face when she turned to the sergeant in charge.

"Are you positive everyone is here? All the guests? You didn't miss anybody?" Toni asked, suddenly feeling a knife-like panic rip at her insides.

"Yes, Lieutenant Underwood, this is everyone."

Toni turned to Kelly. "What villa is Mrs. Marshall in?"

"Number three, down by the pool. Here's the key."

"Let's go, Sal." Toni was already halfway out the door, with fear consuming her, enveloping her in its clutches.

The room was dark and hot. *No one's been here all night.* Toni rushed through the living room area and into the large bedroom. The bed hadn't been slept in. Megan's pink cotton robe was lying in a heap on the floor.

"Her purse and car keys are gone," Sally said quietly, seeing the fear written on Toni's face.

"Megan! Megan!" Toni called out as she headed toward the bathroom.

"Toni." Sally put her hand on Toni's arm. "Toni...she's not here," Sally said, afraid to say what she really thought.

"What do you mean she's not here? That can't be. She knew we were coming to get her today; she wouldn't leave." Fear flooded Toni's face. "Where? Where would she go, Sally?"

Then her eyes narrowed; they were like daggers, her jaw set tight. She suddenly turned without a word, and ran out of the villa and toward the lodge.

"Toni, wait! Don't do anything stupid." Sally ran after her. Catching Toni by the arm, she spun her around and forced her up against the villa wall.

"Let me go, Sal." The look in Toni's eyes was terrifying. "That bitch Clark has her hidden away somewhere as a hostage. I'm gonna kill the mother-fucker if she doesn't tell me where Megan is, right now."

"Listen to me, please," Sally pleaded.

Toni was fighting to free herself. "I don't wanna hurt you, Sal, now let me go!" Toni was screaming, as tears filled her eyes. Fear and rage filled her heart. She knew she was out of control.

"All right, god damn it, go ahead and lose it. Lose the chance of putting Nicky away for good. Lose the chance of ever finding Megan. Go ahead, you damned hothead!" Sally released her grip and stepped back.

But Toni's sobbing was breaking her heart and she softened.

"Come back inside with me," Sally gently urged. She took Toni's arm and led her toward the villa. "Let's sit down for a minute and see if we can think clearly about this, okay?"

Perspiration and tears were streaming down Toni's face; she felt sick. Her shirt was drenched with sweat, her hair stuck to her forehead.

Back in the villa, Sally turned the air-conditioning on, went into the bathroom, got a glass of water and a wet towel. "Here," she said gently, handing them to Toni.

"What are we gonna do, Sal?" Toni sounded like a lost child. It took everything Sally had not to cry.

She sat down on the bed next to Toni and put her arm around her shoulder. "We're going to get Megan back. She's not stupid, you know. I'm sure she's okay. If Clark has her stashed somewhere, we *will* get it out of her, I promise." Sally was going all out in an effort to calm and comfort Toni. "We're going to conduct ourselves like professionals. We're NOT going to let Nicky get the best of us. No matter how hard it is, you are going to hang in there. For Megan's sake, you can't fall apart. You're a police officer, the best, and that's who Nicky Clark and the rest of the department are going to see."

Toni sat on the edge of the bed staring at the floor for a long time, not moving. Finally she sighed, and looked at Sally.

"Okay, Sal, we do it your way. I'll be okay, I promise. For Megan, I'll be okay." Toni took several deep breaths, then stood, pulling her tall body up straight. "Let's find Megan." Slipping on her Raybans, she walked to the door and stepped out into the bright desert sun.

—An excerpt from *Deadly Rendezvous* ($9.99), by Diane Davidson, author of *Deadly Gamble* ($11.99).

These books are available from Rising Tide Press, and from your nearest feminist or lesbian/gay bookstore. Please see ordering instructions.

More Fiction to Stir the Imagination from Rising Tide Press

RETURN TO ISIS
Jean Stewart

It is the year 2093, and Whit, a bold woman warrior from an Amazon nation, rescues Amelia from a dismal world where females are either breeders or drones. During their arduous journey back to the shining all-women's world of Artemis, they are unexpectedly drawn to each other. A Lambda Literary Award Finalist $9.99

ISIS RISING
Jean Stewart

In this stirring romantic fantasy, the familiar cast of lovable characters begin to rebuild the colony of Isis, burned to the ground ten years earlier by the dread Regulators. But evil forces threaten to destroy their dream. A swashbuckling futuristic adventure and an endearing love story all rolled into one. $11.99

WARRIORS OF ISIS
Jean Stewart

At last, the third lusty tale of high adventure and passionate romance among the Freeland Warriors. Arinna Sojourner, the evil product of genetic engineering, vows to destroy the fledgling colony of Isis with her incredible psychic powers. Whit, Kali, and other warriors battle to save their world, in this novel bursting with life, love, heroines and villains. $11.99

EMERALD CITY BLUES
Jean Stewart

When the comfortable yuppie world of Chris Olson and Jennifer Hart collides with the desperate lives of Reb and Flynn, two lesbian runaways struggling to survive on the streets of Seattle, the forecast is trouble. A gritty, enormously readable novel of contemporary lesbigay life which raises real questions about the meaning of family and community, and about the walls we construct. A celebration of the healing powers of love. $11.99

ROUGH JUSTICE
Claire Youmans

When Glenn Lowry's sunken fishing boat turns up four years after his disappearance, foul play is suspected. Classy, ambitious Prosecutor Janet Schilling immediately launches a murder investigation which produces several surprising suspects—one of them her own former lover Catherine Adams, now living a reclusive life on an island. A real page-turner! $10.99

FEATHERING YOUR NEST: An Interactive Workbook & Guide to a Loving Lesbian Relationship
Gwen Leonhard, M.ED./Jennie Mast, MSW

This fresh, insightful guide and workbook for lesbian couples provides effective ways to build and nourish your relationships. Includes fun exercises & creative ways to spark romance, solve conflict, fight fair, conquer boredom, spice up your sex lives & enjoy life together. Plus much more. $14.99

AND LOVE CAME CALLING
Beverly Shearer
The rough and ready days of the Old West come alive with the timeless story of love between two women: Kenny Smith, a stage coach driver in Jackson, Colorado and Sophie McLaren, a young woman forced to marry, then widowed. The women meet after Kenny is shot by bandits during a stage coach holdup. And love blooms when Sophie finds herself the unexpected rescuer of the good-looking wounded driver. $11.99

CORNERS OF THE HEART
Leslie Grey
A captivating novel of love and suspense in which beautiful French-born Chris Benet and English professor Katya Michaels meet and fall in love. But their budding love is shadowed by a vicious killer, whom they must outwit. Your heart will pound as the story races to its heart-stopping conclusion. $9.95

DANGER IN HIGH PLACES
Sharon Gilligan
Set against the backdrop of Washington, D.C., this riveting mystery introduces freelance photographer and amateur sleuth, Alix Nicholson. Alix stumbles on a deadly scheme, and with the help of a lesbian congressional aide, unravels the mystery. $9.99

DANGER! CROSS CURRENTS
Sharon Gilligan
The exciting sequel to *Danger in High Places* brings freelance photographer Alix Nicholson face-to-face with an old love and a murder. When Alix's landlady turns up dead, and her much younger lover, Leah Claire, is the prime suspect, Alix launches a frantic campaign to find the real killer. $9.99

PLAYING FOR KEEPS
Stevie Rios
In this sparkling tale of love and adventure, Lindsay West, a musician, travels to Caracas, where she meets three people who change her life forever: Rob Heron a gay man, who becomes her dearest friend; Her lover Mercedes Luego, who takes Lindsay on a life-altering adventure down the Amazon River; And the mysterious jungle-dwelling woman Arminta, who touches their souls $10.99

NIGHTSHADE
Karen Williams
Alex Spherris finds herself the new owner of a magical bell, which some people would kill for. With this bell, she is ushered into a strange & wonderful world and meets Orielle, who melts her frozen heart. A heartwarming romance spun in the best tradition of storytelling. $11.99

DREAMCATCHER
Lori Byrd
This timeless story of love and friendship introduces Sunny Calhoun, a college student, who falls in love with Eve Phillips, a literary agent. A richly woven novel capturing the wonder and pain of love between a younger and an older woman. $9.99

AGENDA FOR MURDER
Joan Albarella
Though haunted by memories of love and loss from her years of service in Viet Nam, Nikki Barnes is finally putting back the pieces of her life, and learning to feel again. But she quickly realizes that the college where she teaches is no haven from violence and death, as she comes face to face with murder and betrayal in this least likely of all places—her college campus.   [Avail.11/98] $11.99

HEARTSTONE AND SABER
Jacqui Singleton
You can almost hear the sabers clash in this rousing tale of good and evil, of passionate love between a bold warrior queen and a beautiful healer with magical powers. $10.99

SHADOWS AFTER DARK
Ouida Crozier
Fans of vampire erotica will adore this! When wings of death spread over Kyril's home world, she is sent to Earth on a mission—find a cure for the deadly disease. Once here, she meets and falls in love with Kathryn, who is enthralled yet horrified to learn that her mysterious, darkly exotic lover is...a vampire. This tender, beautifully written love story is the ultimate lesbian vampire novel! $9.95

TROPICAL STORM
Linda Kay Silva
Another winning, action-packed adventure/romance featuring smart and sassy heroines, an exotic jungle setting, and a plot with more twists and turns than a coiled cobra. Megan has disappeared into the Costa Rican rain forest and it's up to Delta and Connie to find her. Can they reach Megan before it's too late? Will Storm risk everything to save the woman she loves? Fast-paced, full of wonderful characters and surprises. Not to be missed. $11.99

SWEET BITTER LOVE
Rita Schiano
Susan Fredrickson is a woman of fire and ice—a successful high-powered executive, she is by turns sexy and aloof. And from the moment writer Jenny Ceretti spots her at the Village Coffeehouse, her serene life begins to change. As their friendship explodes into a blazing love affair, Jenny discovers that all is not as it appears, while Susan is haunted by ghosts from her past. Schiano serves up passion and drama in this roller-coaster romance. $10.99

SIDE DISH
Kim Taylor
She's funny, she's attractive, she's lovable—and she doesn't know it. Meet Muriel, aka Mutt, a twenty-something wayward waitress with a college degree, who has resigned herself to low standards, simple pleasures, and erotic fantasies. Though seeming to get by on margaritas and old movies, in her heart of hearts, Mutt is actually searching for true love. While Mutt chases the bars with her best friend, Jeff, she is, in turn, chased by Diane, a former college classmate with a decidedly romantic agenda. When a rich, seductive Beverly Hills lawyer named Allison steals Mutt's heart, she is in for trouble, and like the glamorous facade of Sunset Boulevard, things are not quite as they seem. A delightfully funny read. $11.99

NO WITNESSES
Nancy Sanra
This cliff-hanger of a mystery set in San Francisco, introduces Detective Tally McGinnis, whose ex-lover Pamela Tresdale is arrested for the grisly murder of a wealthy Texas heiress. Tally rushes to the rescue despite friends' warnings, and is drawn once again into Pamela's web of deception and betrayal as she attempts to clear her and find the real killer. $9.99

NO ESCAPE
Nancy Sanra
This edgy, fast-paced sequel to *No Witnesses*, also set in picturesque San Francisco, is a story of drugs, love and jealousy. Late one rain-drenched night, nurse Melinda Morgan is found murdered. Who cut her life short, plunging a scalpel into her heart, then disappeared into the night? As lesbian PI Tally McGinnis sorts through the bizarre evidence, she can almost sense the diabolical Marsha Cox lurking in the shadows. You will be shocked by the secrets behind the gruesome murder. $11.99

DEADLY RENDEZVOUS
Diane Davidson
A string of brutal murders in the middle of the desert plunges Lieutenant Toni Underwood and her lover Megan into a high profile investigation which uncovers a world of drugs, corruption and murder, as well as the dark side of the human mind. An explosive, fast-paced, action-packed whodunit. $9.99

DEADLY GAMBLE
Diane Davidson
Former police detective Toni Underwood is catapulted back into the world of crime by a mysterious letter from her favorite aunt. Black sheep of the family and a prominent madam, Vera Valentine fears she is about to be murdered—a distinct possibility, given her underworld connections. With the help of onetime partner (and possibly future lover) Sergeant Sally Murphy, Toni takes on the seamy, ruthless underbelly of Las Vegas, where appearance and reality are often at odds. Flamboyant characters and unsavory thugs make for a cast of likely suspects... and keep the reader guessing until the last page. $11.99

CLOUD NINE AFFAIR
Katherine E. Kreuter
Chris Grandy—rebellious, wealthy, twenty-something—has disappeared in India, along with her hippie lover Monica Ward. Desperate to bring her home, Christine's millionaire father hires expert Paige Taylor. But the trail to Christine is mined with obstacles, as powerful enemies plot to eliminate her. A witty, sophisticated & entertaining mystery. $11.99

COMING ATTRACTIONS
Bobbi D. Marolt
It's been three years since she's made love to a woman; three years that she's buried herself in work as a successful columnist for one of New York's top newspapers. Helen Townsend admits, at last, she's tired of being lonely....and of being closeted. Enter Princess Charming in the shapely form of Cory Chamberlain, a gifted concert pianist. And Helen embraces joy once again. But can two lovers find happiness when one yearns to break out of the closet and breathe free, while the other fears that will destroy her career? A sunny blend of humor, heart and passion. A novel which captures the bliss and blunderings of love. $11.99

HOW TO ORDER

TITLE	AUTHOR	PRICE

☐ Agenda for Murder-Joan Albarella 11.99
☐ And Love Came Calling-Beverly Shearer 11.99
☐ Cloud 9 Affair-Katherine Kreuter 11.99
☐ Coming Attractions-Bobbi Marolt 11.99
☐ Corners of the Heart-Leslie Grey 9.95
☐ Danger! Cross Currents-Sharon Gilligan 9.99
☐ Danger in High Places-Sharon Gilligan 9.95
☐ Deadly Gamble-Diane Davidson 11.99
☐ Deadly Rendezvous-Diane Davidson 9.99
☐ Dreamcatcher-Lori Byrd 9.99
☐ Emerald City Blues-Jean Stewart 11.99
☐ Feathering Your Nest-Gwen Leonhard/ Jennie Mast 14.99
☐ Heartstone and Saber-Jacqui Singleton 10.99
☐ Isis Rising-Jean Stewart 11.99
☐ Nightshade-Karen Williams 11.99
☐ No Escape-Nancy Sanra 11.99
☐ No Witnesses-Nancy Sanra 9.99
☐ Playing for Keeps-Stevie Rios 10.99
☐ Return to Isis-Jean Stewart 9.99
☐ Rough Justice-Claire Youmans 10.99
☐ Shadows After Dark-Ouida Crozier 9.99
☐ Side Dish-Kim Taylor 11.99
☐ Sweet Bitter Love-Rita Schiano 10.99
☐ Tropical Storm-Linda Kay Silva 11.99
☐ Warriors of Isis-Jean Stewart 11.99

Please send me the books I have checked. I enclose a check or money order (not cash), plus $4 for the first book and $1 for each additional book to cover shipping and handling. Or bill my ☐Visa/Mastercard ☐American Express.

Or call our Toll Free Number 1-800-648-5333 if using a credit card.
CARD # _____ EXP.DATE_____

NAME (PLEASE PRINT) _____SIGNTURE_____

ADDRESS _____

CITY_____

STATE_____ZIP_____
☐ Arizona residents, please add 7% tax to total.
RISING TIDE PRESS, 3831 N. ORACLE RD., TUCSON AZ 85705